THE PRIME SUSPECT

Hayley watched Gloria glance around the room

Books by Lee Hollis

DEATH OF A KITCHEN DIVA

DEATH OF A COUNTRY FRIED REDNECK

DEATH OF A COUPON CLIPPER

DEATH OF A CHOCOHOLIC

DEATH OF A CHRISTMAS CATERER

DEATH OF A CUPCAKE QUEEN

DEATH OF A BACON HEIRESS

DEATH OF A PUMPKIN CARVER

DEATH OF A LOBSTER LOVER

DEATH OF A COOKBOOK AUTHOR

EGGNOG MURDER
(with Leslie Meier and Barbara Ross)

Published by Kensington Publishing Corporation

DEATH of a COOKBOOK AUTHOR

A Hayley Powell
Food and Cocktails Mystery

LEE HOLLIS

KENSINGTON PUBLISHING CORP.
www.kensingtonbooks.com

ISBN-13: 978-1-4967-1384-1
ISBN-10: 1-4967-1384-2

First printing: May 2018

10 9 8 7 6 5 4 3 2 1

Printed in the United States of America

First electronic edition: May 2018

ISBN-13: 978-1-4967-1385-8
ISBN-10: 1-4967-1385-0

Chapter 1

Hayley stared numbly at the inscription that had been scribbled inside her book cover only moments before.

She couldn't believe what she was reading.

"To Hayley, one of my inspirations! Keep writing and cooking! All the best, Penelope Janice."

Inspiration?

Penelope Janice was Hayley's idol. A cooking and lifestyle expert with her own top-rated TV show on the Flavor Network. When Hayley heard the famous part-time summer resident of Mount Desert Island was going to make an appearance at Sherman's Bookstore in Bar Harbor midweek before the long Fourth of July weekend, she was filled with excitement. Hayley owned all of Penelope's cookbooks in hardcover, and they lined the bookshelf in her living room. *Cowboys and Turbans*, Penelope's mouthwatering exploration of Mexican-Indian fusion recipes, was a personal favorite. She had met her idol in person a few times in passing at Penelope's famous Fourth of July barbecues she held every year at her palatial Seal Harbor estate for all the local residents, but Hayley had never worked up the nerve to bring one of her cookbooks and personally ask her for an autograph.

Since it was practically a holiday week, Hayley's boss Sal Morretti, editor in chief at the *Island Times* newspaper, was amenable to her leaving early on a Wednesday in order to get in line for Mrs. Janice's book signing.

By six o'clock when Penelope was scheduled to arrive, the line had already wrapped around the aisles of the store, out the door, and down Main Street, nearly stretching all the way to the Bar Harbor Banking and Trust building blocks away. But thanks to Hayley's careful planning, she was only tenth in line to get her newly purchased hardcover signed.

This latest release, *Making Magic out of Leftovers* was the perfect title to add to her collection, especially now that Hayley's two kids, Gemma and Dustin, were out of the house and living on their own. She suddenly found her refrigerator stocked with leftovers in Tupperware containers. She was used to cooking for a family of three for so many years. Four, if you counted the years her ex-husband Danny was in the picture. But for the record, that period of her life she would just as soon forget.

Hayley chatted with a few locals in line with her while waiting for the official start of the book signing, including Martha Hickenlooper, a culinary fan in her own right who had moved back to the island after years working as a chef in Atlanta and gaining fame in some circles for designing meal plans for Delta Airlines.

Martha also considered Penelope Janice a hero.

"Have you read this latest book?" she asked Hayley, breathlessly.

"No," Hayley said, "I just bought it today. I'm going to curl up on my couch between all the barbecues and fireworks this weekend and tear my way through it!"

"It's genius! Penelope has no peer when it comes to creating gourmet recipes you'd expect at a five-star restaurant—and out of the simplest ingredients you can find in your cupboard any day of the week! I mean, the woman is brilliant. I had some leftover cheeses and a few roasted potatoes on hand, and within minutes I had a heavenly casserole like none I've ever tasted! I'm telling you, she is—"

Martha stopped mid-sentence, her jaw dropped, and her eyes grew wide as her attention was drawn to something happening outside the store window.

Hayley turned to see a maroon Chevrolet SS sedan pull up in front of the store, and a petite, fiery redhead in Dolce & Gabbana sunglasses, a bright pink blouse, and white capri pants jump out. The fans outside the store burst into spontaneous applause, and although she made several modest gestures begging them to stop, Penelope Janice clearly loved soaking up all of the adoration.

Donna, a heavyset Sherman's Bookstore employee, who was known for wearing thick wool sweaters even in the dog days of summer because she was cold all the time, flew out the door to greet the VIP guest, and then ushered her inside the store with all the fanfare she could muster.

"Hello, everyone, I'm so glad you could make it!" Penelope cooed as the doting fans inside the store followed the leads of the less fortunate ones still standing outside and enthusiastically broke into more applause.

"She looks even prettier in person!" Martha gushed, clapping her hands so hard her palms started turning red.

Donna whisked Penelope down the aisle to the back of the store where her table, pens, and stacks of books awaited.

After a few minutes of glad-handing all of the Sherman's Bookstore staff, Penelope plopped down in her leather chair that had been wheeled out from the back office just for this special occasion. She waved over the first person in line to get her book personally autographed.

Hayley had secretly hoped that she might get the chance to have a brief chat with Penelope while having her book signed, mostly because she wanted to tell her just how much she enjoyed her books and TV show, but gatekeeper Donna kept the chatter between the author and her devoted readers to a minimum by shooing them away the second Penelope handed their book back to them with a bright smile.

It took less than five minutes before Hayley found

herself standing before her culinary idol. She clutched her copy of *Making Magic out of Leftovers* to her chest and stared at the attractive woman with the Lucille Ball hair color.

Hayley was at a complete loss for words—a rare occurrence, by the way.

"Would you like me to sign your book?" Penelope asked politely, as Hayley noticed her lipstick matched her hair perfectly.

Martha had to nudge Hayley in order to snap her out of her trance.

"Oh, yes, sorry," Hayley laughed, shaking her head. "Just make it out to Hayley. That's Hayley with a Y. I mean, in the middle, everyone knows Hayley has a Y at the end. Although I did go to summer camp when I was a kid with a girl who spelled it with two E's at the end. H-A-I-L-E-E. But that's rare—"

"Could you please just hand her your book, Hayley, so she can sign it?" Donna barked, quickly losing patience.

"Gosh, I'm just a bundle of nerves. I guess I never thought I would ever meet you in person," Hayley said.

She handed Penelope the book and watched her start to write her name on the title page inside the front cover, but then she stopped and looked up at Hayley.

"Hayley . . . as in Hayley Powell?"

"Yes, that's right," Hayley said, incredulous.

How could this woman possibly know who she was?

"As in Hayley Powell, who writes the Island Food & Spirits column I read *every* week in the local paper?"

"Yes," Hayley said.

"I'm such a *huge* fan!" Penelope yelped.

Martha dropped her book on the floor in shock.

"You know my column?" Hayley asked, her mouth agape.

"Of course I do! You forget I live here during the summer. I like to keep up with all the local news. I stumbled across you a few years ago, and I have to say, I've been hooked on your column ever since. I also must confess, I've lifted a few of your recipe ideas for my show, but please don't sue me!"

"No, of course not! I'm flattered!" Hayley cried, trying to remain calm and not dance around the store in a frenzied euphoric state.

Hayley knew a few notable people who spent the summer months on the island and were aware of her column. There was the late Olivia Redmond, a billionaire bacon heiress, and also Rhonda Franklin, the famous daytime TV hostess of *The Chat* who was an unabashed fan. And there were also more than a few locals who claimed Martha Stewart, a summer resident who bought the old Ford Estate in Seal Harbor, was vaguely aware of her, but Hayley had never encountered her in person.

But Penelope Janice?

Sitting right in front of her with a big toothy grin on her face announcing her devotion to Hayley's obscure small-town musings?

This was a whole other level.

"I've been dying to meet you and talk to you,"

Penelope said, reaching out and taking Hayley's hand to shake it since Hayley was too dumbfounded to offer it herself. "It's such a pleasure to meet you."

"Mrs. Janice, we have a lot of people waiting in line to get their books signed . . ." Donna said softly but firmly.

"Of course, I understand," Penelope said, nodding.

She scribbled a quick note in Hayley's book and handed it back to her.

Hayley stared at it, still unable to comprehend the idea of her being an "inspiration" to someone as talented and accomplished and world famous as Penelope Janice.

Martha pushed Hayley out of the way and took her place in front of the author. "Mrs. Janice, I just have to tell you that I think—"

"Wait!" Penelope shouted as Hayley turned to leave.

Donna grimaced as Penelope waved Hayley back over to her.

"I know this is last minute, but what are you up to this weekend?"

"I—I was going to read your book," Hayley stammered.

"Well, I would never discourage anyone from reading one of my books, but perhaps you can do it at my house in Seal Harbor," Penelope said, smiling.

"I'm sorry, what?" Hayley asked.

"I'm sorry, what?" Martha echoed.

"I don't mean to be forward, but I need you. If I could explain . . ."

Donna checked her watch and sighed.

Hayley stepped forward, all ears.

"I'm hosting an event at my house this weekend, sort of a celebrity potluck, if you will, where famous chefs come together and whip up their signature dishes in a friendly competition. The unveiling of the winner will be taped for a segment on my TV show. Well, as luck would have it, Irina St. Pierre, you know, the French pastry chef, is going through a nasty divorce back in New York. She slapped her husband after a court hearing and it wound up on TMZ, so she's in damage control mode now working with a high-priced public relations firm, and she had to cancel at the last minute. So to make a long story even longer, I need a fill-in. But finding a replacement has been somewhat challenging to say the least, given the short notice, not to mention that it's Fourth of July weekend, so I was wondering—"

"I would love to participate!" Hayley screamed.

"She would love to!" Martha echoed.

"That's wonderful! The guests will be staying for an extended weekend. Most of them are arriving tomorrow and are not scheduled to leave until Monday or Tuesday because they need a couple of days to shop for ingredients and prepare their dishes before the competition. My husband and I have also planned a few outings and excursions, so if it's not entirely inconvenient for you—"

"You want me to stay the entire Fourth of July weekend at your estate in Seal Harbor?"

"It's not exactly an estate. More like a summer cottage," Penelope said, brimming with modesty.

Hayley smiled knowingly, having seen some of the expansive rooms on a few episodes of *Penelope's Cupboard* when she shot segments in Seal Harbor. Penelope's idea of a summer cottage was in reality a normal person's idea of a large sprawling estate.

"No pressure though. I know it's last minute and a very busy time of the year," Penelope purred, knowing full well Hayley would instantly jump at the chance to join her potluck party.

And she did.

With gusto.

"Yes! I would love to!" Hayley blurted out. "I just need to check with my boss to see if I can get Thursday and Friday off."

"Marvelous! You will have full access to my kitchen to prepare your dish," Penelope said. "I can't thank you enough, Hayley. You're a lifesaver! I'll have my assistant call you at your office with the rest of the details."

"Thank you, Mrs. Janice, thank you!"

"Please, it's Penelope."

Martha Hickenlooper pushed her face in front of Penelope and screamed, "I'm a chef too, Penelope! In case anyone else is a no-show!"

Donna folded her arms and glared at Martha,

but Penelope was unruffled and asked with a tight smile, "Who do I make it out to?"

As Martha carefully spelled out her name, Hayley floated out of the bookstore.

Her lazy, boring holiday weekend at home had just turned into the dream of a lifetime.

Chapter 2

Hayley's instincts were right. Penelope's "quaint seaside cottage" boasted spacious dining and living rooms, twelve bedrooms, seven and a half baths, a state-of-the-art kitchen, and stocked pantry. Outside there was also a remarkable combination of covered porches and large sun decks. Surrounding the property were extensive landscaping and colorful gardens with quiet meandering walkways that wind their way to a stunning view of the crystal-blue ocean and the picturesque harbor dotted with fishing boats and summer cruisers.

A perky maid, who introduced herself as Pam, showed Hayley to her room upon her arrival. When Pam swung open the door and Hayley stepped inside, she audibly gasped at the adorable space that had been so lovingly softened by pale pink walls, hanging silk sheers and linen drapes, and an elegant, shell-covered chandelier.

Pam then marched over and dramatically pulled open the curtains, allowing a bright stream of the midday sun to shine through, which lightened the room even more. There was a small dressing table to the left adorned with expensive beauty and skin products and lush towels that matched the walls.

Hayley thanked Pam and reached into her purse to scavenge for a few dollars for a tip, but Pam waved her off, declining any compensation for doing her job. This was a private home, not a hotel. Pam then scooted out the door to give Hayley her privacy.

After looking around and marveling at her gorgeous room once more, Hayley unzipped her bag, unpacked her summer clothing for the weekend, and stored it in the cottage-white antique dresser drawers. Then she changed into a short-sleeve yellow blouse and white shorts, slipped on some low wedge strap-on sandals, and decided to set out to find the kitchen in order to get familiar with it before she started her food prep.

Hayley bounded out of the room, full of excitement over the prospect of hobnobbing with her favorite chefs over a long holiday weekend. But there was also a persistent twinge of nervousness. This whole experience was going to be far outside her wheelhouse.

Halfway down the hall, Hayley got turned around and couldn't find the staircase that led down to the main foyer.

She walked back, turned a corner and headed down another long hallway, but ultimately reached a dead end. She finally stopped to get her bearings.

The house was so big she was now lost.

Hayley smiled to herself.

Cottage? Really?

She suddenly felt something furry brush up against her bare leg, and she jumped with a yelp.

Hayley looked down to see a large fluffy white Persian cat staring up at her with giant copper eyes that seemed to say, "*Of course you are going to love me.*"

"Look how beautiful you are," Hayley cooed, bending down to scratch the top of the cat's head as he closed his eyes, happy, relaxed, and purring, with a proud smile and attitude that said in no uncertain terms, "*Yes, I know.*"

"What's your name?"

Hayley fingered an expensive crystal rhinestone collar around the cat's neck that had a small gold-plated medallion in front with the name Sebastian inscribed on the back.

"Nice to meet you, Sebastian. I'm Hayley," she said, before realizing she still couldn't ditch the habit of talking to animals even though she knew they were never going to talk back unless they were in an animated Disney movie.

"You're being ridiculous!" a man bellowed from behind a closed door just down the hall.

"Do not patronize me, Conrad! I hate it when you patronize me!"

"Well, then stop acting like a petulant child!"

Hayley picked Sebastian up in her arms and he contentedly settled into the crook of her arm, cuddling against her chest, on his back facing up, begging to be scratched. She began to lightly caress his furry white belly as she listened to Penelope arguing with Conrad, whom Hayley knew to be her husband of twenty-six years from her TV show on the Flavor Network.

"I will not be humiliated by that woman this weekend in front of all my peers, do you hear me?"

"What exactly do you think is going on between the two of us?"

"What am I supposed to think? You seem to spend an awful lot of your time with her. She works for *me*, Conrad! Not you! You don't have to take her everywhere you go like some damn service dog!"

"Do not compare Lena to an animal. That's beneath you."

Lena.

Lena Hendricks.

Hayley recognized the name from *Penelope's Cupboard*. She was the star's devoted assistant, although there was a rumor on the Internet that Lena was a very talented author in her own right and actually ghostwrote, or at least contributed heavily to, all of Penelope's number-one best-selling books.

"I gave her the weekend off! Why is she still here? Are you two planning some secret tryst while I'm preoccupied with my guests?"

"Calm down, Pep! I'm *not* sleeping with her," Conrad sighed.

Hayley couldn't resist creeping farther down the hallway toward the door as Sebastian purred loudly, his eyes closed, a euphoric look on his face.

"Don't call me that! You know I hate that name!"

"It's a term of endearment," Conrad argued.

"Well, I hate it!"

"You didn't hate it before you became famous, interestingly enough."

"Oh, please, don't start this again! You always try to make me feel bad about my success. You certainly never complain about the money that comes with my fame!"

"I'm done here," Conrad barked, and before Hayley could even make a move, he slammed open the door, surprising her enough that she dropped Sebastian to the floor. Conrad didn't even acknowledge her as he stomped out of the room, the heel of his shoe catching Sebastian's tail. The startled Persian cat screeched, more from shock than pain.

Conrad didn't bother to even stop, but continued clomping down the hall in a huff until he disappeared around the corner.

Penelope, having heard her cat's surprised cry, shot out into the hall, rearing back at the sight of Hayley skulking outside her bedroom door. "Hayley, what are you doing?"

"Looking for the kitchen," Hayley babbled far too quickly. "I'm hopelessly turned around and have no idea where I am."

Penelope softened and smiled. "Let me show you."

She bent down and patted her cat on the top of his head. "I see you've met Sebastian."

"He's adorable. So good-natured."

"That's because he just ate. The number one rule in this house that we all must follow for our own safety is to never allow Sebastian to get hungry. You never, *ever* want to see him hungry."

Hayley chuckled and followed Penelope to a back set of stairs that she had completely missed before that led them down to the most impressive, top-flight kitchen Hayley had ever seen. Despite the laid-back New England charm of the rest of the house, the kitchen was an organized restaurant-style workspace complete with a multi-unit range with a combination of gas burners, a griddle, a wok burner, and a fryer. Overhead was a full-length hood to provide maximum ventilation coverage, a pasta-filler faucet, and a wall rail for gadgets and utensils. There was also a pizza oven on the opposite side of the room and designated task stations, high-efficiency Sub-Zero refrigeration, stylish work-horse sinks, and hands-free faucets.

It was a cook's dream.

"I hope you'll find everything you need," Penelope said.

Hayley nodded, taking it all in, and thought she might burst into tears with joy. She had never had the privilege of cooking in a kitchen like this.

A back door flew open and a short stout woman with frizzy black hair and a flinty, hard-nosed look on her face barreled inside carrying a bag of fresh produce in a reusable green grocery bag.

"Slim pickings at the market," she said in a thick Maine drawl, setting the bag down on one of the long counters and unloading it. "Everyone must be stocking up for the long weekend."

"Clara, I'd like you to meet Hayley Powell," Penelope said.

Clara slowly turned around and gave Hayley the once-over.

"We've met," she said, scowling.

Clara Beaumont was a longtime local, her family dating all the way back to the mid-eighteenth century according to Mount Desert Island historical records. Very few of her kin ever ventured off the island, most preferring to live a quiet provincial Down East life. Hayley knew Clara mostly from having gone to high school with her son Eben.

Clara was known about town as a good and reliable cook, having worked in a number of high-end restaurants during the summer seasons for most of her adult life. But when Penelope Janice placed an ad in the *Island Times* for full-time kitchen help at her seaside estate, excuse me, summer cottage, Clara applied for the job. She managed to impress Penelope with her mad cooking skills, no small feat, Hayley imagined, and at this point had been working for the culinary queen going on eight or nine years.

Hayley spotted Clara every so often shuffling around in the background during a few episodes of *Penelope's Cupboard.* Clara was extremely camera shy, so whenever Penelope would try and engage her, she would keep her head down and pretend she was whisking or kneading something, or find an excuse to run off to the pantry. It just made Penelope's viewers more curious about her.

Penelope glanced at a text on her phone and then turned to Hayley. "Clara can help you find any ingredients you will need for your dish. I just got word Carol's plane landed at the Bar Harbor

Airport early and there is no one there to pick her up, so I have to send Arthur, my driver, to fetch her."

She had to be talking about Carol Kay, a healthy eating expert with her own show on the Lifestyle Network.

"Excuse me," Penelope said apologetically. "Make yourself at home."

"Thank you so much, Mrs. Janice!" Hayley said.

"Oh, Lord, Hayley, call me Penelope! We're friends now!" she said as she dashed out of the kitchen.

Hayley was still wrapping her head around the fact that Penelope Janice considered her a friend when she noticed Clara glaring at her.

"You must love working in such a beautiful kitchen," Hayley said, attempting to make some small talk.

Clara didn't answer her at first.

She just kept glaring.

Finally, she turned and continued unloading fresh fruit and vegetables from her green grocery bag. "Just because she likes you now doesn't mean you're going to be able to use that to push me out."

"I beg your pardon?"

Clara whipped around, brandishing a stalk of celery, waving it at Hayley.

Hayley would have felt threatened.

If it wasn't a stalk of celery.

"You heard me!" Clara spit out. "I don't take kindly to young women trespassing onto my territory, thinking they can get their grubby little hands on my utensils and take over my job!"

"Clara, I am not here to get a job. I'm just a guest for the weekend," Hayley tried to assure her.

Although she was flattered Clara had referred to her as "young."

Clara was having none of it.

"Others have tried before and failed. I'm a fixture in this house and believe me, I'm not going *anywhere*!"

"I do believe you and honestly I am happy to hear that because I have no interest—"

"She may like you now, but give me a day or two. I'll make sure you don't stay on Penelope's good side," Clara threatened, sneering.

Hayley knew the woman was dead serious, and that there was no convincing her that she was hardly a threat to her revered position in the household.

Only twenty minutes since her arrival and she had already made an enemy.

The Fourth of July weekend was off to a rollicking start.

Chapter 3

Hayley stared at herself in the full-length mirror in her room. She was shocked that she had cleaned up so well. In fact, she never remembered *ever* looking this good. The Lela Rose shift dress with a metallic tweed design and fringe hem that she had borrowed from her far more stylish friend Liddy certainly went a long way in helping shape her look for the evening.

She had been so nervous about fitting in with all these TV bigwigs she almost cancelled the whole weekend at the last minute. But Liddy, who like clockwork flew to New York three times a year for retail therapy, refused to listen to her moaning, and raced over to Hayley's house with some selections in tow. She arrived bearing six or seven dresses from her closet not to mention a small trunk-load of expensive shoes and her prized Chanel white vintage clutch bag as well as a few other high-end accessories.

As for hair and makeup, Hayley was pretty much

on her own, but she managed to dab on some rouge and powder, line her eyes with mascara, and choose a not too flashy pastel peach lipstick color.

She wasn't exactly runway ready but she at least looked presentable.

After giving herself the once-over one more time in order to make sure her mascara didn't make her look like a raccoon and the dress was hanging properly on her frame so she wouldn't have a wardrobe malfunction during dinner, Hayley took a deep breath and walked out of the room, determined not to embarrass herself this evening.

She descended the staircase and could hear the other guests conversing in the large living room just past the foyer. As she entered the dining room she saw everyone paired off and chatting. She shifted uncomfortably, feeling self-conscious as she stood off to the side trying to steady her balance, her feet not trained to support the borrowed Christian Louboutin Apostrophy pumps she was sporting.

Hayley looked around the room, a tight smile fixed on her face, wondering if she should mingle or wait to be approached. She certainly didn't lack self-confidence in her daily life. Only when she was thrown into unfamiliar situations, like a dinner party where she only knew the hostess.

And at the moment, their hostess was nowhere to be found.

Hayley did recognize a few faces. Gerard Roquefort was by a table near the bay window, dipping a large shrimp in a glass bowl of cocktail sauce. Gerard was another top chef star on the Flavor

Network. He was big and boisterous, a true force of nature, with a hearty laugh and a trademark waxed mustache. He was prattling on to a younger man, more fit and muscular but still the spitting image of Gerard, who halfheartedly listened. Hayley knew the younger man was Tristan Roquefort, Gerard's twentysomething son, who was following in his father's footsteps and fast becoming a respected chef in his own right. But he was still a long way away from achieving the kind of massive success his father currently enjoyed.

"That's a lovely dress," a woman said.

Hayley spun around and gasped. The towering, thin, blond Amazon, who was rocking a bright red Herve Leger Sarai sleeveless dress that had to have set her back at least a grand, was Carol Kay. Hayley knew from Penelope that she was going to be a guest this weekend, but now that she was face-to-face with her, Hayley couldn't help but be starstruck.

"Thank you," Hayley managed to choke out before an ill-timed giggle escaped her lips.

"I love the color. So elegant and understated. Mine is so bright it might as well come with an exclamation point!" Carol laughed.

"No, it's beautiful," Hayley said. "It looks perfect on you."

"I'm Carol Kay. I don't think we've met before," she said, holding out her small, bony, freshly moisturized hand.

Hayley pumped it excitedly. "Hayley Powell."

"Oh, yes. Penelope told me all about you. You write those cute little columns in the *Island Herald*."

"*Island Times*. The *Bar Harbor Herald* is our competition."

"Well, I looked you up online to see who I would be competing against this weekend in the celebrity potluck contest."

"I'm strictly an amateur, just here filling in for a no-show, so you have absolutely nothing to worry about."

"I disagree. I thought a few of your recipes were creative and inspired, straight from the heart of a genuine food lover with a fervent imagination."

"There's no question I love food. I was barely able to squeeze into this dress," Hayley said with a smile.

"Yes, and we both know *why*," Carol said, frowning.

Hayley suddenly didn't like where this was going. "We do?"

"As fun and inventive as your recipes are, the bulk of them are loaded with sugar and carbohydrates. Eating too many carbs is like catching the express train to obesity and type 2 diabetes."

"I like to think that trying a little bit of everything is okay as long as you practice moderation," Hayley argued.

"No, sweetie, I'm afraid it's not," Carol said in a singsong voice, shaking her head, as if speaking to a confused and ignorant child. "You should know better as a published food columnist. All kinds of people are reading and trying your recipes. People with heart disease and high blood sugar and slow metabolisms. You have a responsibility not to push them into an early grave."

Hayley nodded. "I guess I never really thought about it. I just write recipes for dishes I've enjoyed over the years."

"Then you should be grateful you're not starring in that TV show *My 600 Pound Life*," Carol said. "Everyone eventually pays a heavy price for their uninformed food choices. You really should order a few of my books on Amazon. I think you may discover a whole new world that could change your life."

Carol Kay then turned her back on Hayley and breezed off, waving as she approached Gerard and gave him a two-cheek air kiss.

Hayley stood there, still concentrating on remaining upright in her fancy pumps, suddenly feeling miserable and fat and no longer an unabashed fan of healthy food expert Carol Kay.

Hayley noticed a plate of crab-stuffed mushrooms on the table near where Gerard Roquefort was standing. Being chastised for her cooking and eating habits only made Hayley more hungry, so she made a beeline for the table. She grabbed a mushroom off the plate and, popping it in her mouth, quickly realized the stuffed mushroom was piping hot and burning the inside of her mouth.

She didn't dare spit the mushroom out, so she started to chew it as fast as she possibly could.

Unfortunately she swallowed too soon and the mushroom went down the wrong pipe.

Now she was coughing and gagging and sputtering.

Gerard Roquefort turned to see what all the commotion was about. Realizing she was half choking, he quickly handed her his glass of champagne. She gratefully gulped it down, and after a little more hacking and wheezing, managed to finally regain her composure.

"Are you all right?" Gerard asked with genuine concern.

Hayley nodded. "Yes, thank you."

She was supremely embarrassed.

"Gerard Roquefort," he said, eyeing her up and down.

"Yes, of course. I know who you are," Hayley said, her voice raspy, as she watched the ends of his mustache go up and down as he spoke.

"And this is my son Tristan," he said, gesturing to the young man standing close behind his father's left shoulder.

"Hello," Tristan said, barely interested.

Tristan was focused on a small camera crew setting up to shoot the dinner for the celebrity potluck episode of *Penelope's Cupboard*. A director of photography checked the camera, a soundman adjusted his boom mic, and a production assistant scribbled on a film slate.

Tristan maneuvered his way toward them to make sure he was in the center of the first shot.

Penelope's producer scuttled around the room

to make sure everyone was placed properly and on camera, and after a few quick instructions to just act naturally and pretend the camera wasn't even there, the cameraman yelled "Rolling!" the director called "Action!" and Penelope Janice swept into the room dressed to the nines in her own Diane Von Furstenberg original, her flaming-red hair styled in a chic chignon.

"Welcome everyone! I am so happy you could join us for our third annual 'Fourth of July Celebrity Potluck Celebration'! We have some heavy hitters in the house, so this year's competition promises to be one for the history books."

Sneaking in behind her, his presence obvious from the strong tobacco smell from the pipe he smoked, was Penelope's husband Conrad. As he puffed on his pipe, he held Sebastian in his arms. The cat was clearly spooked by the lights and cameras and lasted only about twenty seconds in Conrad's grip before he scratched Conrad's arm and wriggled free, landing on all fours on the floor before scurrying out of the room.

Hayley noticed Tristan inching his way closer to Penelope so he would be prominently featured in the shot. It was obvious the ambitious Tristan was fiercely determined not to remain forever in his famous father's shadow.

After some canned pleasantries and obviously scripted moments between the big-name chefs for the camera, Penelope ushered her guests into the dining room to take their seats for the seven-course dinner about to be served.

Hayley grimaced as she was seated between Conrad and Carol. She prayed Conrad would have the good manners to ditch the pipe during dinner and she dreaded health-nut Carol would closely watch everything she ate throughout the entire meal.

A simple clam chowder was served first, much to the delight of everyone. But before they could dig in, their attention was drawn to the dining-room entrance, where a dark-haired beauty in a tight-fitting black dress, unusual for Maine in the summer, stood awkwardly.

Hayley instantly recognized her.

It was Lena Hendricks, Penelope's assistant and suspected ghostwriter.

Penelope's mouth dropped open in surprise.

Conrad was busy slurping his chowder off his soupspoon and didn't notice her at first.

"Lena, *what* are you doing here?"

"Um, I was invited," Lena said, eyeing the extra place setting at the end of the table, but not yet making a move to sit down with the others.

"You *were?*" Penelope asked evenly, her face as red as her hairstyle. She turned to her husband, who absentmindedly wiped his mouth with a white cloth napkin.

"Darling, don't you remember? We discussed this. I suggested we have Lena join us for the weekend because I don't want you running yourself ragged, handling everything by yourself. I thought you could use the extra help," Conrad said, making a big point of smiling in front of the camera.

"Yes, I remember. I just didn't think she was going to join us for meals—"

"Well, the poor girl has to eat," Conrad said, laughing before turning to all of the guests seated around the table. "Am I right, everybody?"

There were a few titters and nods.

Penelope quickly regained control of her emotions, not wishing to appear as some kind of strong-willed, jealous wife on camera. "Yes. Of course. Please, Lena, sit down and introduce yourself to everyone."

Lena did as she was told.

There was a palpable tension in the air for the rest of the dinner.

Hayley dealt with the friction the best way she knew how.

By eating.

Everything that was put in front of her.

A shrimp salad.

A full one-and-a-half-pound lobster.

A rich buttery corn on the cob.

And mussels.

Lots of delicious steamed mussels.

They were Hayley's weak spot.

She loved mussels.

It became the big joke at the table.

Everyone watched and enjoyed Hayley gleefully scarf down her mussels.

Her gluttony certainly brought a little levity to

the table and relieved some of the tension from Lena's clearly unwanted presence.

Even Carol Kay lost her judgmental look for a little while.

Conrad mercifully refrained from smoking his pipe throughout most of the meal, but alas, he couldn't help himself once dessert was served.

Hayley wanted to pinch her nose shut with her fingers, but instead she just held her breath as the puffs of smoke wafted past her face and up her nostrils.

The hired waiter, who had brought out all the previous courses, served blueberry pie and coffee to everyone except Hayley, who wondered if she was finally being cut off.

But then, Clara Beaumont appeared and set another large plate of mussels down in front of Hayley as her dessert.

The camera moved in for a close-up of Hayley's surprised reaction.

"Okay! I love mussels! Guilty as charged!" Hayley said, her face blushing as she raised her hand.

Everyone at the table burst into guffaws.

"I'm sorry, Hayley, I couldn't resist!" Penelope said, laughing. "Please don't feel as if you have to eat them. I had Clara serve them to you as a joke."

But Hayley was already diving into the mussels.

There was no way she was going to allow them to go to waste.

"You can just wrap up my blueberry pie to go," she said, tearing a slimy mussel out of its black salty shell, dipping it into some rich melted butter, and dropping it in her mouth.

Penelope stood up to address her guests. "Everyone, I have a little announcement to make."

The producer signaled the cameraman to wind his way around the table to get a two-shot of Penelope and Conrad.

"As you all know, I have recently been on a book tour for my latest, *Making Magic out of Leftovers . . .*"

There was spontaneous applause at the table.

Well, it wasn't really spontaneous, because the producer standing behind the cameraman started it by clapping her hands wildly, and everyone at the table just followed suit.

"During my travels I have talked to many of my fans, and they've all begged me to do a book on easy-to-make casseroles. Well, truth be told, casseroles are not exactly my specialty. I just can't seem to make a memorable one. But my beloved husband Conrad, believe it or not, is a master when it comes to whipping up a damn good tasty casserole, aren't you, dear?"

Conrad sat back in his chair and puffed on his pipe with a smug look on his face as he soaked up his wife's forced compliments.

Hayley noticed Penelope flinch slightly and followed her gaze over to Lena, who smiled warmly at Conrad. When Lena realized Penelope was staring right at her, she quickly averted her gaze to the blueberry pie in front of her and made a big show of cutting a piece with her small dessert fork.

Penelope returned her attention to her husband seated next to her and gently rested a hand on his shoulder. "Conrad and I have struck a new deal with my publisher. We are going to co-author a book together that will be out next year on how to impress your friends with the perfect casserole!"

All of the guests applauded warmly.

"We welcome any thoughts you creative types may have for a title this weekend," Penelope added before taking her seat again and sipping her coffee.

"That's such a great idea," Hayley said to Conrad, seated to her left. "I *love* casseroles!"

Conrad nodded but didn't verbally respond.

He just blew pipe smoke in her face.

Hayley then turned to her right to see Carol literally counting the number of discarded empty mussel shells in the large wooden bowl that had been placed in front of Hayley.

Yes, she was literally counting how many mussels Hayley had eagerly consumed.

Hayley officially despised Carol Kay at this point, and was going to unfollow her Facebook fan page immediately.

Chapter 4

The rest of the evening was a blur.

An after-dinner cognac.

Lots of conversations about the rigors, trials, and demands of having your own cable network television show. Hayley had nothing to contribute to this topic so she just stood by quietly, nodding and smiling and occasionally choking on Conrad Janice's oppressive pipe smoke.

Finally, as the clock struck eleven, the guests began retiring to their rooms. Hayley, who had been stifling her yawns for nearly an hour, was relieved that her first night at Penelope Janice's estate was finally coming to a close. She was tired and cranky from Carol Kay's obnoxious digs, and her belly was so stuffed she wondered how she would ever sleep through the night.

Gerard Roquefort bounded off to bed, and Conrad lit his pipe and headed out to the porch. Carol had turned in almost an hour ago so she could be up early for her morning yoga routine, and Penelope had made a warm speech about how happy she was to be hosting such an esteemed group of culinary dignitaries before saying good night and hurrying off to the kitchen.

In the parlor, Tristan Roquefort was eagerly chatting up the lovely young Lena Hendricks. Lena smiled politely at the aggressively smitten young man, but her mind was clearly somewhere else.

Hayley excused herself, although Tristan and Lena barely acknowledged her as she clattered out of the room, her high heels making a lot of noise on the hardwood floors. It was impossible to walk softly in Liddy's shoes so she just gave up.

She made her way up the grand staircase and was halfway to her room when she ran into Penelope ascending the back stairs that led up from the kitchen.

"I hope you enjoyed dinner, Hayley," Penelope said.

"Oh my God, I'm going to remember that meal for the rest of my life. I hope I didn't embarrass myself wolfing down all those steamed mussels."

"Of course not. You're a chef's dream guest. You have no pretenses and you don't hold back when it comes to enjoying good food."

"Which is why I have to periodically attend a Weight Watchers meeting," Hayley said.

Penelope chuckled.

Hayley noticed she was holding a glass of milk in her hand.

"My nightly ritual," Penelope said, taking a sip

from the glass. "Warm milk with a sprinkle of nutmeg. My mother used to serve me a glass every night before bed when I was a little girl. She said it would bring me sweet dreams. She was right for the most part. It's a habit I've never been able to give up."

"Thank you for inviting me, Mrs. Janice . . ."

Penelope raised an eyebrow.

"I mean Penelope. It's a real privilege to be here. And I hope my potluck dish doesn't disappoint."

"You wouldn't be here if I didn't think you could seriously compete with the other guests. One of these days I wouldn't be surprised if you have your own cooking show on the Flavor Network."

"Coming from you, that's a *huge* compliment!"

"Good night, Hayley."

"Good night," Hayley said as Penelope took another sip of her warm milk with nutmeg. "Sweet dreams."

Penelope smiled and padded off to her room.

Hayley turned to head off to her own bedroom, but got turned around and walked around for five minutes before she just happened to stumble across it.

The house was so big and confusing to navigate, but she wasn't going to start complaining about spending five days living in the lap of luxury.

After removing her makeup, she shimmied out of her designer dress, tossed off her shoes and rubbed her sore feet, and then slipped on a short lacy cream-colored nightgown and crawled into bed.

She lay there, stretched out under the plush goose-feather comforter, wide awake. Just as she feared, she was so full from eating so much at dinner she couldn't fall asleep. She tossed and turned, sighed, and tried counting dogs and cats because she was never a big fan of sheep.

Finally, she gave up, threw off the covers, and slipped on some khaki shorts, a bulky sweatshirt, and sneakers. Maybe a midnight stroll around the expansive property would help her digest and tire her out enough so she could finally get some shut-eye.

After a few minutes wandering around trying to find the main staircase that led down to the foyer, Hayley managed to get out the front door and into the crisp, breezy night air. The lush gardens were lit at night and as Hayley sauntered through them, she was awed by the beauty of her surroundings. She followed the sound of the crashing waves to a peak that overlooked the rocky Atlantic coast.

That's when she noticed Conrad Janice standing there at the cliff's edge, smoking his pipe.

"Good evening," she said over the din of the angry tide pushing its way toward the shoreline.

Conrad jumped, startled by her sudden presence. He swallowed some of his pipe smoke and coughed.

"I'm sorry. I didn't mean to startle you," Hayley said, reaching out to touch his arm. "Are you okay?"

Conrad nodded as he coughed and gagged some more and dropped his pipe on the ground.

"Would you like me to go back to the house and get you some water?"

Conrad shook his head, and then said in a wheezy, gravelly voice, "No, I'll be fine. Just give me a second."

He tried clearing his throat a few times until the hacking cough mercifully subsided.

"I didn't expect to find anyone out here so late at night," Hayley said.

"I always like to come out here before bed to free my mind from all of the day's stresses," Conrad said, bending over to retrieve his pipe and firing it up again with a lighter from his coat pocket.

"Congratulations on the new book," Hayley said.

Conrad laughed derisively. "Please. I can't cook a casserole to save my life."

"I don't understand."

Conrad was still a little drunk from consuming too much merlot at dinner and was probably a little looser and chattier than he might normally have been.

"That cookbook was all Penelope's idea. She's just humoring me."

"*Humoring* you?"

"Our working together on that silly book is just her way of keeping me busy because she knows when I have too much time on my hands, I tend to get into trouble."

Hayley didn't have to ask what kind of trouble.

She already knew from her eavesdropping earlier in the day that the trouble undoubtedly involved the gorgeous young assistant/ghostwriter Lena Hendricks.

Conrad suddenly realized he was probably talking too much. He sucked on his pipe, and then gruffly pushed past Hayley.

"Good night," he said, leaving her alone near the cliff as he marched back toward the house.

Island Food & Spirits
BY HAYLEY POWELL

Let me just get this out of the way. I love casseroles! As far back as I can remember there was always something about the combination of a number of different ingredients in one baking dish along with a cheesy topping or some kind of creamy sauce, baked and served hot and bubbly straight to the table, that just got me so excited!

As a kid whenever I waited impatiently in the kitchen for one of my Mom's casseroles to fully bake, I was a bundle of hyperactive energy. I kept asking, "When's it going to be done? When's it going to be done?"

My mother remarked that I was less enthusiastic about running downstairs to pore over the wrapped presents Santa placed under the tree on Christmas morning. That's because Santa never ever left behind a cheesy, gooey, big bowl of pure comfort food. Usually it was just ankle socks or a Barbie doll.

Those days from my childhood sparked my life-long love of collecting casserole recipes. I've written enough recipe cards over the years to write my own cookbook! Several volumes, in fact. Just on casseroles alone.

My friends thought I was crazy since none of

them loved casseroles like I did. They just associated the word with a slop of old brown aging meat and canned vegetables covered in a dark gravy that they were served at the dinner table when their mothers were too lazy to prepare a more elaborate meal.

When I was first married to my ex-husband Danny, money was tight, but I was good at making the few dollars we did have stretch at the grocery store and farmers' market so we lived on many casseroles during the early years of our marriage.

Luckily Danny truly loved all of my creations, and actually bragged to his buddies that I was the only person he knew who could make a plain old hamburger casserole taste like an expensive beef stew, the kind served at a fancy steakhouse.

So when we were at church one Sunday, and it was announced that the ladies of the congregation were planning to self-publish a casserole cookbook to raise money for new choir robes and needed people to submit their favorite recipes, I nearly screamed out loud. Actually I did scream out loud, which caused Reverend Staples to throw his bible in the air, barely missing the organist's head as it came crashing down.

Even more thrilling was the announcement that the church would host a benefit supper in two weeks. Anyone who wanted to participate could bring their own casserole for the congregation to taste and vote on a winner that would be featured on the front cover of the cookbook. There was also a cash prize of one hundred dollars! Danny nearly screamed out loud at that one himself. Okay, he did, which caused Reverend Staples to lose his bible again just after he picked it up off the floor.

The next two weeks were a beehive of activity at

my house as I tried to narrow down my casserole choices to my top favorites. I enlisted the help of my friends and family, who were asked to taste the casserole of the day and give me a thumbs-up or thumbs-down.

Finally, only two days before the church supper, I was down to two choices—my Overnight Summer Breakfast Casserole and my Summer Vegetable Chicken Pot Pie Casserole.

I was torn. Both had received high marks from everyone, but they were split evenly on which one should be entered into the competition.

So I did what any native Bar Harbor resident would do.

I packed up both casseroles, paper plates, and plastic forks and drove straight to the Bar Harbor Police and Fire Department. I filled each plate with a heaping helping of each casserole and proceeded to pass them out to everyone working there that day, including the dispatcher, all the firemen and police officers on duty, the two local female painters hired to repaint the fire chief's office, and even one beloved local (I won't mention his name) who had a small mishap the night before and was spending the night in the jail cell for disorderly conduct.

I paced nervously around the freshly washed fire trucks parked inside the big bay on the fire department side of the building, anxiously awaiting a verdict.

Finally, the police dispatcher, Sharon, came in with my two empty casserole dishes and announced that the winner by a landslide was my Overnight Summer Breakfast Casserole.

On the day of the benefit I needed to be at the church an hour before the supper started so I loaded everything I needed into the car. My two best friends Liddy and Mona showed up at my house to wish me luck. They would join me later along with Danny and a couple of his buddies, who were at the house watching a ball game and snacking on my casserole leftovers.

Everyone came out to the front lawn to see me off, and crossing my fingers tightly hoping for a big win, I climbed in the car, turned up the radio, and backed out of the driveway.

I had a good feeling, and already was mentally picturing my breakfast casserole on the front cover of the cookbook, not to mention a hundred dollars in my pocket that I planned to use to buy that new set of pots and pans I had been eyeing in the Sears catalog for almost a year.

I waved to my neighbors who were out in their yards cheering me on, and glancing in the rearview mirror as I drove off, I saw all of my friends, my neighbors, my husband, my kids, all jumping up and down and waving their arms in the air. It choked me up that I had such strong support.

When I arrived at the church and began to unload, I froze suddenly because I didn't see my casserole that I was sure I had carefully placed in the backseat. I must have left it at home!

Just as I was rummaging through my L.L. Bean tote bag for my cell phone to call my husband and have him bring it, I heard a familiar truck horn honking, and turned with relief to see Danny, Liddy, and Mona pulling in to the church parking lot. They must have seen the casserole sitting on the kitchen counter where I had left it and raced over to deliver it to me before the contest.

I thanked them profusely as they all climbed out

of the truck, but their faces told me they hadn't brought my prize-winning casserole.

My heart sank.

Something bad must have happened and they didn't want to tell me.

"Did your bonehead friends eat my casserole, Danny? I will tear them limb from limb, I swear!"

Danny raised a hand. "Nobody ate your casserole. You left it on the roof of your car, and since you had your music turned up, you could see us waving but you couldn't hear us yelling at you to stop! When you turned the corner at Park Street it flew off the roof and splattered all over the sidewalk."

There was momentary silence as it dawned on me that my dream of being featured on the front cover of the church cookbook (not to mention my brand-new set of stainless steel pots and pans) was fast disappearing.

At least I could still turn in my recipe card so my casserole could be included, but for me, the competition was officially over.

On a happier note, my recipe was featured on page five and I received many compliments from a number of locals who tried it out and loved the results! Oh, and one more thing, under the Christmas tree that year I found a brand-new set of stainless steel pots and pans straight from the Sears catalog with no name on the tag. But I think I know a couple of elves who may have been involved.

This week I'll be sharing my Overnight Summer Breakfast Casserole, but first, how about a yummy cocktail to get you in the mood? Last summer my brother Randy and his husband Sergio hosted two very good friends named Ivan Jackson and Stephen Jenkins, who traveled all the way over from Bristol,

England. I had the four of them over for a brunch and served my delicious (if I do say so myself) breakfast casserole. Well, the Brits were in charge of the cocktails, and Ivan made us the most scrumptious drink called the Aviation. I can honestly say that after enjoying a couple of them, I was certainly ready for takeoff myself!

Ivan and Stephen's Aviation Cocktail

2 ounces gin
½ ounce maraschino liqueur
¼ ounce lemon juice
Dash of crème de violette

Shake all ingredients in a cocktail shaker and strain into a cocktail glass.

Overnight Summer Breakfast Casserole

1 pound ground sweet Italian sausage
½ large sweet onion, diced
1 cup sliced mushrooms
2 cloves garlic, minced
3 cups frozen shredded hash browns
2 cups shredded sharp cheddar cheese, divided
1 small green bell pepper, diced
1 small red pepper, diced
12 eggs
2 cups milk
1½ teaspoons dried parsley
1½ teaspoons dried basil
¼ teaspoon cayenne
1 teaspoon freshly ground pepper
1 teaspoon salt

Cook your sausage, onions, peppers, mushrooms, and garlic in a large skillet over medium heat, stirring occasionally to break up your sausage into crumbles. Cook until sausage is no longer pink. Remove from heat and drain any liquid and set aside.

Spray a 13-by-9-inch baking dish with cooking spray and place your hash browns evenly over the bottom of the pan (you do not have to defrost the frozen hash browns). Next spread your sausage mixture evenly over the hash browns.

Crack all the eggs into a large bowl and add your milk, parsley, basil, cayenne, salt, and pepper and whisk until well combined. Now pour your egg mixture over the ingredients in your baking dish. At this point cover with plastic wrap and place in the refrigerator overnight.

When ready to bake in the morning remove the casserole from the refrigerator and preheat your oven to 375°F. Bake the casserole 60–70 minutes, until eggs are set and a butter knife inserted in the middle comes out clean. Let cool 10 minutes. Slice, serve, and enjoy at a leisurely brunch with good food and good friends!

Chapter 5

When Hayley suddenly awoke, she couldn't breathe.

There was something on her face suffocating her.

Like a furry pillow being held tightly over her nose and mouth.

Was someone trying to kill her?

In a panic, she coughed and sputtered and reached up to grab at her assailant, but her hands just sliced through empty air. She then focused on the heavy weight on top of her face. As she came in contact with a long tail that was swishing around, she grabbed the end of it and yanked hard. There was a screech as the big, woolly blob quickly detached from her face, finally allowing her to breathe.

Hayley quickly flipped on the light next to her on the nightstand, and immediately made eye contact with a giant white Persian cat who did not at all seem pleased to have been so violently roused from his peaceful slumber.

"Seriously, Sebastian, you couldn't just curl up next to me? You had to pick my face as your cat bed?"

Sebastian sized her up with his big brilliant copper eyes that seemed to say, "*Please, you should feel lucky I chose you for my company tonight.*"

Hayley couldn't deny that he was a beautiful cat. He certainly knew it himself, given his spoiled attitude and entitled demeanor.

She reached over and scratched Sebastian gently underneath the chin and then behind his left ear.

He seemed to enjoy that, closing his eyes and emitting a soft purr.

She noticed the door was open a crack, which had allowed Sebastian to enter after she had fallen asleep. She must not have closed it all the way when she came back to bed after getting some fresh air and running into Conrad.

"So I take it we're going to be roommates for the weekend," Hayley said, petting his soft luxuriant coat of white fur.

Sebastian answered in the affirmative by walking in a circle and then plopping down at the foot of the bed, lifting a leg, and giving himself a tongue bath one more time before going back to sleep.

Hayley smiled at his determination to keep himself clean.

And then she was overcome with an abrupt wave of nausea.

She felt the bile quickly rising in her throat, and

she clasped a hand over her mouth to keep it from spurting out all over the expensive comforter.

She managed to keep it down and get control of it momentarily.

Hayley slowly lay back down, flat on her back, and stared at the ceiling for a few minutes, hoping it might pass.

A summer fever was the worst.

And of all times to be hit with it, the one weekend she had been invited to a posh celebrity powwow at her heroine Penelope Janice's swanky estate.

Maybe it was nothing.

Just a fleeting queasiness.

It could just be nerves.

She had been slightly worried about competing in the potluck contest.

After all, she was a rank amateur among a cadre of world-class master chefs.

Yes, she was sure of it.

Just a case of the nerves.

But then she started shivering and shaking.

Sweat beads drizzled down her cheek from her forehead.

And suddenly the nausea returned like an unforgiving destructive tsunami on an unsuspecting quiet seaside village.

The mussels.

She was the only one at dinner who had gorged on that last plate of steamed mussels.

She must have eaten one that was spoiled.

She had downed them so fast and vigorously it

was hardly surprising she didn't have the time to thoroughly inspect each one before dousing it in butter and popping it in her mouth.

As she threw off the thick silken comforter, which covered Sebastian much to his extreme consternation, Hayley jumped out of bed, tossed on her powder-blue bathrobe, and raced for the door, banging her foot on a wooden dresser on her way.

She yelped in pain, but didn't have time to inspect her throbbing toe.

She needed to find a toilet pronto.

As the least important VIP staying at the house this weekend, she was the only guest who was assigned a room without an attached bathroom.

Hayley threw open the door and hurled herself out into the hallway in search of a bathroom somewhere in this vast, cavernous house.

She guessed left, but halfway down the hall she found herself at a dead end with no bathroom in sight. She reversed course and hurried back down the hall, past her room, and around a corner that led her to the staircase. She had noticed a half bath just off the foyer as she entered the front door of the house when she first arrived.

Hayley rushed headlong down the stairs, her hand thrown protectively across her stomach as if commanding it not to give up just yet, and as she reached the foyer, she breathed a heavy sigh of relief as she spotted the familiar-looking door that led to the half bath. She dashed inside, feeling around with her hands, unable to find the light switch.

She was out of time.

Hayley dropped to her knees, one hand over her mouth as she removed her other hand from her belly to grab the wooden toilet seat cover that she could just make out from the moonlight streaming through a tiny leaded window above the small sink.

She raised the lid and it banged against the porcelain tank and she quickly dropped her head inside the bowl.

When she was finished, she weakly washed her face and hands, drying herself off with a pink towel next to the basin, and leaned against the wall to catch her breath before heading back upstairs.

As she retraced her steps back to her bedroom, she suddenly overheard two voices, a man and a woman, whispering in the dark.

"I love you. You know I would do anything for you," the man said

"Even murder?" the woman whispered.

"I said *anything*."

"How do you plan on getting rid of her?"

"She won't suffer. I'll make it as painless as possible."

"And you're sure she doesn't suspect?"

"No, she's completely clueless," the man said, chuckling. "You know what they say, the wife is always the last to know."

It was like a movie.

Well, not a good one.

Not one you would go to see in the theater with big stars like Ryan Gosling and Emma Stone.

No, this was more like one of those Lifetime movies starring vaguely recognizable actors from a daytime soap opera.

And Hayley had spent many Sunday afternoons binge-watching dozens of those with a big bowl of buttered popcorn on her lap as she stretched out in her living-room recliner.

Except this wasn't a cheesy TV movie. This was real and actually happening.

And it was not a joke. These two sounded deadly serious.

"You better get back to your room before she notices how long you've been gone," the woman said in a hushed whisper.

Suddenly Hayley was overcome by a nasty odor, like a strong tobacco.

The man was puffing on a pipe, and the smoke had floated its way over to her nostrils. She threw a hand over her mouth as the vile smell nauseated her all over again.

Hayley pressed herself against the wall as much as she could and held her breath. She knew if the man suddenly came bounding around the corner he would bump right into her.

She prayed he would walk off in the opposite direction.

She heard a smacking, slurping sound.

The man was sucking the woman's face like a Hoover vacuum.

It must have gone on for almost a minute before he stopped and finally pulled away from her.

"Sweet dreams," he said softly.

"Of course. I'll be dreaming of *you*," the woman cooed.

Hayley rolled her eyes, but then immediately squeezed them shut, praying she would not be suddenly discovered.

But she wasn't.

Luck was on her side.

The man headed off in another direction.

The woman waited until he was gone and then sighed, and sailed right past Hayley, not turning the corner, but instead hurrying off toward the other end of the wing, never even realizing she was standing there.

She waited a few seconds making sure the coast was clear before scampering off to her room where she found Sebastian waiting for her on the bed, blinking, trying to assess her condition without showing her he cared too much.

Hayley crawled into bed, her body wrecked and tired from all the heaving and running back and forth from her room to the bathroom downstairs.

She tried to think about what she had overheard in the hallway.

Had she just imagined it?

She was, after all, overcome with fever, and hallucinations are not uncommon when you are running a high temperature.

But before she could come to any conclusions, she drifted off into a deep sleep, her stomach settling down at least for the moment, with Sebastian nestled next to her head, having inched his way up from the foot of the bed.

Chapter 6

Hayley awoke with a start, choking and gagging, unable to breathe.

Sebastian was once again perched on top of her face.

She shoved him off her, and he skittered back to the foot of the bed with a low growl, unhappy over being so rudely awakened as she spit out cat hair.

"Are you actually *trying* to smother me to death? Is that your plan?" Hayley asked, suddenly embarrassed that she was accusing a cat of nefariously plotting her demise.

She suddenly remembered the events from last night.

Desperately searching for a bathroom.

Stumbling upon the whispered conversation of a mysterious disembodied couple, who were in the midst of hatching a treacherous plot to off the man's poor unsuspecting wife.

She knew in her bones it was Penelope's husband Conrad from the foul smell of his pipe. The woman was obviously Lena Hendricks. It was quite clear to even the most casual observer that there was friction in the marriage, and that the focal point of their discontent was the attractive young assistant/ghostwriter.

Hayley slid out of the bed and threw on some jeans and a sweatshirt as she contemplated her next move.

She checked the clock on the nightstand.

It was early.

Only six thirty.

Most of the other guests were probably still sleeping.

She was feeling much better. Her debilitating food-poisoning symptoms had mostly subsided. Her body was still in a weakened state and she was still mind-numbingly tired, but the nausea was finally gone.

Hayley sat on the edge of the bed as she debated with herself what she should do. Sebastian stared glumly at her, disappointed not to have her face as a sleeping cushion.

Should she go directly to Penelope and inform her about what she had overheard?

Maybe she should call the police?

Or would the wise thing to do be to confront Conrad and Lena directly?

Hayley sighed, not sure which option would be the best one.

She had been dreadfully sick while she bumbled about in the night, lost in the dark.

Perhaps she had hallucinated the whole incident.

But it seemed so real. The pipe smoke was so strong.

No, it had *not* been some kind of fever dream. It had actually happened. She was certain of it.

Hayley made a decision.

She grabbed her cell phone and called her brother Randy's house. It rang a few times before Randy answered and groaned groggily, "Hello?"

"Randy, I'm sorry to call you so early, but it's very important."

"It better be," he barked. "I was at the bar until two in the morning and I just got to sleep."

"Can I speak to Sergio?"

"Hold on. He's just coming out of the shower."

Hayley waited, glancing over at Sebastian, who wasn't even mildly curious as to what she was doing.

"Hayley, what's wrong?" Sergio asked in his deep Brazilian-accented voice.

Randy's husband Sergio Alvares was Bar Harbor's chief of police.

And in her opinion, the perfect person to get some advice from at the moment.

"Good morning, Sergio, I hate to bother you. I know you're very busy, but I need to talk to you. I want . . . gosh, I really don't know how to say this, but I want to report a crime."

"What kind of crime?"

"A murder."

"What?" Sergio gasped. "Where are you?"

"I'm at Penelope Janice's estate in Seal Harbor."

"Who is the victim?"

"Penelope Janice, I think."

"You think? Did you see the body?"

"No. She's not dead. Yet."

"Hayley, you are not making any sense."

"I know! I'm just really nervous. I overheard Penelope's husband and her assistant talking in the hallway last night, and I believe they are going to try and kill her."

"So this crime you want to report hasn't happened yet?"

"That's correct."

"But you're sure it was Penelope's husband and assistant you heard in the hallway."

"Yes. Absolutely. I think."

"What do you mean you *think*? You cannot call me at six in the morning and report a murder conspiracy and not be one hundred percent certain about your information."

"Well, you see, I had some bad mussels last night at dinner and I was running a fever and not thinking clearly, and so there is a slight chance I imagined the whole thing, but I'm pretty sure I didn't because the memory is so vivid and the pipe smell was so strong."

"Pipe smell?"

"Conrad smokes a pipe."

"I see."

"I know this sounds crazy, Sergio, and I apologize for dragging you into this, but if I'm right, and what I overheard actually happened, then Penelope's life could be in danger and I would never forgive myself if something happened to her and I didn't say anything."

"I understand your concern. You did the right thing by calling me. You're being a concerned Cinnabon."

Hayley paused, chewing on that one.

Cinnabon.

The baked goods chain that sold various kinds of frosted cinnamon rolls.

What did that have to do with . . . ?

"Oh, you mean citizen! Concerned citizen!"

"That's what I said," Sergio said, annoyed.

Sergio's first language was Portuguese, so on rare occasions he had a habit of mixing up his words.

Okay, full disclosure, it wasn't so rare.

It happened all the time.

"So what do you think I should do?" Hayley asked.

"Did you talk to Penelope?"

"No. I decided to call you first. I mean, I don't even know what I would say to her! Something like, 'Good morning, Penelope, may I have a little cream for my coffee? And oh by the way, your husband of twenty-six years wants to kill you!' It sounds so absurd!"

"Let me get dressed and drive over there. I can be there in half an hour. Wait for me outside and then we will go speak to Penelope together."

"Thank you, Sergio. You're a peach."

"I know I am gay, Hayley, but you do not have to call me a fruit."

"No, it's just a term of endearment, it doesn't mean anything derogatory."

"Crazy Americans," he barked as he hung up.

True to his word, thirty minutes later Sergio was pulling up in front of the main house in his police cruiser where Hayley waited for him outside in the morning cold.

He stepped out, the two of them hugged, and then they went to find Penelope. It was still early and the house was eerily quiet, but they did happen upon one of the household staff, who pointed them in the direction of the kitchen.

When they arrived, they found Penelope in jeans and a blue plaid flannel shirt with the sleeves rolled up and a white apron tied around her waist, chopping vegetables, while her devoted cook Clara spiced some meat at a food station behind her.

Penelope looked up at Hayley and smiled. "My, you're up early, Hayley!"

She suddenly noticed Sergio hovering behind Hayley in his police uniform. "Good morning, Chief."

"Morning, Mrs. Janice," Sergio said grimly, nodding.

"Since when do you require a police escort, Hayley?" Penelope asked, curious as Clara glared at her just behind Penelope's left shoulder.

"I was hoping we might be able to speak privately," Hayley whispered, glancing at Clara, who

s a dream, Hayley," Penelope said, shaking
l. "You woke up with a fever and you were
ted."

sidered that possibility, really I did, but
s that horrible smell, the same odor that
om Conrad's pipe, it was so heavy, and I
lidn't imagine *that*," Hayley said.

e it *you* believe her fantastical story?" Penel-
d Sergio pointedly, almost implying that
t not be sending her annual check to the
epartment's charitable foundation this

, Hayley is a very reliable witness, and I
e remiss if I did not follow up on every
receive . . . although this one did sound a
fetched, I must admit," Sergio said, throwing
n apologetic look.

y wasn't mad at Sergio for practically throw-
nder the bus. She knew Penelope wielded
nfluence, and there was the matter of town
o be considered.

, I appreciate you coming all the way out
ief Alvares, but let me assure you, there is
to her story. Conrad was with me in our
n all night. He never left. I'm a very light
I wake up when he stirs even slightly next
would have known if he tried to sneak out
ret rendezvous."

," Sergio said, eyeing Hayley.

f it would make you both feel better, I think
ld go talk to Conrad directly, just to clear

sneered before pounding the slab of meat harder
with her fist.

"I'm sorry, Hayley, I have a houseful of guests, a
TV show to get in the can, and a lunch menu to
prepare. Every minute is precious so whatever you
need to talk to me about, you're just going to have
to do it here."

Hayley hesitated, glancing at Sergio, who nodded,
encouraging her to just spit it out.

Hayley cleared her throat and said softly, "I had
food poisoning from a bad mussel last night and—"

Penelope nearly sliced off her finger with the
knife she was using to chop her vegetables. "*What
did you say?*"

"I had food poisoning . . ."

Penelope whipped her head around and glared
icily at Clara.

The suddenly nervous cook raised her wet oily
hands from the meat and stammered, "I inspected
all the mussels myself before serving them! I swear
there wasn't a bad one in the batch!"

Penelope stared daggers at Clara and hissed,
"Well, obviously you missed one if that's what made
Hayley sick!"

Clara glowered at Hayley, who shifted uncomfortably.

Penelope turned back to Hayley, her face full of
concern. "Are you sure it was food poisoning, dear,
and not just some horrid stomach flu?"

"Well, I can't be sure, but no one else seems to
have been affected that we know of, and I was the
only one who ate that last plate of mussels."

"You're right about one thing," Clara hissed. "You *can't* be sure!"

"Clara, please," Penelope sighed, signaling her cook to shut up and get back to work.

Clara pounded her meat some more, keeping a watchful eye on Hayley, her disdain painfully obvious.

"I am mortified that anyone would get food poisoning dining at my house. I would appreciate your discretion, Hayley, because if anyone were to find out . . ."

"Of course. I have no intention of telling anybody. That's not why we're here."

Penelope smiled at Sergio, almost flirtatiously. "Good. I would hate to think the chief was here to arrest me for serving a bad mussel."

"The mussels weren't bad! I checked every shell before I put them in the steamer!" Clara cried, agitated her reputation was now on the line.

"That's enough, Clara!" Penelope said sternly before adopting a more cheery tone. "Now what seems to be the problem?"

Hayley recounted what she heard.

All of it.

Every last detail.

Penelope listened, her face a mask of calm though the veins in her neck began to noticeably pop out. She was obviously a master of controlling her emotions, but it was inevitable a few clues to how she was really feeling on the inside would manifest themselves.

When Hayley finished, there in the kitchen.

Clara had stopped pounding stood there, mouth agape.

Sergio stood quietly next to

Hayley held her breath, waiti do something, say something, sta ing, maybe throw a few pots and the enormity of her husband's began to sink in.

But she did none of that.

She just stood there, staring i over what she had just heard.

And then she began to laugh.

Really hard.

Her face turned beet red, and howling, gripping the side of her she wouldn't collapse to the floo in a fit of unabated giggles.

This was not exactly the rea Sergio had been expecting.

When she finally got contro scooped up a dish towel from the it to wipe the tears away from he

"I take it you don't believe Hay said, a stoic look on his face.

"Believe it? It's the most prep ever heard!" Penelope wailed, n with Clara, who had a tight smi sure what she should do at this

"I know I was sick and not con mind at the time, but it felt very

"It w her he disorie

"I c there v came know I

"I ta ope as she mi police year.

"We would repor little f Hayle

Hay ing he a lot o politic

"We here, nothin bedro sleepe to me. for a s

"I s

"Bu we sho

up this whole matter now so there are no further misunderstandings this weekend," Penelope said firmly.

"Yes, I think that would be a good idea," Sergio said. "And I want to personally thank you for your cooperation."

"Well, you know I'm a big fan of the police department, and specifically you, Chief. You have such an inspiring life story. Traveling all the way here from Brazil with just the shirt on your back, working your way up from dispatcher to chief of police. Very impressive," she said, touching him on the arm like a high school cheerleader trying to snag the star quarterback. "Let's go find my husband, shall we?"

Sergio took her gently by the arm like a military escort serving as a consort at a debutante ball, and the two of them glided out of the room, leaving Hayley behind.

It was official.

She had now lost the whole room.

Nobody believed her.

Hayley glanced over at Clara, who stood there, grinning, relishing Hayley's utter humiliation.

Chapter 7

"This is outrageous!" Conrad spit out, his cheeks red with fury, his eyes blazing. "How on earth did you come up with that wild story, Ms. Powell? I thought you only wrote recipes! Are you some kind of aspiring author hoping to pen the next *Fifty Shades of Grey* or something silly like that?"

Hayley stood silently by as Conrad berated her and tried to embarrass her in front of Penelope and Sergio on the back porch of the main house with sweeping views of the quiet harbor and dark blue Atlantic beyond.

He was taking Hayley's accusation about as well as she had expected.

It didn't help that Penelope had barged in on him sunning himself while having his coffee and browsing headlines on his mini iPad on the porch, and without any sort of gentle run-up, simply announced "Hayley thinks you're going to murder me! What do you have to say for yourself?"

His wife's sudden and unexpected pronouncement had caused him to spill his coffee all down the front of his white polo shirt. After angrily wiping himself off, Conrad clamored to his feet to face his accuser.

"Murder? What are you talking about?"

"Are you conspiring to do away with me with your secret lover in order to take charge of my affairs and become the de facto head of my company?"

Conrad was speechless, eyeing Sergio nervously, assuming the police chief was there to place him under arrest.

But then Penelope burst into laughter, guffawing so hard, tears streamed down her cheeks.

Conrad failed to see the humor.

"I don't understand what's going on here," he growled.

Penelope was happy to bring him up to speed.

The bad mussels.

A nauseated Hayley wandering about in the dead of night in search of a bathroom and accidentally stumbling upon the hushed voices of a pair of wicked lovers scheming to free themselves of the harpy wife who was the only thing keeping them apart.

Conrad listened with rapt attention, eyes wide, horrified, his bottom lip quivering.

He finally raised his hand and bellowed, "I've heard enough!"

"It's a rather intriguing tale, wouldn't you say, Conrad?" Penelope said, watching her husband and loving the fact he was so discombobulated.

"It's pure fantasy! She's obviously making the whole thing up!" he cried, after finishing his tirade against Hayley.

"*Why* would she do that, dear?" Penelope said, sighing.

"I don't know! Maybe to get attention for herself or a juicy headline for that local rag she works for! Frankly I don't care why she did it, I just want her gone!"

Conrad moved menacingly in Hayley's direction as if he was going to eject her from the premises himself, and got so close to her Sergio casually stepped forward to send a clear message to Conrad to not even think about laying a hand on her.

Taking the hint, Conrad retreated. He fumbled in his pants pocket and pulled out his pipe. He flicked a lighter a few times before it finally lit up, and then he calmed down after taking a few laborious puffs.

He collected himself and then quietly said to his wife, "Did you tell them you're a light sleeper and that if I tried to sneak out you would have heard me?"

"Yes, I did," Penelope said calmly.

Conrad raised his eyes to face Hayley, who defiantly stood her ground.

She knew what she had heard, and she had no intention of backing down.

He stared menacingly at her, never blinking once.

"I don't know what kind of game you're playing, Ms. Powell," he seethed. "But I refuse to allow you to besmirch my reputation. I want you packed and out of this house in five minutes!"

"Darling, don't be such a drama queen!" Penelope cracked, before turning to Hayley and smiling. "He uses big words like besmirch when he's really angry."

Hayley tried hard not to smile.

But she couldn't stop the corners of her mouth from curling up just a bit and Conrad unfortunately caught it. She could almost see the steam blowing out of his ears as he stormed into the house, slamming the screen door behind him.

"Maybe he's right. I should go . . ." Hayley said softly.

"Nonsense. You're already part of my Fourth of July special and it's too late to replace you. I need you here. Besides, I believe you."

"You do? You believe Conrad wants to kill you?"

"God, no! Conrad isn't capable of planning a picnic let alone a murder. He's too stupid. And I say that with all the love in my heart. But I do believe you ate some bad mussels and were in a foggy state from the food poisoning and you heard *something* in that hallway, just not what you think. A feverish mind can sometimes play tricks on you."

"I'm just not sure I'm going to be comfortable around Conrad for the rest of the weekend . . ."

"I'll talk to him and make sure he behaves. Don't you worry about that. And if anyone tries to mess with you, I want you to come directly to me."

Hayley nodded. "Thank you for giving me the benefit of the doubt, Penelope."

Penelope gently touched Hayley on the arm and said warmly, "Anything for my number one fan."

And then she breezed inside the house, leaving Hayley on the porch with Sergio.

"Do you know what I think?" Sergio asked, ready to tell her whether she wanted to hear him or not.

"You think I should just go home and forget this whole thing."

"Yes! You're asking for trouble staying here. Penelope can not protect you twenty-four hours a day and that man now holds a grudge, and he is not going to make things easy on you. Why put yourself through that? Come over to our house instead. We will celebrate the holiday together and barbecue some steaks. Doesn't that sound like a lot more fun?"

"It's certainly tempting. Randy grills the most perfect steaks," Hayley said, wistfully picturing herself outside of this tornado of tension she was suddenly caught up in at this swanky estate.

She seriously thought about throwing in the towel but then she turned to Sergio. "I'm staying. What if what I heard wasn't a fever dream? What if it was real and Conrad is lying and once I'm out of the picture he and Lena manage to carry out their plan and Penelope winds up dead? I can't have that on my conscience, Sergio. I'm going to tough it out."

"Tuxedo yourself," he said, shrugging his shoulders.

"I'm sorry, what?" she asked, a puzzled look on her face.

"Do whatever you want."

"Yes, but that's not what you said. You said . . ."

It suddenly dawned on her.

"You mean suit yourself! It's suit yourself! But tuxedo is really close, Sergio. It totally makes sense when you think about it."

Sergio shook his head. "You confuse me, Hayley."

He ambled down the porch steps and around the side of the property toward the front where his police cruiser was parked.

Hayley headed back inside the house, mentally preparing herself for whatever trials were ahead of her, determined to prove that she was not some kind of crackpot conspiracy theorist.

She was convinced the pompous pipe-smoking Conrad was a bona fide would-be killer.

Chapter 8

Later that afternoon, Hayley was still feeling a bit under the weather. She was no longer battling nausea, but had been hit with a throbbing headache, probably from the overabundance of tension she had endured all morning confronting Penelope and then her tightly wound husband Conrad over what she had overheard the previous evening.

She rummaged around in her toiletry bag for some aspirin and caught a glimpse of herself in the full-length mirror across from the bed hanging on the wall. She looked drawn and tired and completely spent from her bout with food poisoning. She pulled the skin around her eyes back giving her a self–face lift and didn't look much better so she just let her face sag back into its normal position.

She was under too much stress.

That was the only reason she was looking prematurely old.

Yes, that had to be it.

If she was at home and relaxed she would absolutely look decades younger.

At least that's what she told herself.

And by golly, she was convincing.

Hayley still had an hour before she was to report to the kitchen to start the prep work for her potluck dish she was making for the competition so she decided to take another brief stroll around the property, as she had the night before, hoping the fresh air might do her some good.

It was a chilly day so she wrapped herself in a bulky white wool sweater and put on some long thick pants and sturdy sneakers, and set out along the gravel trail through the picturesque gardens and lush foliage.

The farther Hayley walked away from the house, the colder and breezier it became, especially as she got closer to the ocean. She folded her arms and squeezed tightly trying to keep warm. She was about to turn around and head back when she heard a woman laughing. She looked around and didn't see anyone nearby. She listened for a few more moments, and then heard the woman's cackle again. It was a rich, melodious laugh, flirtatious and feminine, and it was coming from behind a row of tall husky bushes.

Hayley inched her way closer to get a look at the woman laughing, squeezing herself between the bushes and creeping through in a crouch position, then lying flat on her stomach in order to peek through and observe what was going on without being seen.

On the other side of the bushes, near the cliff's edge that led down to the rocky coastline, she could see Lena Hendricks playfully slapping the arm of another man and giggling like a coquettish teenager.

But it wasn't Conrad.

She was cavorting, however innocently, with a much younger man, Tristan, the strikingly handsome son of celebrity chef Gerard Roquefort.

Hayley watched as Tristan suggestively took Lena's hand in his own as he entertained her with a story. She laughed at all the right places, and Hayley was close enough to see Tristan's eyes sparkling, mad with desire for this attractive, slightly older woman.

When he finished his story, Lena threw her head back and laughed again. He couldn't take it anymore. He slipped a hand around the back of her waist and pulled her to him, gently stroking her face with the palm of his other hand.

There was a moment of stillness as the two stared into each other's eyes, but then, Lena seemed to snap out of her reverie and gently extricated herself from his grasp. She took a few steps back, putting some safe distance between them.

Tristan looked confused and hurt, but tried to cover as Lena spoke softly to him.

Hayley strained to hear what she was saying, but a breeze had kicked up and it was drowning out the sound of their voices.

Behind her, on the other side of the bushes, she heard a man clearing his throat.

She froze, not daring to move, hoping that whoever was hanging about the row of bushes wouldn't see her.

No such luck.

She felt a strong finger tapping her on the back of her leg, which undoubtedly was sticking out of the bushes in plain view on the other side.

Hayley inched her way back out until she was able to stand up and brush the dirt off her sweater and pants.

"I'm curious to know what was so interesting on the other side of these bushes?" a familiar voice asked.

Hayley turned around and gasped. "Lex?"

Lex Bansfield smiled and nodded, tipping his ball cap like a true gentleman.

Lex had worked as a caretaker at several island estates over the years mostly because he was good at fixing things and making the properties look lush and pristine year-round.

He had a sterling reputation around town.

He was also Hayley's ex-boyfriend.

They had dated on and off for a couple of years before drifting apart and ultimately going their separate ways.

Still, she had many fond memories of their time together.

Her kids adored him and were both still in touch with him.

He would slip them some cash to help pay for schoolbooks and expenses, and once in Gemma's case, Hayley learned, even paid for a ski trip to Sugarloaf with some of her college pals.

Lex had many good qualities.

But he was a tough nut to crack.

He rarely allowed his emotions to surface, and that made it challenging for Hayley to know what he was thinking. And the frustration from that and the pressure of not knowing what was going on in his mind eventually caused them to break up.

"What are you doing here?" Hayley asked.

"I work here."

"Since when?"

"A few months. Got hired by Penelope herself. She said she liked my laid-back attitude and effortless charm."

"She said that?"

"Yup."

Well, it was undeniable that Lex Bansfield possessed both of those qualities, and he certainly knew how to turn them on when he needed to, especially in a job interview.

"Do you like working here?" she asked.

"Yeah, it's a good gig. The pay is decent and they pretty much leave me alone when they're here in residence, which is only a few months out of the year. The rest of the time, I run the place on my own."

"I'm so happy for you," Hayley said, adding quickly, "Really, I am."

Lex grinned. "You look good."

"Thanks," Hayley said, resisting the urge to pull

back the skin around her eyes with her fingers again to look a few precious years younger.

"So I heard through the grapevine you're no longer seeing the vet," Lex said casually, though the words dropped like a bomb.

"No, we tried awfully hard, but it just wasn't in the cards, you know how it goes," Hayley said.

"I sure do," Lex said wistfully.

There was an awkward silence.

Lex cleared his throat again.

Hayley stared down at her now mud-stained sneakers.

"So I'm single again," Hayley felt the need to add.

"Good to know," Lex said with a wink. "I better get back to work and leave you to your . . . spying."

"Oh, I'm not—!"

Lex gave her a withering look as if to say, *"Don't even try to con me. I know you too well."*

He tipped the visor of his ball cap one more time and trotted off to his pickup truck parked nearby with some gardening tools stacked in the back.

As he jumped in and pulled away, Hayley realized her headache was gone and she wasn't feeling so tense anymore.

Still, the air around her was filled with plenty of tension.

Only this kind of tension was more of a sexual nature.

Hayley sighed.

Like it or not, Lex Bansfield was back in her life.

Chapter 9

When Hayley arrived in the kitchen to start prepping her potluck dish, Spaghetti Pie Casserole, she was surprised to find all the necessary ingredients including noodles, ground beef, spicy Italian sausage, onion, cheese, garlic, and all of her required spices and vegetables for her homemade tomato sauce carefully laid out on the large island in front of the massive stove and oven. Penelope had reserved three whole hours for Hayley to have exclusive use of the kitchen with orders that she was not to be disturbed.

After a quick inventory to ensure she had everything she needed, she filled a pot with water and set it on the stove and fired up the burner full blast to get the water boiling for the pasta. Then, she greased a large pie pan with a stick of butter and set it aside and searched for a skillet to cook her meat.

She was just about to tear open the package of ground beef when she spotted Clara, wearing a dowdy coat and worn red hat, suitcase in hand, quietly heading for the back door, which led to the grounds outside.

"You off to do some food shopping, Clara?" Hayley asked.

Clara spun around and stared daggers at Hayley, fire in her eyes.

"No, I'm not off to do some food shopping," she said in a mocking tone. "I'm going home. I've been fired."

"What?"

"Well, what the hell did you expect to happen after you accused me of trying to poison you with bad mussels?"

"Penelope *fired* you? I don't believe it!"

"Not Penelope. Conrad," Clara spit out, barely able to contain her rage. "He stormed in here this morning and gave me a real dressing-down before ordering me to pack my things and vacate the premises immediately!"

"Oh, Clara, I'm so sorry . . ."

"Yeah, I'll just bet you are," Clara said with a sour look on her face.

"No, really, I am. I never meant for you to get the blame because I got a bout of food poisoning. I mean, it's not like you deliberately fed me that bad mussel . . ." her voice trailed off as she watched Clara's mouth turn up into a derisive sneer.

"Well, I guess you will never know for sure, will you?" Clara said.

Clara had to be joking.

She wasn't evil enough to serve Hayley a rotten mussel on purpose.

Or *was* she?

"Clara, did you really . . . ?"

Clara let the possibility hang in the air long enough to get the reaction she wanted, which Hayley dutifully provided by slowly backing away from her.

Clara scoffed and vigorously shook her head. "Of course I didn't! I love this job. I would never do anything to jeopardize my position here. But then you came along and ruined everything!"

Clara gripped the handle of her suitcase and charged out the door. "This isn't over, Hayley Powell! You better watch your back!"

Hayley chased after her but stopped in the doorway. "Clara, please let me talk to Conrad . . ."

"It's too late! He's made up his mind!" Clara shouted back at her.

Hayley watched her run off, dragging her scuffed suitcase behind her.

This was a disturbing development.

She had to at least try and make things right.

Hayley left her ingredients on the counter, and headed out to find Conrad. After speaking with a housekeeper, who saw him strolling outside with his pipe in hand, Hayley knew she would find him in his usual spot near the cliffside, smoking.

As she made her way through the end of the garden where it opened up to the beautiful ocean view, she spotted Conrad exactly where she expected to find him, but he was not alone. In his arms, her head resting on his broad chest, was Lena Hendricks. He was stroking her hair and reassuring her about something. Lena's previous suitor from earlier that morning, Tristan Roquefort, was nowhere to be seen.

Hayley slowly approached them. She had no intention of hiding this time. She wanted them to see her. When Conrad caught sight of her out of the corner of his eye, he almost shoved Lena away from him. As she stumbled back, her face full of surprise, Hayley could see Conrad signaling her that someone was approaching.

Lena turned her head and upon seeing Hayley marching toward them, grimaced. She said something quickly to Conrad, and then scampered off in the opposite direction down a path that led to the shoreline and disappeared.

"Do you make a habit of spying on people, Ms. Powell?" Conrad asked, annoyed.

"No, I just came to talk to you about Clara."

"Well, you don't have to worry about her anymore."

"I know. And I feel awful about that. I was hoping you might reconsider . . ."

"What if it had been the governor, or a senator, or a big-name actor or some other VIP who ate those mussels . . . ?"

"Instead of a lowly local food columnist?"

"You know what I mean. What if it got out that someone at one of Penelope's dinner parties got food poisoning? It would be the most talked-about story on social media. She'd be more of a pariah than Paula Deen! We can't afford mistakes like that and risk tarnishing Penelope's reputation."

"But don't you think everyone deserves a second chance?"

"No. Frankly, I don't."

"But Clara has been with you and Penelope for such a long time . . ."

"My wife tends to honor loyalty more than I. Which is why I am in charge of the hiring and firing these days. Penelope is too much of a softie. And we need to rule our staff with an iron fist in order to stay focused and competitive. I'm thinking of our company's long-term goals."

Hayley could see that Conrad was not going to budge.

"Okay, then, well I'm sorry I interrupted you and . . ." she said quietly, letting her voice trail off as she glanced in the direction where Lena had fled so quickly from the scene.

Conrad stiffened. "I admit, I am very fond of my wife's assistant, Lena, and I consider myself a friend and mentor to her . . ."

Hayley nodded, trying desperately not to show any judgment in her face, but she failed miserably because she could see Conrad frowning at her and getting more defensive by the second.

"But let me assure you, Ms. Powell, there is no hanky-panky going on between the two of us," Conrad said forcefully, although his words rang hollow. It was as if he had rehearsed what he was going to say and was just going through the motions, hoping his performance might be adequately convincing.

"Understood," Hayley said.

"And let me be perfectly clear. I do not have some kind of nefarious plan to kill my wife so I can be with her assistant. I love Penelope and would never do anything to harm her. And if you suggest otherwise, to anyone, especially the press, I will sue you for defamation of character!" Conrad seethed, stepping forward forcefully, throwing Hayley off guard.

"Got it! Thank you for taking the time to talk to me!" Hayley said, slipping past him and scurrying off back toward the house. Her only thought was getting as far away from the cliff's edge as possible in case Conrad lost it and tried shoving her over the side.

Something deep down in her gut told her that he would have had no compunction in sending her hurtling to her death if it meant salvaging his reputation and keeping his seat secure on the Penelope Janice gravy train.

Island Food & Spirits
BY HAYLEY POWELL

A few years ago we had one of the hottest Fourth of July weekends on record. Normally I would brave the heat and watch the town's annual parade go by from the sidewalk, but this year that low-profile plan was squashed when I was enlisted by my brother Randy to help him with his float representing his local bar Drinks Like a Fish. It was his way of showing the community just how much he appreciated their business. We spent the night decorating and sorting out all the T-shirts, ball caps, and bumper stickers we planned to toss out from the back of the truck to the large crowd of locals and tourists, who would be lining every inch of the parade route, which traveled from the ball field down Main Street, then along Cottage Street and onto Mount Desert Street, and finally down Ledgelawn Avenue, where everyone would finally disperse and head over to the ball field for the next main event, the Rotary Lobster Feed and assorted activities and games.

Ivan and Stephen, two pals of Randy and Sergio who were visiting from Bristol, England, and my best friends Mona and Liddy, as well as myself, had overnight completely transformed Sergio's black

Dodge Ram truck into a mirror image of Randy's actual bar with a couple of small tables, stools, and a completely stocked bar set up in the bed of the truck. We accented the sides with red, white, and blue crepe-paper trim.

After only a few hours of sleep before the parade, everyone gathered at my house for my world-famous—okay maybe a few blocks-famous—French Toast Casserole and a large pot of coffee laced with a bottle of amaretto. I added the amaretto because what's a holiday if you can't celebrate?

After polishing off two pots of spiked coffee and the casserole, it was time to go. Someone got the bright idea to fill a few thermoses full of the amaretto laced coffee so we didn't get thirsty during the parade, and off we went fully prepared for the two hours it would take to get from start to finish on the parade route.

We were all in incredibly high spirits, despite the scorcher of a day we were having, and by 10 A.M. we were rolling along Main Street and could already see the cheering crowd ahead of us!

Stephen insisted on driving the truck since Sergio could not do it himself. As police chief, he had to bring up the rear of the parade in his cruiser. We briefly worried about putting Stephen behind the wheel since he was used to driving on the opposite side of the road in England, but he assured us he was fully capable of driving in America. Since the parade moved along at a snail's pace, what harm could he really do?

Liddy, Mona, Ivan, Randy, and I took our places in the back of the truck, pretending to have a wonderful time at the faux bar, waving and throwing our loot out as children rushed forward to grab our goodies.

As we moved along, the sun climbed higher and hotter in the sky. I tried to ignore it at first, but it was so sweltering and overwhelming, I thought I might get heatstroke from the oppressive humidity. My head was pounding, and I was choking on the diesel exhaust pouring out of the tailpipe of the truck in front of us, where the First National Bank employees excitedly threw little plastic piggy banks at the crowd. Behind us, the Mount Desert Island High School award-winning marching band played "The Theme from *Shaft*" and it was deafening.

I noticed Liddy wiping her brow and swaying from side to side, about to faint. She pitched forward, passing out, and I rushed forward to catch her and we both fell to the floor of the truck. Mona sank down too, overcome by the heat. Ivan tried steadying himself but he forgot to put sunscreen on his bald head and face and he was completely red and feeling sick as well.

Randy, who was also burned and nauseated, pounded on the back window of the truck to get Stephen's attention, but with his windows up, the air conditioner blasting, and Rihanna's latest hit jacked up to full volume on the radio, needless to say he didn't hear anything. He just caught a glimpse of Randy waving frantically in the back window and gave him a smile and a thumbs-up.

Randy was the last one to collapse next to the rest of us. We were all officially sick from drinking too much amaretto coffee and not preparing properly for the harsh rays of the beating sun. The crowd watched our float pass by, puzzled to see no one in the bar that was erected in the flatbed since we were all lying down, moaning and complaining and covering our heads from the sun.

When Stephen glanced at his rearview mirror again, and didn't see any of us, he immediately thought we had somehow fallen out of the back. He slammed on the brakes, tossing us around, threw the truck in park, and jumped out to find us.

Unfortunately the MDI High School marching band wasn't quite able to stop as fast as Stephen, and the band director, who was marching backward so he could conduct the band, ran right into the back of the truck. After that, according to eyewitnesses, it was like watching a game of dominoes as the poor marching band began running into the line in front of them and crashing to the ground, falling down row by row with instruments flying everywhere! The last one to go down were the cymbals, crashing to the ground and making a clanging sound so loud it seemed like the song's finale! The crowd didn't know whether they should applaud or rush to help.

Meanwhile, unbeknownst to us, poor Stephen was running up and down the parade route screaming that there had been a horrible accident and people were missing! This set off a panic in the crowd of people, and many of them whipped out their cell phones and called 911.

Fortunately Sergio arrived promptly at the scene since he was already riding at the end of the line of parade floats, and quickly realized the missing people were all accounted for in the back of the truck, sunburned and sick from too much amaretto.

One must always have a good strong cup of coffee and a hearty hot breakfast to begin the day. Suffice it to say, a shot of amaretto in your coffee is sure to make you want to celebrate something, even if it's not an official holiday. Just stay indoors if it's a hot day!

Amaretto Coffee

1 cup hot coffee
1½ shots amaretto
Whipped cream
Sliced almonds

Pour your hot coffee into your favorite coffee mug.

Add 1½ shots of amaretto and stir.

Top with whipped cream and a few sliced almonds, kick back, and enjoy!

Easy Breezy French Toast Casserole

4 tablespoons butter (½ stick), melted
¾ cup packed brown sugar
1 loaf brioche bread cut into 1½ inch slices
8 eggs slightly beaten
1 cup whole milk
1 tablespoon vanilla extract
1 tablespoon cinnamon
¼ teaspoon ground ginger
¼ to ½ cup chopped pecans (to your liking)
½ teaspoon salt

Combine your sugar and melted butter in a small bowl and pour into the bottom of a 9-by-13-inch baking pan. Lay your slices of bread on top of the mixture, overlapping if necessary.

Combine your milk, beaten eggs, vanilla, cinnamon, ginger, and salt in a medium bowl. Pour the mixture evenly all over the sliced bread in the baking pan.

At this point cover your French toast tightly with plastic wrap and refrigerate for at least 4 hours and up to 12 hours.

In the morning take the casserole out of the refrigerator at least 15 minutes before baking. Preheat your oven to 350°F and bake the casserole 30–35 minutes, until a knife comes out clean. Remove from oven and cool slightly. Yummy!

Chapter 10

It was no surprise when Gerard Roquefort's Cod, Potato, and Fennel Casserole easily took first prize in Penelope Janice's celebrity potluck competition that evening. Carol Kay came in a distant second with her Oyster Casserole, which everyone agreed was tasty, but ultimately inferior to Gerard's heavenly dish. Hayley's Spaghetti Pie Casserole didn't even place, even though she was quite proud of her final effort. Penelope said it was "tasty" on camera as she swept through, fork in hand, trying all of her esteemed guests' entries, having dramatically disqualified her own dish, a simple Spinach Gratin, when she revealed on camera that she, in fact, would be the deciding judge. Hayley never seriously thought she had a shot at actually winning the contest, but she was happy knowing she had been invited to participate.

The small camera crew followed Penelope around as she congratulated everyone on their individual impressive culinary achievements, making sure the cameraman didn't miss Gerard's son Tristan pouting in a corner, a sore loser, whining to his father that his Chicken and Swiss Chard Enchilada Casserole, in his opinion, had been unfairly judged. Penelope loved any drama she could squeeze out and exploit on her show, and bad sport Tristan was handing her a great promotional spot with his sullen attitude.

Still, poor Penelope got a lot more drama than she bargained for when she chose to ignore her husband Conrad spending too much time refilling his glass with scotch at the bar during the post-competition interviews.

Hayley had been eyeing him all evening, and he appeared tense and angry, even storming out at one point when his own dish, a simple Root Vegetable Gratin, was summarily dismissed by his wife as "humdrum and pedestrian." A producer had to chase him down and coax him back, which took almost a half hour.

Hayley had tasted Conrad's casserole herself and, though not a huge fan of root vegetables, thought it was quite flavorful and yummy and undeserving of such pointed criticism.

She had to assume Penelope was purposely punishing her husband for his boorish behavior and possible dalliance with her ravishing assistant. Penelope's harsh words did not sit well with Conrad, and he showed it by getting rip-roaring drunk, quietly at first, but then as his inhibitions melted away, he steadily became more combative and abusive.

"This is all a farce," he slurred, jiggling the ice in

his glass before downing what had to have been his seventh or eighth scotch on the rocks.

Penelope whirled around, a furious look in her eyes, as she sized up her hopelessly inebriated husband. "I think you've had quite enough to drink, Conrad. Perhaps it's time you turned in for the night."

"The Queen of the Kitchen has issued her decree and has ordered me exiled from the castle," Conrad bellowed, playing it up for the camera which was recording his every word and movement for posterity.

Penelope eyeballed the camera nervously.

This was not a scene she wanted featured on her special Fourth of July holiday episode.

"I'm not a child you can send off to bed before the party is over like one of those cloying von Trapp kids in *The Sound of Music*," Conrad blustered, nearly tripping over his own feet as he made a beeline for the bar and sang off key, "*So long! Farewell! Auf Wiedersehen . . .*"

"Conrad, enough!" Penelope cried, marching over and physically pushing the lens down so the cameraman couldn't capture any more of the embarrassing scene.

She hissed in the producer's ear, "I don't want to see *any* of this in the editing room."

"God forbid the public gets an accurate picture of what really goes on around here," Conrad scoffed, stumbling over an ottoman.

Gerard lunged forward to catch him before he fell, but Conrad managed to balance himself and shook Gerard off, raising his arms and accidentally elbowing Gerard in the face.

Gerard flew back and crashed into the long table with all the potluck dishes, knocking it over and causing all the half-empty casserole plates to smash to the floor.

There was stunned silence.

Tristan rushed over to help his father to his feet.

Penelope flashed a panicked look at her producer and them calmly announced, "I think we should call it a night."

The guests and camera crew silently filed out of the room as Penelope signaled to one of her kitchen staff, who was hovering near the entryway. "Gloria, could you please clean this mess up for me?"

"Of course, Mrs. Janice," the young girl said, racing to find a broom and dustpan.

Penelope traipsed past Hayley, her face tight, trying desperately not to lose it in front of her. "Good night, Hayley."

"Good night," she answered, watching Penelope disappear around the corner, leaving her all alone in the dining room.

Hayley walked over and lifted the table upright before kneeling down and picking up shards of broken glass off the floor.

Gloria returned and began sweeping the smaller pieces of glass into her dustpan, shaking her head.

"That was quite a show," Hayley said.

Gloria nodded, not eager to gossip with a stranger, something that could potentially backfire on her in a big way.

"Does this kind of thing happen often?" Hayley casually asked.

Gloria shrugged. "No, not really. He only drinks too much when he's upset about something."

Hayley dropped the broken pieces of glass she had gathered in a small wastebasket. Gloria kept sweeping vigorously, trying to scoop up every last remnant of food and glass that littered the hard-wood floor.

"What do you suppose he was upset about?"

"Beats me. But believe me, she gives him plenty of reasons to be upset. She's terribly tough on him."

"Penelope wears the pants in the family, huh?"

"Yeah," Gloria said, chuckling. "It's no wonder he—"

"It's no wonder he what?"

Gloria realized she had said too much and suddenly sealed her lips and bent down to pick up the dustpan full of casserole bits and shattered glass. She then dumped it in the wastebasket.

"Gloria, you were going to say something . . ."

"I shouldn't be talking to you. I don't want to get fired like Clara."

"Whatever you tell me will be in the strictest confidence," Hayley promised.

Gloria wavered, debating with herself. She wanted to get something off her chest, but wasn't sure Hayley was the right trusted confidante.

"Please, Gloria, I won't tell anyone, I promise."

Gloria sighed, making a decision.

She glanced around the room to make sure no one else was within earshot.

"Last night Penelope was in a pretty nasty mood and was taking it out on Conrad and . . ." Gloria said, hesitating.

"And . . . ?"

"Well, I saw him in the kitchen and he had a bottle of pills . . . he was crushing some into a powder and stirred it into her warm milk with nutmeg."

"Which she has every night before bed."

"That's right."

"Did you see the bottle? What kind of pills were they?"

"Sleeping pills, I think."

Sleeping pills in her milk.

Penelope was admittedly a very light sleeper.

But those pills would no doubt have knocked her out cold for the entire night allowing Conrad to slip away freely and rendezvous with Lena.

In order to secretly discuss Penelope's murder.

After helping Gloria clean up the mess and thanking her for confiding in her, Hayley retreated to her room, exhausted from the evening's intense drama.

On her way up the stairs she spotted Lena slipping out of her room and quietly tiptoeing down the hall.

Was she meeting Conrad?

Or Tristan?

Or some other secret courter?

Hayley debated following her, but was overcome with exhaustion, still weak from her nasty bout of food poisoning the night before, and so she just trudged into her room, peeled off her clothes, threw on her nightgown, and crawled into bed.

She was asleep within seconds.

When she awoke hours later in the early morning, everything was still dark and she was having trouble breathing again. As she tried to open her mouth and suck in some air, she inhaled a wad of fur and started choking. Realizing Sebastian the cat was parked on her face again, she pushed the hefty feline off her, causing him to emit a short abrupt hiss and then a growl. Sebastian huffily marched to the end of the bed, tail high in the air to signal his disapproval, and then circled the comforter a few times before plopping down into a big round fur ball.

Hayley leaned down and patted him gently on the head. "I don't mind us being roommates, Sebastian, but I'm sorry, pal, you can't sleep on my face."

As much as he wanted to maintain his distant and cold demeanor, Sebastian simply couldn't resist Hayley's magic fingers scratching his head and soon he melted into a euphoric state, purring like the hum of a motorboat's engine.

Suddenly Sebastian's blissful mood was shattered by a woman's screams. The sharp shrieks were so startling he flew off the bed and skittered underneath it to hide.

Hayley jumped up and raced to the window, tugging open the curtains, unhooking the latch, and throwing open the window. Down below, by the cliff's edge, she could see Carol Kay, in a loud pink sweat suit, presumably out for an early morning jog, yelling and pointing over the rocky drop-off.

"There's a body down there!" she wailed.

Hayley struggled into her clothes that were strewn across the floor from the night before and bolted out of the room, down the stairs, and out the front door, running as fast as she could to reach Carol, afraid her worst fears were about to be confirmed, and Conrad and Lena had made good on their diabolical plan to kill Penelope.

If only she had followed Lena the night before, perhaps she could have somehow prevented this, found some way to save Penelope from her husband's deadly machinations.

When Hayley finally reached Carol, who by now was on her knees, hugging herself, weeping uncontrollably, Hayley stopped to comfort her for just a moment, rubbing her back and telling her it would be all right, and then she slowly, carefully stepped over to the cliff's edge and peered down at the body.

She gasped as she stared numbly at the corpse, lying broken on the jagged rocks far below as the rush of water from the crashing waves washed over it, threatening to pull it far out to sea.

It wasn't Penelope Janice.

It was her husband Conrad.

Chapter 11

Police Chief Sergio Alvares was back on the scene at the posh Seal Harbor estate in record time after Carol Kay finally collected herself enough to call 911 on her cell phone between sobs and tears. The other houseguests, alerted to the commotion outside, quickly dressed and gathered together in a huddle as Penelope, hand over her mouth, her whole body shaking, insisted against the advice of her friends to see the smashed body of her husband for herself.

After peeking over the edge, she howled, and then collapsed into Sergio's arms, hanging onto him as she buried her face in his broad, muscled chest.

It was quite a performance.

One Hayley didn't buy for a second.

Especially when she spotted Penelope, supposedly grief-stricken, cover her eyes with her hands as she moaned and blubbered in the arms of Sergio, but peering through her splayed fingers at her houseguests' reaction to her grieving, as if she wanted to make sure her emotional display was thoroughly convincing enough for all the witnesses on the scene, especially the chief of police.

Penelope clearly wanted to put on a good show leaving no doubt in everyone's mind that she was sufficiently heartbroken over Conrad's untimely death, whether she truly felt that way or not.

Sergio managed to peel Penelope off him and consult with his officers who were canvassing the area for clues. Hayley noticed a pipe lying on the ground near the cliff's edge. She knelt down to inspect it, and sure enough, it looked as if it had been discarded. There was some recently burnt tobacco in the small round bowl of the pipe. She signaled Sergio, who trotted over to take a look at what she had just found.

He bent down to examine the pipe.

"Do you think it belongs to Conrad?" he asked.

"Yes, he must have dropped it when he tripped or stumbled, before falling over the side of the cliff," Hayley said solemnly.

Sergio waved over Officer Donnie to bag and tag the pipe in the event Conrad's death was ruled a homicide and the pipe needed to be submitted as evidence.

"What do you suppose happened?" Hayley asked Sergio, who surveyed the area near the cliff's edge where Conrad presumably fell.

"I'm leaning toward an accident. So far, everyone I've talked to has told me Conrad was blisteringly drunk last night when he left the dining room. I can only assume he took a stroll along the property, something he did every night before bed according to his wife and the household staff. He stopped here to smoke his pipe, and accidentally slipped on some rocks, which were wet from a brief rain last night. He probably stumbled, tried regaining his balance, dropped his pipe here, and just tumbled over the side, dying instantly when his body hit the rocks."

It all made perfect sense.

And yet, Hayley believed, given the previous events that had already unfolded during her stay here, the friction between Conrad and Penelope and the murder plot she had heard discussed between Conrad and Lena meant that this horrific occurrence was far more than just a simple tragic accident.

She was still convinced Conrad had every intention of murdering his wife to be with Lena.

But somehow the tables had suddenly turned.

And she was determined to get to the bottom of it.

"Excuse me, everyone, please, will you all accompany me back to the house?" Penelope called to her guests who were milling about the scene. "The police have a lot of work to do, and the coroner's office and fire department have just arrived to bring up Conrad's body, so I think it would be wise for us to all get out of their way. Breakfast will be served in the dining room in fifteen minutes."

Nobody moved at first.

Everyone was still in shock.

But as Penelope took the lead and marched back up the trail to the main house, they all slowly, like herded cattle, followed her back inside.

Penelope led the guests into the main dining room, where the kitchen staff had laid out a beautiful buffet of breakfast options including scrambled eggs, sausage, roasted potatoes, a vat of oatmeal, toast, an array of yummy baked goods, and several different kinds of coffees and teas as well as fruit juices. There were also four bottles of pricey champagne to make mimosas.

Everyone quietly and obediently picked up a plate and formed a line. Hayley noticed Carol hang back, still shaken over her grisly discovery just a couple of hours earlier. When Penelope passed by, Carol reached out and touched her arm.

Penelope, who seemed far more relaxed and calm and had no lingering signs of wet tears now that she was no longer under the watchful eye of Chief Alvares, stopped and smiled. "Yes, Carol?"

"I think it would be a good idea if, after we've all had breakfast, we go to our rooms and collect our things and call the airlines to rebook our flights so you can have some privacy."

"I don't think that's a good idea at all," Penelope said, shaking her head. "I don't need any privacy."

Carol was taken aback by Penelope's matter-of-fact demeanor, which was so unlike the emotionally distraught breakdown she had apparently suffered outside, falling into the arms of the police chief, overcome with grief.

It was as if none of that had even happened.

"But surely given the circumstances . . ." Carol said, taking Penelope's hands into her own. "What you must be going through right now . . ."

Penelope slipped her hands out of Carol's grasp and turned to her other guests, who were standing around the buffet table, pretending not to listen.

"May I have your attention, everyone, please, I'm sorry to interrupt your breakfast, but Carol here thinks we should cut the weekend short. She thinks I'm being insensitive for wanting you all to stay . . ."

"I never said that," Carol murmured.

Gerard stepped forward. "We would totally understand . . ."

"A lot of money and planning have gone into this weekend, and I have every intention of seeing this through. Conrad was a big part of my show, and I know he wouldn't want us to abandon our special holiday episode just because he died."

The room stood in stunned silence.

Hayley couldn't believe what she was hearing.

"I know he would have wanted us to keep a stiff upper lip, power through, and get the job done. Now who's with me? Let's see a show of hands!"

Gerard and Tristan both shot their hands up in the air in an instant.

Carol hesitated, but then shakily raised her hand, not wanting to be odd woman out.

Penelope's loyal producers and crew also enthusiastically gave her a thumbs-up. They were being paid to agree with whatever their star wanted.

Hayley was the last one wavering, and she suddenly noticed all eyes in the room were fixed on her, especially Penelope, whose face seemed to be daring her to defy her wishes.

Although she really wanted to just go home at this point, the pressure to stay was overwhelming.

After a few more tense moments of will-she-or-won't-she drama, Hayley found herself raising her hand, joining the others.

"It's unanimous! The show must go on, as they say!"

There was an awkward moment as everyone stood there, waiting to take their cue from Penelope, who breezed over and picked up a shiny white plate off the pile and stood behind Hayley to wait her turn.

"I'm certainly not going to cut to the front of the line just because I own the place. Come on, people. Move it. I'm starving!"

There were some titters and smiles as everyone resumed filling their plates with breakfast food and taking their places at the large dining room table.

Hayley sat next to Carol, who kept her head down, eating silently, still obviously disturbed by the image of Conrad's broken, twisted body on the rocks.

Hayley took a swig of her mimosa and then began cutting into her sausage. Carol turned her head slightly in Hayley's direction and muttered, "Look at her. You'd never know in a million years that she just saw her husband's shattered corpse."

Hayley glanced over at Penelope, who was holding Gerard's hand flirtatiously as he entertained her with some story about a disastrous restaurant opening in France.

Carol was right.

Penelope had never looked more relaxed and happy.

"Their marriage was a sham, you know," Carol whispered, keeping one eye on Penelope to make sure she didn't see them gossiping about her.

"I was starting to get that impression," Hayley whispered, smiling at Penelope's producer, who was watching her suspiciously.

"She *despised* him," Carol said between bites of fresh grilled tomatoes. "I heard the only reason she decided to co-author that casserole cookbook was to bribe him. It was a payout. A way for her to help him get his own brand as a chef established so he would be out of her hair and finally leave her alone."

Carol made perfect sense.

Judging from their "George and Martha from *Who's Afraid of Virginia Woolf?*" antics only hours before he died, there was certainly not a lot of love left in their tenuous marriage.

Perhaps Penelope knew about Conrad's affair with Lena and didn't really care? Maybe she just pretended she did. But now that he was dead, Penelope would no longer have to endure working with him so closely on a cookbook.

She was free of him.

Hayley wondered if that might have been motive enough to give him a violent shove off that cliff.

Penelope was undoubtedly aware that he went there every evening to smoke his pipe and clear his head.

She could easily have snuck up behind him and surprised him.

Sergio believed it was an accident. A drunken fall.

But Hayley wasn't so sure.

In a way, she was grateful that Penelope was so insistent on carrying on with the holiday weekend shoot for her TV show.

It would give her more time to figure out just what was going on behind the gates at this palace of intrigue.

Chapter 12

On the official schedule of events for the weekend that Hayley had received prior to her arrival at the estate was a late Saturday afternoon excursion on Penelope and Conrad's luxury sailboat christened with the name *The Foodie,* a pricey forty-four-foot midsize cruiser that would comfortably accommodate six guests along with a two-man crew including a captain and one deckhand.

Hayley had been excited about the sailing trip, but assumed it had been cancelled given the somber mood that hung over the estate after the devastating and troubling death of Penelope's husband Conrad.

Penelope, however, had no intention of shying away from any of her meticulously laid-out plans, especially a boat ride on her posh yacht that would look so good on camera for her TV show as it sailed majestically in the harbor. She sent a personal note to each of her guests requesting that, in honor of Conrad's memory, they continue enjoying the weekend's festivities since the weather was so beautiful, and it would be such a shame to waste the clear skies and balmy temperatures.

Oh, and "it would have been what Conrad wanted" was scribbled at the end, almost as an afterthought.

Hayley was taken aback by the callousness of the note. Penelope seemed to be skipping over the "grieving widow" part of the program that under normal circumstances she was expected to play, and steaming right ahead to the "moving on with her life" phase.

Conrad's body had barely been recovered and shipped off to the morgue.

If Penelope actually did give her cheating husband a brutal shove off that cliff, then she was doing a terrible job of feigning innocence. Or more likely, she was indeed innocent, and just didn't care to mourn the fresh corpse of a husband she so obviously despised.

Either way, Hayley did what she was told, and rummaged through her luggage for a passable sailing outfit. She managed to scrounge up a nautically inspired blue striped shirt, white capri pants, a pink windbreaker, Sperry Top-Siders, and in a daring move, a cute, decorative, floppy crochet lace sun hat she had borrowed from Liddy's closet. She probably looked utterly ridiculous wearing it, but she decided to go for it anyway.

Hayley arrived at the dock, which was located about half a mile from the estate, a short walk from the main house. She found Gerard, Tristan, Carol, and Penelope already there. A grizzled white-bearded captain right out of a Herman Melville novel, smoking a pipe just like Conrad's, gave *The Foodie* a quick inspection while a muscled deckhand in his early twenties, who introduced himself as Tommy, stood by to assist the VIP passengers aboard the vessel.

"It's such a beautiful day for a sail," Penelope exclaimed, shading her eyes from the sun with a hand as she took in the crystal-blue harbor stretching out to sea before them.

There was an unspoken tension as the others struggled with how to deal with this odd and awkward situation. They filed up the plank and aboard the boat, with a welcoming smile from Tommy, to find champagne, orange juice, baskets of muffins and croissants, and a plate stacked with strawberries, blueberries, melon, and pineapple awaiting them, along with a piping hot pot of fresh coffee.

After a quick safety rundown from the captain, who kept winking at Carol while he demonstrated how to secure a life vest around your chest and torso in the unlikely event that the boat sank, *The Foodie* chugged slowly out of the harbor and farther out into the deep blue sea as the passengers began picking over the muffins and fruit plate.

Penelope chatted amiably with Gerard and Tristan while Hayley hovered by the food table with Carol.

"The muffins look delicious," Hayley said to

Carol, trying desperately to make conversation and pretend everything was normal.

Carol shook her head and scowled. "Probably five hundred calories a pop, but go ahead and knock yourself out!"

Carol opened up a large wicker picnic basket she had brought aboard with her, and pulled out wrapped containers of fresh veggies including carrots, celery, and sliced cucumbers, her signature homemade gluten-free dips, which she sold at her online store, a small bottle of honey mustard, and a garlic herb hummus.

Hayley kept a watchful eye on Penelope as they sailed along the coast. At one point, they spotted a whale thrashing along just a few hundred yards out at sea. Penelope remained poised and bouncy and in remarkable high spirits.

Hayley also noticed that Lena Hendricks had not been seen nor heard from since Conrad's body had been discovered. Either she was sequestered in her room crying, or she had been ordered to vacate the premises immediately.

At this point, it was anyone's guess.

Hayley glanced over to see Tristan wandering off toward the far end of the boat by himself as Penelope, Gerard, and Carol gossiped about a network executive at the Lifestyle Network who had greenlit Carol's show and was currently cheating on his wife with a major Food Network on-camera talent.

Uninterested in that conversation, Hayley picked up her half-full champagne glass and tiptoed away, smiling at the handsome young deckhand Tommy, who nodded as she passed while he practiced tying a bowline knot with a thick piece of rope. He was obviously still in training.

The captain was parked behind the wheel, re-lighting his pipe, as he gazed upon the horizon, his already deeply red pockmarked face that wasn't hidden by his bushy white beard getting more burnt by the harsh rays of the sun as each minute passed.

Hayley casually joined Tristan in the stern of the boat.

He glanced at her next to him, and gave her a half smile, not appearing to be annoyed that she was crowding his personal space. It wasn't a very big boat to begin with so there weren't many places to go for privacy.

"What a strange day," Hayley said, leaning against the back railing and staring out at sea.

Tristan nodded. "I still can't believe it. Conrad sure had his faults, but overall he was a pretty decent guy. Nobody deserves to go like that. I can't imagine what went through his mind in those last few seconds after he fell."

"So you agree with the police that he fell and it was a just a horrible accident?"

Tristan stared at Hayley, stupefied. "Of course. Why? You don't?"

"No, it sure appears that way. I mean, it all makes sense. It rained for a short time last night and the rocks were slippery, and we all saw how drunk Conrad was earlier in the evening . . ."

"Exactly," Tristan said. "The facts speak for

themselves. And there is no point in trying to make more of something when there's nothing there."

He glanced sideways at her pointedly.

Hayley nodded and sipped her champagne.

"Are you still trying to sell that wild story you told everybody about Conrad and Penelope's secretary secretly plotting to do away with her?"

"I wasn't trying to sell anybody a story. I know what I heard," Hayley said defensively before adding, "but I admit I was very sick and disoriented at the time . . ."

"You want my advice? There's enough drama going on this weekend, and you're only going to make things worse by fanning the flames."

"So you believe I made the whole thing up?"

"No, it has nothing to do with me. I just met Conrad and Penelope. They're my father's friends, not mine. I have no investment in any of this."

"What about Lena?"

"I don't know her either."

"Funny, I saw the two of you talking yesterday."

Tristan scrunched up his face, putting on a big show of trying to remember. "Are you sure it was me?"

Hayley gave him a sideways glance. "Yes, and I was fully recovered from the food poisoning and can say with full confidence I was not hallucinating anything at the time."

"Oh, right, yeah, we did have a very brief exchange," Tristan said, suddenly remembering. "We ran into each other out in the garden and chatted for a few minutes. Mostly about the potluck contest and what I was going to make. I didn't even remember her name at the time. I think I called her Laura by accident and she had to correct me."

"Interesting," Hayley said flatly.

"What do you mean? Why do you say that? There was nothing to it."

"You just seemed to be more familiar with each other, that's all. I saw the two of you holding hands at one point."

Tristan's face froze for a moment, but then he quickly recovered and forced a smile. "She's a very beautiful woman. Any man would have trouble keeping his hands to myself. But trust me. There's no secret affair going on between us."

"I see Miss Marple has been peppering you with her nosy questions, son," Gerard Roquefort blared, loud enough for everyone on the boat to hear.

"We were just talking," Hayley said softly.

"Why must you insist on stirring up trouble, especially on this day, when Penelope is going through such heartbreak?"

Hayley glanced at Penelope, who had been happily drinking her champagne at that moment, but then on Gerard's cue, like a trained actress, she slapped on a feeble look of despair.

"She thinks I'm sleeping with Penelope's secretary, and I'm guessing her theory is that Conrad was too, and so I killed him in order to get him out of the way so I could be with my one true love, the exquisite and voluptuous and seductive Lena Hendricks," Tristan joked.

But it didn't sound like a joke.

It sounded like a perfectly plausible theory.

Out of the mouth of a very plausible suspect.

And it was also suspicious that just moments before Tristan claimed he couldn't even remember Lena's first name, and now not only did he get it right, but he also easily rattled off her last name as well.

"I think it would be wise if you would stop all this nonsense, Hayley," Gerard bellowed, making as big a scene as he could to embarrass her. "Before you get poor Penelope even more despondent than she already is!"

Hayley was mortified and shaking and just wanted to shrink away as all eyes on the boat were laser focused on her, awaiting her reaction to Gerard's tirade, including the venerable old captain and his cute, shaggy-haired deckhand Tommy.

"Can you do us that one favor, Hayley?" Gerard spit out.

Hayley stared at him, speechless.

"Well, *can* you?" Gerard shouted.

Hayley nodded and turned away from everyone, downing the rest of her champagne, turning her back to all of those judging eyes, and gazing out at the island in the distance behind them, wishing she was back on dry land, away from these miserable, odious people she had once idolized—one of whom, she was convinced, was a cold-blooded killer.

Chapter 13

Hayley let out a huge sigh of relief when the captain steered the boat around and finally headed back to shore. After her dressing-down from Gerard Roquefort, she had managed to keep her distance from the others, mostly staying put near the stern of the boat while the other passengers socialized and finished off the champagne and breakfast items up in the bow of *The Foodie.*

None of Penelope's other guests made any attempt to engage Hayley in any further conversation. It was as if she were contagious with some social disease, and nobody was willing to get too close to her.

Finally, as Tommy the deckhand lowered the sails, and the captain stood steadfastly at the wheel, guiding the boat in the direction of the harbor's dock, the engine chugging, Penelope herself walked from the bow to the stern along the starboard side and joined Hayley.

"I'm sorry you didn't enjoy our little outing

today, Hayley," Penelope said, pursing her lips in a fake pout.

"I didn't mean to cause a scene, Penelope," Hayley said.

"You didn't cause a scene. Gerard did. He can be very protective of me. We go back a long time," Penelope said.

"I'm just very troubled by what has happened."

"Yes. I'm still in shock over Conrad's death too, and maybe I'm pushing to proceed as if everything's normal in order not to think about it, or talk about it, or figure out what I'm going to do now. If I do, I'm afraid I'll just crumble, and I can't allow that right now. I have responsibilities to the show, the network, and my fans. And I know Conrad would agree."

"But the circumstances—"

"Hayley, my husband has a long history of being a clumsy drunk," she said, placing a hand on top of Hayley's, which gripped the brass rail of the boat. "He was always staggering around and breaking things and falling down whenever he guzzled too much liquor. Did you know he recently had his hip replaced because he got so blotto on whiskey he fell off the porch and landed on his side, smashing his hip *and* his pelvis to pieces? That's just one example of the consequences of his behavior."

"I understand, but based on what I heard the other night, or what I think I heard, and then his sudden death the very next evening . . ."

"You're conflating the two incidents. You were

suffering from a wretched case of food poisoning, and you were stumbling about the house unsure of where you were. And quite frankly you cannot even say definitively that what you heard actually transpired. Conrad's fall had nothing to do with any of that. It was just a tragic coincidence."

"Maybe I should just pack up my things when we get back to shore and—"

"Nonsense. Please, we still have some shooting to do for my Fourth of July holiday special and I need you to be very much involved in that, especially when we as a group attend the fireworks in town on Sunday night. It's a must for the episode's teaser."

"Aren't you worried about blowback from just powering through this shoot instead of making funeral arrangements for your husband?"

"I've always been a multitasker. I'm already in contact with McFarland's Funeral Home, and I have an appointment to pick out a casket and order flowers once we're back on shore. I also just got off the phone with your paper about the obit before we all piled on this boat and set sail. Trust me—I've got everything covered. Journalists will write what they're going to write. Probably that I'm a cold bitch more worried about her career than losing her spouse of twenty-six years. But those jackals have been writing nasty things about me ever since I made a name for myself, so I'm used to it. I'm just adding to the myth of Penelope Janice," she said with a smirk. "So promise me you will see this through, Hayley. For me. As a personal favor. I will have Gerard come back here and apologize."

Hayley shook her head. "No, there is no need for that. I'll stay."

The truth was, she didn't want to have any more contact with that pompous, egotistical jackass.

"Thank you," Penelope said. "I guarantee if you just play along and help me out with this special, when it's all over, I will make you a household name."

Penelope gave Hayley a quick peck on the cheek, and then turned and strolled back up the starboard side to join the others.

Hayley watched her go, and slowly turned around and leaned against the cold chrome rail fitting, staring out at the vast ocean behind them as they slowly motored toward the dock, navigating past scores of moored boats bobbing up and down in the choppy current.

Hayley wondered why Penelope was so determined not to believe her story of Conrad and Lena Hendricks conspiring against her. How could she be so sure that what Hayley heard was just a simple hallucination caused by a bad mussel?

It didn't make any sense.

Anyone would be disturbed by it, especially the person who was the supposed targeted victim in the malevolent plot. But Penelope had remained so disturbingly calm and unusually skeptical, and she made no secret of her desire for Hayley to just stop talking about it.

Why?

What was she missing?

What else was going on here?

Hayley couldn't hide in the back of the boat forever so she decided it was time to be brave and join the others for the remainder of their voyage.

Insults and attacks be damned.

But before she had the chance to turn around, she suddenly sensed someone rushing up fast behind her. Something hard slammed into her back, knocking the wind out of her before she could let out even a yelp. She lost her balance and stumbled as someone bent down, grabbed her by the legs, and forcefully heaved her up and over the railing.

She splashed into the ocean, sinking below the surface, and swallowing seawater. Her first thought was the fear of getting caught in the sailboat's fast-spinning propellers, so she frantically flapped her arms and legs with all her might to push herself away from the boat and the whirlpool of water its motor was stirring up.

When her head broke the surface, she coughed and sputtered, trying desperately to suck in air. She caught a glimpse of the boat moving away from her toward the shore.

"Help!" Hayley cried, swallowing more salty water, trying to stay afloat.

She didn't see anyone in the stern of the sailboat.

The passengers were all up front in the bow and the crew were at their stations for docking, unable to hear her calls for help. And her screams were drowned out by the running motor.

There were no other people on the moored boats in the harbor, nor were there any other boats sailing in the vicinity.

She was all alone.

At least she prayed she was all alone, and there were no sharks down below swimming up to feed off her kicking legs as she tried treading water.

Hayley was still about a mile out from shore and hardly an expert swimmer. It would be another ten minutes before *The Foodie* reached the dock and anyone noticed that she wasn't on board. Then, more time would be needed to get the boat back out to search for her.

She wasn't sure if she could keep her head above water for that long.

She started swimming, dog-paddling, toward shore, which she deemed closer than the nearest moored boat, but after a few minutes she stopped, exhausted.

This was not going to end well.

But then, a miracle.

She saw Tommy, the quiet, shy young deckhand with the shaggy hair, in the back of the boat, looking around for her. She waved her arms and screamed at the top of her lungs. She could see him standing at the railing in the stern, staring out to sea, a hand cupped above his eyes to block out the blazing sun.

And then she saw him react and spring into

action. He grabbed an orange-and-white lifesaver and dove headfirst into the deep frigid water.

As he swam like an Olympian toward her, Hayley finally relaxed a little, still coughing up water and wary of winding up shark food, but a little more confident that she would make it out of this ordeal alive.

Chapter 14

Hayley's eyes were puffy and red and she had been coughing for the better part of an hour. She felt the nasty cold coming on just minutes after being hauled out of the ice-cold water and back aboard the yacht. Her rescuer Tommy valiantly raced belowdecks and instantly reappeared with a pile of warm blankets, wrapping them around her as she shivered so hard she had to sit down on the floor of the deck.

Penelope and her guests had now gathered at the stern of the boat to watch as she hacked and sputtered and pulled the blankets tighter around herself.

None of them said a word.

In Hayley's eyes, they *all* looked guilty.

The captain gently put a hand on Hayley's shoulder and asked, "How did you fall, dear?"

"I didn't fall. Somebody pushed me," Hayley whispered.

But it was loud enough for everyone to hear.

Penelope rolled her eyes, but resisted the urge to challenge her again. Her face clearly betrayed what she was thinking. That Hayley was a klutz who had obviously had too many mimosas, tripped over something, and tumbled overboard accidentally.

And now, like the boy who cried wolf, she was once again claiming foul play.

Penelope wasn't alone in her opinion.

Gerard, Carol, and Tristan all exchanged skeptical looks, Gerard even suppressing a smile.

"Who do you think pushed you?" Carol asked, trying her best to maintain a straight face. "We were all up in the front of the boat, the captain was at the wheel, so that only leaves Tommy."

"And he was the one who jumped into the freezing water to save you! Why would he do that if he was the one who pushed you?" Gerard asked pointedly. "Unless his evil plan was to shove you overboard and then dive in to rescue you in order to make himself out to be the big hero!"

Tommy's eyes widened and his mouth dropped open as he was filled with fear that the group might actually start taking this wild theory seriously.

He need not have worried.

None of them were buying it.

And neither was Hayley.

Tommy was a good kid.

And she would forever be grateful to him for saving her from drowning.

Hayley didn't believe for a second that Penelope, Gerard, Tristan, and Carol had all been glued to the front of the boat, chatting amiably. One of them had obviously slipped off for a few seconds, snuck up behind her, and shoved her over the railing. She was dubious about wispy Carol's physical strength despite her devotion to yoga. Her assailant had physically hoisted her off the ground before chucking her overboard. Penelope was stronger and more stouthearted. But the more likely suspects were Gerard or his son Tristan, both strapping, able-bodied men, both of whom could have effortlessly lifted her up like a sack of potatoes and launched her into the sea.

When they arrived back at the estate, Hayley immediately retreated to her room, where she crawled into bed with a box of Kleenex to recuperate. After an hour of blowing her nose and taking shots of cough syrup, she was feeling slightly better.

Hayley was just about to doze off when she heard a scratching at the door.

It had to be Sebastian.

Her feline roommate.

Hayley threw back the comforter and slipped out of bed, padding over to open the door.

Sure enough, Sebastian was outside, looking up at her, tail flapping, annoyed she took so long to answer.

Directly behind him was a pair of men's brown work boots.

She jumped back, startled.

The sudden move spooked Sebastian and he flew into the room and scooted underneath the bed.

Hayley looked up to see Lex Bansfield standing in the doorway.

"Sorry, I didn't mean to scare you," Lex said.

"No, it's fine. I've just been a little jumpy ever since I got here," Hayley said, smiling. "Please, come in."

"With good reason. A lot's been happening this weekend," Lex said, casually entering the room and looking around.

"That's putting it mildly," Hayley said, kneeling down to see Sebastian glaring at her with his glowing copper eyes under the bed, not ready to venture back out anytime soon.

She stood back up and faced Lex, who appeared slightly nervous.

"I heard about your midafternoon swim earlier today," Lex said. "It's all anyone is talking about around here."

Hayley sneezed and wiped her nose with a wad of Kleenex. "Well, I'm sure Penelope is selling her official version. Her bungling clown of a guest is just trying to make a name for herself by spinning wild stories about secret affairs and murder conspiracies."

"Yes, but for what it's worth, the kitchen staff believes you. But then again, they still watch daytime soap operas religiously between preparing and serving all the meals," Lex said, chuckling.

"I didn't make *anything* up," Hayley said quietly.

"I know," Lex said somberly, taking a step forward and putting his hands on her still shivering shoulders. "And I want you to know that I am here, and if you feel alone, or need someone to talk to, or even if you feel the slightest sense of danger, you can come to me."

"Thank you, Lex."

She hugged him tightly, resting her head on his broad chest.

Hayley had done this countless times when they had been together as a couple, but now, years later, she found herself still drawn to the safety of his strong arms.

And it felt good.

They stood there embracing for almost a minute.

Sebastian finally inched out from underneath the bed, jumped up on the bedcovers, and kneaded the comforter with his paws until he found a satisfactory napping spot. He plopped down, his eyes half-closed as he purred, and watched Hayley and Lex's rekindled affection for one another.

Hayley fought back tears. She couldn't believe that she was suddenly getting so emotional. She certainly did not want to dissolve into a blubbering mess in front of Lex. But the last couple of days had taken quite a toll on both her psyche and her physical stamina, and she wasn't sure how much longer she could endure it all.

But knowing Lex was around improved her spirits. She was now determined to see this whole crazy weekend through, and she was not going to allow anyone, least of all a pompous ass like Gerard Roquefort or his lying, sniveling, butt-kissing son to drive her away.

Hayley gently pulled away from Lex, who kept

his hands firmly on her shoulders, almost as if he was unwilling to let her get away again. They stared at each other for a few seconds, both shyly smiling, their minds racing with the various possibilities of how this awkward yet tempting moment could go.

Lex snapped out of it first. He yanked his hands back to his side, and gave Hayley a nod. "Let me know if you need anything."

He hustled out of the room leaving Hayley shaken. And not from her dramatic dunk in the ocean.

She had been so certain, up until this very moment, that this chapter in her life, her relationship with Lex, had been over for a long, long time.

But now she was not so sure.

Island Food & Spirits
BY HAYLEY POWELL

"The Ladies Who Lunch" was a popular song from the Broadway show *Company*, which Liddy went to see with her family in New York during its 1995 revival. When she arrived home, she sang the song in front of me over and over to the point where it just stuck with me. I'd find myself humming it over the years, not as good as the defining Elaine Stritch version, may she rest in peace, but I can at least carry a tune. Since the title of the song fed into, pardon the pun, my obsession with food, I even considered calling my food and cocktail column here at the Island Times "The Lady Who Lunches," but Sal thought it was too weird and artsy for our local paper so he suggested I stick with something a little less fancy, hence the far more staid and straightforward "Island Food & Spirits."

For years there have been rumors and gossip floating around Bar Harbor that during the summer months there exists a secret society of very chic, very wealthy women, who arrive on the island every year like clockwork to spend the summer months at their various sprawling estates, and who call themselves, coincidentally enough, "The Ladies Who Lunch."

Now to be perfectly honest, no one can really say that they have met or even seen this clandestine group of women, but rest assured, just about everyone on the island has heard a story or two about them.

I know I have. This coterie of hush-hush billionaires supposedly boasts a long list of impressive last names such as Rockefeller, Stewart, and Ford to name a few, and even one summer the name Kennedy (gasp!) was whispered in certain gossip circles. Well, what all these wealthy private women shared in common besides oodles of money was a pure passion for dining on the delicious mouthwatering local seafood and farm-fresh ingredients that our island and other places around Maine have to offer.

Rumor also has it that a summer tradition for the "Ladies Who Lunch" is to choose one lucky local chef to cook for them in the privacy of one of their stately manors. But none of us yokels have ever been able to officially offer any proof of this, or even the existence of the group, for that matter.

However, the stories continue to swirl, and we do hear every so often about one favorite chef in town who suddenly went off the grid for a few days only to reemerge with vague excuses and a self-satisfied look on his or her face like a cat who swallowed a canary. Eager to talk, but bound by either promise or even a contract to remain tight-lipped. All of this just fired up the town gossips, and even yours truly, about how those ladies had struck again and claimed another favorite chef around town as their own.

The rumor mill did bring a lot of young chefs with stars in their eyes and dreams of hosting their own Food Network show to town with the hope that the ladies might pluck them from obscurity and request a sit-down meal, firmly cementing their desire to be "a top chef to the fabulously rich and famous!"

Of course, I've never been a gossip, and yes I say

that with a straight face, nor have I ever known anyone who was ever contacted by this secret society.

That is, until they reached out to me personally!

On Monday, August 22, 2016 at 7:45 A.M. I arrived at the *Island Times* office to find a beautiful cream-colored envelope with gold trim all around the sides and my name printed on the front lying in the middle of my desk. Since I was the first one to arrive at the office, I had no idea where this fancy envelope could have possibly come from, but I immediately plopped down at my desk and carefully opened it, my heart pounding with anticipation.

Inside was an engraved invitation.

My eyes nearly popped out of my head as I read it.

Was this Liddy and Mona pulling some kind of prank?

Or was this actually real?

Dear Ms. Powell,

We would like to request that you prepare for us
a favorite dish of yours
for this Friday, August 26th, 2016,
using of course a local ingredient(s) of your choice.

A car will arrive at your residence
at promptly 12:00 P.M.

We ask that you keep this request to yourself,
and if you would like to accept our invitation,
please take this card outside and hand it
to the gentleman standing
at the front door of your office.

Warmest Regards,

The Ladies Who Lunch

Utter shock would be an understatement. How did these VIPs even know who I was? The only possible answer was that they had read my column, but I couldn't imagine that could be true.

I jumped up from my desk and raced to the front door, swinging it open to find a well-dressed, quietly understated man I had never seen before standing on the front step.

With a warm smile, he plucked the invitation out of my hand and said he would see me Friday at the appointed time. I opened my mouth to thank him but no words came out. I was still too thunderstruck by what was happening. He turned and marched back to an extravagant silver sedan. I wasn't sure of the make or model, just that it was expensive looking. He slid in the driver's seat and pulled away, leaving me standing in the doorway of the *Island Times* office, mouth still agape.

How on earth was I going to get through today and the rest of the week knowing Friday at noon was looming? And more important, how was I going to make it through without telling *anyone*? Not even my brother Randy, or BFFs Mona and Liddy? I tell them *everything* going on in my life! This was going to be torture!

I decided to plow ahead and just keep my mouth shut and make a family favorite—a creamy Goat Cheese Mac and Cheese casserole. I purchased the goat cheese from a local dairy farm I often frequented in order to stay within the rules.

After pleading with Sal to allow me a personal day on Friday even though I had already used them up and it was only August, I nervously prepared my dish. I still could not believe that I was now one of the chosen few, and that soon the mystery of the

"Ladies Who Lunch" would be solved! I would finally know their true identities!

Right on schedule, Friday at noon, the same silver sedan pulled up in front of my house, and with the bubbling, hot Goat Cheese Mac and Cheese casserole fresh from my oven and packed in a carrying case that I cradled in my arms, I headed down the driveway.

The same gentleman who took my invitation card stepped out and gave me a polite nod. He opened the back door, and I was about to climb in when I suddenly noticed four other dishes packed for travel sitting on the backseat. It suddenly dawned on me that my Goat Cheese Mac and Cheese casserole was going to meet the "Ladies Who Lunch" but *not* me! That's why their identities had remained such a closely guarded secret. None of the other chefs they approached had ever met them in the flesh either! I laughed as the gentleman took my carrying case from me and set it down on the backseat along with the others. He then tipped his hat at me, walked back to the driver's side of the sedan, slid in, and drove away.

The next morning, on my doorstep, I discovered my freshly washed casserole dish and a note thanking me for my delicious and decadent contribution. I was assured it had been enjoyed immensely by the ladies, and as an added bonus, there was a gift certificate to a local high-end restaurant. The amount was so generous I was able to treat my two best friends along with my brother and his husband to a spectacular and memorable meal. Let's just say we did it up in style, and had plenty of toasts with our Rum Sunset cocktails to the "Ladies Who Lunch."

Rum Sunsets

6 ounces orange juice
2 ounces light rum
1 tablespoon grenadine
Lime slice for garnish

Pour your orange juice, rum, and mix into a glass filled with ice. Add your grenadine on the top and add a slice of lime for garnish. Now sit back and enjoy the sunset!

Creamy Baked Goat Cheese Mac and Cheese

2 tablespoons butter
1 clove garlic, minced
2 tablespoons chopped fresh basil leaves
1 cup panko bread crumbs
1¾ cup freshly grated Parmesan cheese
1 pound (16 ounces) pasta shells (or feel free
   to use your favorite pasta)
2 cups heavy cream
16 ounces goat cheese
½ cup pesto sauce, store-bought or homemade
1 teaspoon kosher salt
1 teaspoon freshly ground pepper

Spray or butter a 2-quart baking dish and set aside.

Melt the two tablespoons butter in a small saucepan and then add your garlic, basil, panko, and ¼ cup of the grated cheese. Mix well and set aside. Bring a large pot of salted water to a boil and cook your pasta according to the directions on the box.

Meanwhile simmer your 2 cups of cream in a medium saucepan over low heat 5–6 minutes, until a little thick and reduced. Save at least ½ cup of the pasta water and then drain your pasta in a colander and set aside. Place your pasta pot back on the stove on low and add the warm cream and goat cheese and whisk until smooth. Then add the rest of the Parmesan, whisking until melted.

Turn off heat and add the cooked pasta and pesto, mixing until everything is coated, adding your pasta water a little at a time if mixture is too thick. Salt and pepper to taste.

Pour the pasta in the greased baking dish and top with the reserved butter and panko mixture.

Place under a preheated broiler until the crust is brown and the top is bubbly.

Cool for a few minutes then dig in and enjoy!

Chapter 15

Later that afternoon, Hayley stumbled down to the kitchen in search of some canned soup in the pantry that she could heat up on a burner, hoping it might warm her up and make her feel a little better.

She found some of the kitchen help, the pretty young girl Gloria, who had previously been so helpful with her account of witnessing Conrad crushing up some mysterious pills in Penelope's warm milk before bed, and another staffer Rose, about the same age, plump, rosy-cheeked, with frizzy black hair that she had tightly tied up in a bun. They were plopped down on a pair of kitchen stools next to the island, whispering and giggling until they noticed Hayley approaching.

They quickly hopped off the stools and snapped to attention.

"Hello, Ms. Powell," Rose chirped, a forced smile

on her face. "We heard you were a bit under the weather."

"Yes, I am . . . I fell off the boat during our outing earlier today, and now I'm fighting a nasty cold," Hayley said.

Gloria relaxed, and gave Rose a furtive look, signaling her that she needn't worry.

Hayley was not an enemy.

"I'm looking for some soup," Hayley said, heading toward the pantry.

"Oh, there's some leftover homemade chicken noodle soup in the fridge that Penelope made herself. It's quite delicious. Let me warm some up for you," Rose said, scurrying off to the refrigerator.

"Thank you so much. I'm hoping I feel better by dinnertime since I'm sure our esteemed hostess will have the camera crew recording us eating every bite of whatever she's preparing," Hayley said, regretting ever jumping at the chance to spend the weekend here.

And then she sneezed.

And sneezed again.

And again.

Gloria tore a bunch of paper towels off a thick roll on the counter and handed them to Hayley, who accepted them gratefully and blew her nose.

"If not, I may just give up and go home," she said, balling up the used towels when she was finished and tossing them in the trash bin.

"Who was on the boat with you today?" Gloria asked casually.

"Penelope, Gerard, Tristan, Carol . . ."

"So all the usual suspects," Rose said as she stood at the stove, slowly stirring the soup in a copper saucepan.

"Yes, plus the crew," Hayley added.

"Oh, that Tommy is *so* cute!" Rose cooed, lost in her fantasies, probably of young Tommy tenderly ravishing her during a romantic afternoon sail.

"She's got such a *huge* crush on him," Gloria said, laughing.

But then Gloria suddenly got serious, and leaned into Hayley and whispered, "So which one do you think pushed you overboard?"

Hayley was taken aback.

She hadn't expect this line of questioning from one of Penelope's employees, but then again, she and Gloria had somewhat bonded the night before, cleaning up the mess from Conrad's drunken hissy fit, so she probably felt at ease and comfortable talking freely to her.

"So you heard about the crazy lady screaming about someone shoving her over the railing, leaving her to drown at sea?"

"You bet we did!" Rose said breathlessly, as she poured the steaming soup from the saucepan into a bowl, peppering it with a few spices before grabbing a spoon from the cupboard and delivering it to Hayley.

"Thank you," Hayley said, gratefully accepting the soup.

"I'm Rose, by the way. I work with Gloria."

"I'm Hayley, nice to meet you."

"Pleasure. I've only been working here for a few weeks. Gloria got me the job. We're best friends so it's nice we get to work together."

"We tell each other all our secrets," Gloria said, smiling at her buddy, before turning back to Hayley. "And I mean *everything*!"

They both giggled like schoolgirls.

Gloria stepped forward closer to Hayley, full of anticipation. "So?"

She noticed Hayley's hesitancy as she made a sideways glance toward Rose.

"Seriously, you don't have to worry about Rose. We both know not to blab what we hear down here. We only tell each other things when we know we're alone," Gloria said. "You can get canned pretty quick if you're not careful."

"It was Tristan!" Rose said, slapping the palm of her hand down on the island countertop as if all the suspects had been gathered in the drawing room and Miss Marple was finally unveiling the culprit.

"I was going to say him too!" Gloria cried, thrilled to be on the same page with her bestie.

"Why? What makes you say that?" Hayley asked.

"Do you want to tell her?" Gloria asked Rose.

Rose shook her head. "No, you tell her!"

Hayley wanted to scream "*Please, just somebody tell me!*"

But she remained calm, and casually sipped her soup.

"Well, it was no big secret Conrad was obsessed with Penelope's ghostwriter, I mean secretary, which is what we've all been told to call her since

Penelope thinks nobody knows that Lena actually writes all of her books . . ."

Rose jumped in, unable to contain herself any longer. "We'd see the two of them together, taking quiet strolls around the property, it was *so* obvious he was head over heels in love, and one time I even overheard him say he wanted to leave Penelope to be with Lena."

"Well, you *thought* you heard that, but that was the night we stole what was left of the dessert wine after one of Penelope's big dinner parties and you were pretty wasted . . ."

"I know what I heard!" Rose yelled.

Hayley was entirely sympathetic to Rose, having her own hearing questioned on her first night at the estate.

"But apparently Lena was resistant, and didn't want Conrad leaving Penelope because she was interested in someone else," Gloria said in a hushed tone. "*Not* Conrad!"

"Tristan?" Hayley asked, not at all surprised after she saw them canoodling in the garden.

"Yes, and Conrad found out, and was enraged," Rose piped in as if excitedly recounting the plotline of her favorite soap opera. "And the gardener overheard Conrad tell Lena that he would go out of his way to make her life miserable if she didn't dump this other guy immediately and just be with him!"

"We think Lena and Tristan were in cahoots to get Conrad out of the picture so they could finally be free of him and his threats!" Gloria said in an urgent whisper.

"That would be so romantic," Rose sighed, completely forgetting the fact that their little love story involved them committing cold-blooded murder.

"Chop, chop, girls, we have a lot of work to do before dinner and we're already hours behind schedule," a familiar voice bellowed, causing Gloria and Rose to quickly back away from Hayley and pretend to be busy.

Clara appeared, her crisp, clean linen apron tied around her waist and a clipboard with a pad of paper in hand. She tore off a piece of paper and handed it to Rose. "Here you go, Rose. These are the items I need at the grocery store. I want you back here in an hour with everything on that list! No flirting with the stock boys!"

"Yes, Clara!" Rose squeaked before rushing out of the kitchen.

"Penelope wants to use the Royal Copenhagen china tonight, Gloria. You'll find the key to the Bramley Hall chest in the left-hand drawer. I want it all cleaned and the silverware polished," Clara said, as Gloria scooted to the drawer, grabbed the key, and hauled butt out the door.

Clara finally noticed Hayley standing there, empty soup bowl in one hand and a big spoon in the other.

She grimaced but kept her cool.

"Penelope hired me back this afternoon," Clara said triumphantly, as if Hayley had actually been the one advocating for her dismissal. "She's hosting a barbecue on the estate that's open to the public on the Monday after Fourth of July so she needs all the help she can get."

"Welcome back," Hayley said.

"Thank you," Clara sneered. "She's depended on me for years, and now that her husband is gone, may he rest in peace, she needs me more than ever."

"Well, I'm happy it all worked out," Hayley said, growing more uncomfortable with each passing moment.

"In many ways, I'm much closer to her than her late husband ever was," Clara said, a smug look on her face. "And nothing or no one is going to get in the way of that."

Hayley shuddered as Clara glared at her with unbridled scorn.

Hayley agreed with Gloria and Rose that there was a strong plausibility in their theory of Lena and Tristan conspiring together against Conrad, who if the rumors were true, was threatening them if they didn't end their relationship.

But there was another theory slowly coming into focus.

Right here in front of Hayley was a woman who had been unceremoniously fired by the murder victim, tossed out of the house after years of hard work and fierce loyalty over one bad mussel in a batch of a dozen. And then suddenly, the tables had turned. Conrad was now just a stiff tagged and logged in at the morgue while Clara was happily back at work, once again reunited with her beloved boss, a world-famous household name, her power position in the kitchen once again firmly secured.

It was highly suspicious.

Clara gave Hayley a crooked smile as she snatched the bowl and spoon out of her hands. "Here, let me take these and clean them for you."

Clara had a strange look in her eye.

It was as if she was daring Hayley to just try and mess with her again.

She could plainly see that Clara was feeling confident that she would never be fired again now that Conrad was out of the picture.

And she was happy to be rid of him.

Chapter 16

"All I've been hearing from my sources is that Conrad was a hopeless drunk who probably lost his balance while trying to light his pipe and accidentally fell over the side of the cliff to his death," Bruce Linney said on the phone when Hayley called him at the *Island Times* between coughing and sneezing fits.

"Well, I'm convinced there is a lot more to it than that, Bruce. There are a number of people here with very good reasons to want to see Conrad dead, including our hostess Penelope Janice!" Hayley said before covering the mouthpiece of the phone and coughing.

"Hayley? Hayley? Are you still there?"

She set the phone down and coughed a few more times, unable to speak, blew her nose into a wad of Kleenex, and then picked up her phone again. "Yes, I'm still here. I have a terrible head cold."

"It sounds like you're on to something big,"

Bruce said, excited. "Maybe it's time I join the investigation."

"What are you talking about?"

"Ask Penelope if it would be okay if your boyfriend joined you for the remainder of the weekend."

"I don't have a boyfriend."

"You do now."

"Bruce, my head is fuzzy, my nose is stuffy, my throat is scratchy, and try as I might, I just don't understand what you're saying."

"I'm going to pack a bag and head over there and pretend to be your boyfriend so I can help you get to the bottom of what really happened to Conrad."

"Bruce, I'm not feeling well, and I'm ready to forget this whole thing and just go home and crawl into my own bed . . ."

"You can rest in bed there in the lap of luxury and let me do all the poking around. Plus if I'm there as a guest, I'll have access to the whole property, and nobody will suspect what I'm really up to," Bruce said.

"Bruce, no, I don't think that's a good idea . . ."

"What's the harm in asking?"

He was going to strong-arm Hayley until she agreed, and they both knew it.

Hayley dropped the phone and coughed some more.

"Hayley, are you there?"

She picked up the phone, cleared her throat, and growled, "I'm here. I'm not sure Penelope is going to want a stranger around, especially a journalist who writes about true crimes, given all that's

happened. But okay, Bruce, you win, I'll ask her.
But I can't guarantee she is going to go for it."

"Great. Should I bring a jacket and tie? Are the
meals semiformal?"

"No, Bruce, but just hold on until I ask her."

"Fine. Call me back when you get the all clear."

He hung up.

She had to admire his optimism.

As if just the name Bruce Linney would ensure an
invite.

Hayley started coughing again.

Well, much to Hayley's surprise, Penelope jumped
at the idea of Hayley's "boyfriend" Bruce joining
them when she found her in the kitchen going over
the evening's menu with Clara.

Clara perked up too. She claimed to be a fan of
Bruce Linney's crime column in the *Island Times*,
and casually mentioned how handsome he was in
his byline photo, having never had the pleasure of
meeting him in person.

Neither seemed even remotely concerned that
Bruce's job involved covering local crimes.

Penelope told Gloria, who was hovering by the
stove eavesdropping, to find Pam the maid and
have some extra towels delivered to Hayley's room.

That's when it dawned on Hayley that she and
Bruce would be sharing a bedroom.

Of course it made total sense.

After all, Bruce was posing as her boyfriend.
Penelope would naturally assume they would want
to share the same bed.

How on earth were they going to manage that?

Penelope's obvious enthusiasm over Hayley having a date also made perfect sense. She was most likely hoping his presence might keep Hayley distracted and out of trouble for the rest of the weekend.

Bruce arrived within the hour, overnight bag in hand, and bounded into the house like he owned the place, pumping hands and cracking jokes. Penelope was instantly charmed by him and welcomed him as if she had known him for years. Despite his sometimes grating personality, Bruce could slip into any social situation with ease and win over whomever he needed in order to get the information he wanted. That's what made him such a great reporter.

Hayley showed him to their room, and he dropped his bag on the floor, grabbed a towel and robe, and headed off to find the bathroom to take a shower as it was already close to dinnertime.

Hayley changed into a floral print short-sleeved blouse, her white capri pants, and some low-wedge strap sandals and spritzed some perfume on her neck. She stuffed a wad of Kleenex in her pants pocket because she knew she would never make it through dinner without succumbing to a coughing or sneezing fit.

Bruce returned freshly showered and wearing his plush white robe. He bent over to fish through his bag for a change of clothes. Hayley turned her back to him while he slipped on some khaki pants and a smart blue polo shirt and some Ralph Lauren canvas slip-on sneakers with no socks. He also sprayed on some Calvin Klein cologne, too much in fact, so the scent was overwhelming. Hayley made a point of waving it away as she coughed, more from the cologne this time than from her cold.

Bruce checked his watch. "Come on. We don't want to be late for cocktails."

They headed downstairs to the dining room, and just as they rounded the corner, Bruce reached out and grabbed Hayley's hand.

She flinched at first.

It felt so weird holding hands with Bruce.

But she finally relaxed into it and smiled, pretending it was the most natural thing in the world, as the other guests greeted them.

It took Bruce less than five minutes to bond with Gerard. He complimented him on a recent episode of his show, a culinary excursion to Thailand, a country Bruce had traveled through extensively and knew much about. Gerard lit up, and quickly engaged Bruce in a long conversation about his various adventures, allowing Gerard to talk about his favorite subject—himself.

Gerard eventually waved over his son Tristan, who had been making small talk with Carol, and all three men huddled together in deep conversation.

Left with no one else to talk to, Carol bounced over to Hayley.

"How are you feeling, Hayley?"

"Fine, thank you, Carol."

"I heard you have a bit of a cold after paddling around in the ocean for so long today."

"It wasn't a late morning swim, Carol. I *fell* overboard," she said, hitting the word "fell" hard enough so as not to cause another stir by insinuating that she had been violently pushed.

"You know, the proper diet goes a long way in optimizing your health . . ."

"I'll be sure to pick up one of your books," Hayley said dismissively.

She was tired of Carol's rants about the proper foods that she should consume. Her advice only made Hayley want to chow down on a cheeseburger and French fries.

Penelope swept in the room at the appointed hour, smartly dressed in a shrimp-colored button-up tunic, gazebo pants, and high heels. She had a glow about her as if she hadn't been this happy in years, the death of her husband a distant memory even though he had only died that morning. On her heels were the camera crew hustling into the room behind her, trying to catch various guests greeting her.

Penelope immediately homed in on Bruce, catching his eye, and making a point of welcoming him to the party loudly enough for everyone to hear. The producer signaled the cameraman to get a shot of the new face on the scene.

When the guests all took their places at the table, Penelope insisted Bruce sit next to her and across from Gerard, who was now his best buddy, the two already planning a foodie trip to China. Hayley was shunted to the end of the table between Carol and an empty seat that had probably been reserved for Conrad before his unexpected plummet over the side of a cliff.

Carol managed to turn her back slightly to Hayley, and spent most of the meal chatting with Tristan, so Hayley ate quietly, nodding and laughing at the jokes made closer to the head of the table, pretending to be enjoying her meal when what she really wanted was to be in bed recovering from this beastly cold.

Bruce, on the other hand, was having the time of his life. He soaked up the attention and relished entertaining everyone with his maverick journalist stories. Some of them were actually true. Bruce had a knack for embellishing his accomplishments from time to time. Once when he located a local embezzler who had fled Maine to a condo in Fort Myers, Florida, he called the local authorities and they went over and arrested him without incident. But by the time Bruce published his story, he made it appear in his article that he had gone down there himself, wrestled the perpetrator to the ground, and personally handcuffed him and delivered him with much fanfare back to the local courthouse to stand trial for his crimes. There was also no mention that the guy was eighty-seven years old and needed an oxygen tank because of his emphysema.

Hayley managed to struggle through the evening until dessert. Clara arrived, her eyes dancing at the sight of Bruce, and offered him one of her small homemade eclairs from a tray of sweets she had personally prepared. Bruce popped it in his mouth, the cream filling oozing out onto the sides of his mouth. He moaned rapturously, and paid Clara the utmost compliment by immediately grabbing another. Everyone laughed, and Clara nearly toppled over from swooning.

It was more than Hayley could take.

She was about to excuse herself when Clara, having gone around the room, finally landed next to her.

She stiffly held out her tray. There were only two sweets left since Carol had demurred, not wanting that much sugar in her delicate system.

A cream puff and a fudge nut brownie.

Hayley eyed them both, but she knew her stomach was still weak from the food poisoning, and so she just smiled slightly and shook her hand. "No, thank you, Clara."

Clara's eyes flared, insulted at being so overtly disparaged. She leaned down and whispered in Hayley's ear. "What's the matter? Do you think I poisoned these too?"

Hayley locked eyes with her.

Did she just admit to poisoning the mussels?

And was she trying again, hoping to finish the job this time?

"Or would you prefer it if I brought out a fresh batch of mussels?" Clara sneered.

Just the idea of mussels made Hayley's stomach

turn, and she stood up quickly, excusing herself, and made a mad dash to the bathroom, coughing and hacking the whole way.

Would this weekend *ever* end?

And when it did, would she still be alive?

Chapter 17

By the time Hayley finally made it back to the room, Bruce was already there rifling through his overnight bag for a Ziploc bag of his toiletries.

Hayley stumbled toward the bed ready to do a face-plant right into the center of it.

"Want to flip a coin to see who gets the bed?" Bruce asked casually. "You have a fifty-fifty chance of winning."

"I don't need to flip for it because there is a one hundred percent chance that I will be under those covers fast asleep in less than a minute."

"I was joking. Of course you can have the bed!"

"Where are you going to sleep?"

Bruce looked around. "I don't know. Probably the floor."

He knelt down and tapped the floor gently with the palm of his hand.

"Now I know why they call them hardwood floors . . . because the wood . . . it's really hard."

Hayley felt a twinge of guilt.

She didn't want him up all night tossing and turning on a hard, dusty floor.

Sighing, Hayley waved at Bruce to get up.

He stood upright again and looked at her expectantly.

"You can share the bed with me. Just stay on your own side."

"No, I don't want to do anything that might make you feel uncomfortable."

"Honestly, I don't mind you sleeping in the same bed with me."

"No, I mean staying on my own side," Bruce quipped.

"Very funny, Bruce! Can't you see how hard I'm laughing?" Hayley quipped, stone-faced.

"The floor's fine. Really," Bruce said getting down on his knees and walking around on all fours to find the perfect spot. He turned around in a few circles while he debated.

"You're worse than my cat Blueberry trying to find a spot to lie down," Hayley said, yawning. "Are you sure you're okay down there?"

"Yes, no worries. I'll be fine."

"You're absolutely sure?"

"Yes, Hayley, I'm sure."

"All right then," Hayley said, watching Bruce stretch out on his back on the hardwood floor. "Good night."

"Good night," Bruce said, staring at the ceiling.

Hayley shut off the lamp that was on the dresser next to the bed and slid deeper underneath the covers and burrowed her head in the stack of lace pillows.

"Oh, this is going to kill my back!" Bruce cried in the darkness.

Hayley sat up and snapped the light back on.

"Get in the bed, Bruce," she sighed.

Bruce popped up to his feet with a big grin on his face. "Thanks, Hayley."

He began unbuttoning his shirt.

"What are you doing?" Hayley asked.

He was now shirtless and working on his belt buckle.

"Getting undressed."

"Well, how far are you planning to go?"

"Actually, all the way. I like to sleep in the nude."

Hayley opened her mouth to protest but Bruce held up a hand.

"Relax, I'll stop at my underwear."

"You didn't pack pajamas?"

"What am I, twelve? No, Hayley. I obviously didn't think this through. I never expected to be sharing a room with you."

Bruce shimmied out of his pants and stood before Hayley in nothing but his Calvin Klein briefs.

"I always pictured you as a boxers kind of guy," Hayley said, unable to resist staring at his surprisingly well-worked-out body.

"Yeah, well I'm a briefs man. You got a problem with that?"

"No, not at all."

Bruce went around the side of the bed and

climbed in, drawing the comforter up over him and turning his back to Hayley.

"Good night, Hayley."

"Good night, Bruce."

Hayley reached over and once again shut the lamp on the dresser off.

She shut her eyes and snuggled deep inside the covers and was just about to drift off to sleep when Bruce sneezed.

The sound and force of it nearly caused her to fly out of the bed and find shelter underneath a doorway as if she were in the middle of an earthquake, but she remained in her sideways sleeping position.

She closed her eyes to try again.

Bruce sneezed, even louder this time.

And then he sneezed three more times in quick succession.

She could hear him rummaging around for a tissue.

Hayley sat up in bed, reached over, and once again turned on the light. "Don't tell me I gave you my cold already?"

Bruce was sitting up in bed, covering his face with a wad of Kleenex.

He shook his head.

"This isn't a cold. This is my allergies."

"What are you allergic to?"

"Cats."

Hayley shot out of bed and searched the room. "Sebastian! He must have snuck in here and is hiding somewhere."

Bruce sneezed again and rubbed his watery eyes.

"Oh, this is bad. Hayley, you have to find that cat or it's just going to get worse!"

"I'm looking! I'm looking!"

She dropped to her knees and peered under the bed.

Sure enough, there was Sebastian, crouched down, staring out at her, incensed over the intrusion of this unwanted guest.

"Come here, Sebastian! Be a good kitty and come to Hayley!"

Hayley stretched her arms out to try and pull Sebastian out, but he backed away out of her reach, growling and hissing.

"Did you get him?"

"Not yet. He's not being very cooperative," she said before making kissing sounds as if that might entice him to come out from underneath the bed.

"Well, hurry! I'm dying here!"

"I'm doing my best!" Hayley was flat on her stomach, shoving herself farther underneath the bed, trying to get within reach of Sebastian. Her fingers managed to wrap around his swishing tail. Sebastian hissed some more and took a swipe at Hayley with his claws, which caught the tip of her finger, drawing blood.

"Ouch! All right, you have officially worn out your welcome!" Hayley wailed, quickly withdrawing her hand and scooting back out from under the bed. She looked at Bruce, who had splotches of red on various parts of his arms and legs and looked miserable as he continued to sneeze and blow his nose.

"Bruce, do you have something to lure him out with, like a feather or something?"

"Yes, Hayley, I have my complete collection of feathers in my overnight bag. No, I don't have a frigging feather! I wasn't expecting to share a room or have playtime with a cat tonight!"

"Okay, calm down! I'll find something!"

Hayley remembered something.

Her laser pointer that her son Dustin had given her one Christmas.

Cats loved those!

She raced to her bag and foraged through it for the pen. Unable to immediately locate it, Hayley, flustered and frustrated, upended the bag and spilled the contents all over the bed. A cascade of loose change, keys, chewing gum, paper clips, rubber bands, lip gloss, sunglasses, chocolates, and pepper spray poured out. Finally, the last item out, as if not wanting to see the light, was the pen. It tumbled out and landed softly on the comforter.

Hayley scooped it up, dropped back down to her knees, and began jiggling the pen around so the red light danced around Sebastian, whose head was spinning at a dizzying pace as his eyes followed the laser. He tried stopping it with his paw but it was frustratingly elusive. Hayley moved the light slowly so Sebastian could keep his eyes glued on it as it moved out from under the bed.

Unable to resist, Sebastian scampered out after it.

Hayley dropped the light and made a mad grab

Chapter 18

Hayley was startled awake by the sound of men's voices in the distance, yelling at each other. She tried to move, but seemed to be pinned down. She felt a weight holding her across the waist. She shifted and turned her head to see the unconscious face of Bruce Linney, eyes closed and mouth open with short grunting snores escaping past his lips. He was sound asleep. He also had an arm slung around her waist and was cuddling with her.

Hayley wriggled free from his thick muscled arm and slipped out of bed. She padded over to the window and peered out. She didn't see anyone outside, but could still hear the men shouting.

Suddenly there was a loud banging on the door. "Hurry! Everybody out of the house now!" a man hollered, and then he was gone.

Hayley spun around to Bruce, who was hugging pillow and still snoring softly, his bare leg hanging out over the edge of the bed.

Hayley rushed over and tried to shake him awake.

for Sebastian, but he slipped through her fingers and darted across the room right in Bruce's direction.

Bruce recoiled at first, but he knew he was the only chance to stop the cat before it circled around and scurried back underneath the bed.

He reached down and plucked the Persian cat right off the floor. He squeezed his eyes shut and looked away, holding the cat at a full arm's-length distance, letting Sebastian dangle in front of him, as Bruce raced to the door. Sebastian was so stunned by his sudden capture he became completely submissive and didn't even try to struggle.

Bruce fastened him to his chest with one arm and reached out to open the doorknob with the other. When he yanked open the door, Lex Bansfield stood there, his knuckles up as if he was just about to knock on the door.

Lex stared at Bruce, who was holding a cat in his arms and wearing just his underwear.

"I swore I was at the right room," Lex said, dumbfounded.

Hayley suddenly appeared next to Bruce. "No, it's the right room, Lex. What are you doing here?"

"I just came by to see if you needed anything. I'm heading into town early tomorrow morning. Maybe some more cold medicine or aspirin?" he asked, glancing at Bruce, who was tensing up and about to let loose with a massive sneeze.

And then he did.

Right in Lex's face.

Bruce was still holding Sebastian, who was now wriggling to free himself, so he didn't have a hand free to cover his mouth. Bruce set Sebastian down on the floor and then tapped his butt, which surprised the cat enough to send him hurtling out the door and down the hall in a panic.

Bruce looked at Lex. "Sorry."

Lex wiped his face with a handkerchief he had pulled out of his back pocket. "Guess you caught Hayley's cold."

Hayley could only imagine what Lex must be thinking as he considered just *how* Bruce had caught Hayley's cold.

"It was the cat! Bruce is allergic to cats!" Hayley blurted out, a bit too quickly.

Lex nodded. "Allergic to clothes too apparently."

Bruce, who had slightly recovered from his allergy attack now that Sebastian had dropped the mic and left the stage, put an arm around Hayley and with a sly smile, said to Lex, "I'm her boyfriend."

"Oh, I see," Lex said, eyeing Hayley disappointedly, now convinced she had lied to him when she had told him she was single.

Bruce tightened his grip on Hayley's shoulder and pulled her closer to him either protectively or possessively, she couldn't tell which one it was.

"Sorry to bother you, folks. You have a good night," Lex said, slowly backing out of the room.

"Night," Bruce said, waiting until Lex had cleared the doorway and was safely out in the hall before he slammed the door shut.

Exasperated, Hayley spun around "Why did you tell him you're my boyfrie

"Because I am," he said. "At least tonig Hayley, it's very important we maintain You never know who he might talk to or could tell them," Bruce said, not the leas cerned that he might have damaged a fu mantic prospect for Hayley.

Especially one with whom she had a comp history.

No, Bruce wasn't concerned at all.

In fact, he appeared to be loving every m of it.

Bruce jumped under the covers and pla motioned for her to join him.

"Keep dreaming," she said, rolling her ey she crawled into the other side of the bed an off the light one last time.

"Oh, don't you worry, I will," he said in the Great.

Her mind would be racing all night wor just what he had meant by that comment.

Now she was never going to get any slee

"Bruce, something's happening! We need to get out of the house!"

He snorted and turned away from her, and was now flopped on his back, not happy to be roused out of his slumber.

Hayley grabbed his arm and shook harder.

"Bruce! I'm not kidding! Wake up *now*!"

He grumbled and moaned to himself before he reluctantly opened his eyes, surprised to find himself staring into Hayley's face.

"What?" he asked sleepily.

"Come on! We have to get out of here!"

Hayley ripped off the comforter and sheets, leaving his nearly naked self lying on top of the mattress, arms and legs spread out to the four corners, like he was making a snow angel.

Hayley noticed a strong smoky smell in the air, not quite like the smell of a pipe, but rather a fire pit burning.

Suddenly her entire body shook with fear.

"Oh my God! The house is on fire! Bruce, let's go!"

She grabbed his arm and hauled him out of bed.

He crashed to the floor, and was finally fully awake.

"Fire? What?"

Bruce sniffed the air a few times, and when it finally clicked in his brain that the house was burning down and their lives were in danger, he jumped to his feet, grabbed Hayley's hand, and hightailed it out of there with Hayley in tow.

He forgot he was still only wearing his underwear.

Hayley and Bruce scrambled out the door to the

immaculately landscaped front yard of the main house on the estate, visible by the porch lights which had all been turned on, and quickly realized they were the last ones to escape as all of Penelope's other guests were already huddled together in various stages of dress. Penelope was directing her household staff to make sure everyone was accounted for, and to report back to her immediately.

They were suddenly bathed in flashing red lights as two fire trucks arrived, careening down the dirt road from the main gate, sirens wailing.

Hayley looked back at the house and saw thick clouds of black smoke billowing up over the rooftop, but no flames.

She still didn't know where the fire was burning.

Penelope wrapped her silk baby-blue bathrobe tighter around her as she raced up to the four firemen jumping down from their truck and frantically spoke to them while gesturing wildly toward the house. The firemen jogged around the side of the mansion while the remaining men worked feverishly to unhook the hose from the truck.

A few minutes later, the group of firemen emerged, walking calmly, but all with somber looks on their faces.

They spoke to Penelope in hushed whispers, and from the reaction on Penelope's face, it wasn't good news.

Bruce, who was now freezing in the chilly night temperatures, wearing only his underwear, hugged himself as he sidled up next to Hayley.

"What do you think is going on?"

"I don't know, but I think the fire was already out by the time they got here," Hayley said, watching the scene unfold.

Penelope hugged the fire chief, thanking him profusely, and then wiped a tear away from her eye. She glanced over at her houseguests, all of whom stood numbly in the cold, confused and disoriented.

Hayley couldn't stand the suspense anymore.

She walked briskly over to Penelope, who stood with a hand over her mouth as she stared at the house, lost in deep thought.

"Penelope, do you know what started the fire?"

Penelope shook her head.

"Where was it?"

"The pantry."

"But it's out now so we have that to be thankful for," Hayley said, trying to get some kind of reaction out of Penelope, who remained in a trance-like state. "It could have been much worse."

Penelope's eyes brimmed with tears. "Lex and his crew managed to put it out before the fire department could get here."

"Well, you're lucky they were here to stop the blaze before it spread to other parts of the house," Hayley said, watching Penelope, who seemed on the verge of some kind of breakdown. She stepped forward and gently placed a hand on Penelope's shoulder. "Penelope, what is it? What's wrong?"

"Lex and his men smelled smoke and realized

there was a fire, but they didn't know where the smoke was coming from, so it took them a while to locate the source. They finally saw it pouring out from underneath the door of the pantry so they got buckets of water to put it out, but the pantry door was locked and they had to bust it down. After they doused the fire and some of the smoke cleared, that's when they saw her . . ."

"Her? Who?"

"Lena. She was lying on the floor. They think she may be dead."

"What?"

Hayley heard a police siren in the near distance fast approaching.

Somebody had called 911.

As Hayley comforted Penelope, the police cruiser sped down the road along with the emergency ambulance right on its tail. Both vehicles screeched to a stop. Sergio and two of his officers, Donnie and Earl, bolted from the cruiser while a pair of paramedics rolled a gurney out of the back of the ambulance, and they all raced around the side of the house to the entrance in the back where the kitchen and pantry were located.

Bruce casually strolled up to Hayley and Penelope and cleared his throat. "So does the fire department have any idea when it might be safe to go back inside the house?"

"Not now, Bruce!" Hayley barked.

"I just want to put some pants on! I'm not asking for the world, Hayley!"

"It shouldn't be too long," Penelope whispered. "I'm so sorry for the inconvenience."

"It's no inconvenience, Penelope. He's *fine*!" Hayley exclaimed, giving Bruce the evil eye as he stood barefoot in the dirt, shivering and hugging himself.

"I can't lose her, Hayley. Please tell me she's going to be okay," Penelope said, her voice cracking, as she buried her face in Hayley's chest.

"She's going to be fine," Hayley said.

There was that word again.

Fine.

Everything's going to be fine.

Hayley never knew why she said things like that.

Very rarely was everything fine.

Especially right now at this moment.

And more important, she had no idea what she was talking about. She had no idea what the hell was going on in the pantry.

But she did know one thing.

Penelope Janice seemed far more upset over her assistant's possible demise than she did over her own husband's death just hours before.

She could barely muster even the slightest frown for that one.

Lena was reportedly embroiled in an affair with Penelope's husband.

Wouldn't that have drastically changed Penelope's opinion of her?

Put a marked strain on their working *and* personal relationship?

But right now Penelope was sobbing and weeping as if she was on the verge of losing her own daughter.

The paramedics reappeared swiftly, rolling the gurney toward the ambulance. There was a supine body strapped in to it. Penelope broke away from Hayley and rushed over to the paramedics, running alongside them.

"Is she going to be okay?"

"Out of the way, ma'am!"

Penelope reached down and stroked Lena's black-smudged face. "Lena, speak to me! Are you all right?"

"Out of the way, please, ma'am!" the paramedic screamed again as they tried to load Lena and the gurney into the back of the ambulance. "She has severe smoke inhalation and we need to get her to the hospital."

Gerard Roquefort finally had the good sense to run over and pull a near hysterical Penelope off the gurney so the paramedics could transport Lena to the hospital for urgent care.

Bruce finished talking to the fire chief and quickly turned and yelled to the other guests, "Hey, everybody! It's safe to go back inside!"

And then he turned and trotted off inside to find some clothes.

The guests slowly filed back into the house, but Hayley remained outside.

She was going to wait for Sergio.

Hayley knew in her gut that he had been called to the scene for a reason.

When Sergio finally reappeared nearly half an hour later, Hayley made a fast beeline for him. "Why did they call you if it was just a pantry fire?"

Sergio glanced around to make sure no one saw him talking to her, but with the exception of Donnie and Earl, who were too busy teasing each other over something silly, there was no nobody else around.

"The fire department did a routine sweep of the pantry after they got here. The fire was already out thanks to Lex and his crew, but they found a few suspicious items so they thought it would be wise to call me" Sergio said.

"What kind of suspicious items?"

"A cat food dispenser," he said, straight-faced.

Hayley waited a moment, letting that one hang in the air.

"Okay, I'll bite. How is a cat food dispenser suspicious?"

"Not just the cat food dispenser, but the other items that were close by. I also found a timer, some chlorine tablets, a bottle of brake fluid. Now separately, I wouldn't give them a second thought, but together . . . ?"

"What do they do together?"

"There's a way you can rig a cat food dispenser with a timer that releases chlorine tablets and brake fluid, which when mixed causes a small explosion. And then you've got yourself a fire."

"So we're talking arson?" Hayley gasped.

"No, Hayley, somebody locked that poor girl

inside the pantry from the outside having already rigged an explosion to cause a fire around the same time, knowing she would be trapped in there. She swallowed a lot of smoke and might not make it. If she dies, we're not talking arson, we're talking murder!"

Chapter 19

"That's preposterous!" Penelope snorted, sipping a cup of coffee on her back porch that looked out over the dark blue waters of the Atlantic just as the sun was creeping up over the tip of Cadillac Mountain in Acadia National Park, bathing the whole island in a golden hue. Penelope was still in her cream-colored silk nightgown, most of which was covered by a cherry blossom and crane kimono robe she had probably picked up while doing a sushi special in Japan for her TV show. "Who on earth would get the wild idea to rig my cat food dispenser with some kind of bomb? For what possible purpose?"

"Someone who wanted to cause a lot of damage either to you, or your home, or anyone near the pantry—like Miss Hendricks," Sergio said, stone-faced.

Hayley hovered behind him, watching Penelope, who on the surface appeared genuinely perplexed and upset about this whole disruptive and disturbing situation.

"It's just such a wild notion. Why would anyone want to hurt poor Lena?"

There was a long pause.

Penelope's own motive for eliminating Lena Hendricks was the elephant in the room, and she was not about to acknowledge it.

"We are not sure whether Miss Hendricks was the intended victim, or if she just happened to be in the wrong place at the wrong time when the timer went off causing the chemical explosion," Sergio said.

"But the chief does know that someone purposely locked Lena inside that pantry just before the fire started," Hayley said, before catching herself, realizing she had just broken her own vow to stay silent and allow Sergio to do his job.

Penelope stared at Hayley, her mouth dropped open, her lip quivering. "Someone . . . locked her . . . inside?"

"Your groundskeeper Lex Bansfield and a couple of his men had to break down the door to get to her. There's no telling how long she had been trapped in there, and there was no one around in or near the kitchen who would have heard her cries for help, not until people in the house began smelling smoke and realized there was a fire," Sergio said solemnly.

Penelope sat down in a wicker rocking chair as if the wind had suddenly been knocked out of her. Sergio studied her behavior closely, trying to determine if her obviously pained reaction was natural or a well-rehearsed performance from a seasoned TV performer used to being in the spotlight and having a camera follow her around to record her every action and emotion.

Hayley was already convinced Penelope wasn't faking it, having witnessed firsthand how genuinely distraught she was when she first learned Lena had been seriously injured.

"Is there any word yet? Is she going to make it?" Penelope asked, her voice cracking.

"I honestly don't know," Sergio said quietly, shaking his head. "They're still treating her at the hospital."

"I just don't understand why anyone would do such a horrible thing . . . to Lena, of all people, she was such a sweet girl . . ."

"It could be the same person who pushed Conrad over that cliff," Hayley said, unable to stop herself.

Penelope's eyes narrowed, focusing squarely on Hayley, and she growled in a low voice, "By all accounts, Hayley, my husband had too much to drink and fell off that cliff. Correct me if I'm wrong, Chief, but there is absolutely no evidence to suggest anyone shoved him. This fire is an entirely different story. If someone deliberately locked Lena inside that pantry with a rigged cat food dispenser set to go off and cause a fire, then that is premeditated murder."

"You're right, I'm sorry," Hayley said, neither

believing Penelope was right nor that she was sorry for saying it.

In her gut, Hayley was still convinced they were now dealing with two murders, not just one.

"Mrs. Janice, who has a key to the pantry?"

"The entire kitchen staff. We keep a key hanging on a hook by the door. Everyone knew where it was but nobody used it because we always just kept the pantry unlocked."

"Did anyone else besides the kitchen staff have access to the area?"

"Just about everyone. People were in and out of there all the time getting coffee, grabbing a snack, all sorts of deliverymen were sent back there. I encouraged everyone to help themselves to any food in the pantry if they were on the property working."

"What about the cat food dispenser?"

Penelope blanched and threw a hand to her mouth.

"What is it, Penelope?" Hayley asked.

"No. She would never . . ."

"Who?" Sergio asked, stepping forward.

Penelope struggled with herself, not wanting to divulge any more, but she knew the chief of police would not leave her alone until he got all the information he wanted.

She sighed and whispered, "Clara."

"The cook you recently fired?" Sergio said, almost accusingly.

"My husband fired her. I *rehired* her after . . ." she

said, making sure her eyes were locked on Hayley before she continued. "After his tragic *accident*!"

"So it was Clara's job to feed the cat," Sergio said.

"Yes, but Clara wasn't even here last night. I saw her leave after dinner. She went home to her family, and I'm sure if you call them, they will confirm that she was with them the whole night," Penelope said confidently, unwilling to believe her devoted cook was capable of such a heinous crime.

"Yes, but she could have set the timer on the cat food dispenser *before* she left," Hayley murmured.

Still, it was loud enough for Penelope to hear and she clearly did not appreciate Hayley's on-the-fly theories and less-than-expert opinions.

Too much had happened in the short span of this holiday weekend for Hayley to even care anymore what Penelope Janice thought of her.

"It would have been possible for Clara to rig the cat food dispenser with the chemicals and set the timer, but if her alibi checks out, then it would have been impossible for her to have locked Lena in the pantry before the explosion. It had to have been someone else," Penelope said.

Penelope folded her arms, happy with herself for stomping all over Hayley's attempts to indict Clara, convinced in her mind that Hayley was still blaming Clara for her rough bout with food poisoning.

In her own mind, Penelope must have believed she had just outsmarted them both. But the cold hard fact remained that even if it had been impossible for Clara to have locked Lena in the pantry before the fire, she could have easily been working with someone else who did.

Which meant Clara the cook was hardly in the clear for Lena's attempted murder.

And neither was Penelope.

Island Food & Spirits
BY HAYLEY POWELL

What kid doesn't look forward to summer vacation? I know my brother Randy and I sure did! Especially since it meant going to our grandparents' house and staying longer than just the weekend and a few nights over school vacations. Mamie and Grandpa lived in Trenton, Maine, which was located just on the other side of the bridge that connects Mount Desert Island to the mainland about twenty-five minutes out of town.

The lure for us, of course, was our kind loving grandparents spoiling us rotten! But we also enjoyed the make-believe adventures we played on their sprawling farm with a large barn complete with hidden rooms and horse stalls. They didn't own any horses anymore, but we always pretended there were some there for when we created make-believe scenes from the Old West.

There was also a large upper loft that housed secret treasures inside old rusted trunks, including hundreds of old black-and-white photos, newspaper clippings, and assorted documents—basically a history of our family dating back to the first settlers in Maine in the mid-1600s. We also played in the two large old-fashioned horse sleighs that were over a hundred years old but had held up remarkably well.

Grandpa had even tied a long thick rope from one

side of the loft to the other inside the barn and carved a swing seat for the rope so we could swing to our hearts' content all day long, even when it was snowing or raining outside.

Behind the farmhouse was a huge field with acres upon acres of open land and woods. We would spend hours exploring, and every year, without fail, one of us would get lost, and Grandpa would have to gather a search party of neighboring kids to come find us.

So you can imagine our excitement when our mother Sheila suddenly announced that she was meeting some old childhood school friends in Boston to go on a cruise through the Caribbean for a girls-only getaway, and that we would be staying at Mamie and Grandpa's for two whole weeks, from late June right through the Fourth of July holiday weekend!

That meant Randy and I would be front and center at our grandparents' annual Fourth of July Barn Party that they held every year for their close friends and neighbors, which also included a few kids close to our ages so we were guaranteed an army of playmates for our made-up adventures.

As usual, Mamie would be making her now famous Tomato Casserole Pies with her fresh-from-the-garden tomatoes that she had been carefully watering and tending to all summer, waiting for just the right moment to pick for her pies. Everyone in the town of Trenton just swooned over Mamie's mouth-watering tomato pies!

The day before the party, after almost two weeks of sharing the same bedroom, Randy and I were on each other's last nerves. We had endured way too much togetherness, and we spent the day picking at each other to the point where we couldn't stand being in the same room with the other anymore. The last straw was in the barn when Randy selfishly refused to put on the horse halter and pull me around the yard in an old wheelbarrow. He told me in no uncertain terms that he was not there to amuse me by pretending to be a horse and dragging me around all day.

As the older sibling who should be rightfully in charge of all the fun activities, I thought his obstinacy was inexcusable! Both of us kept running to the kitchen to complain about the other to Mamie, who was desperately trying to get her pie dough made for the ten or so pies she was planning on serving the next day at the party. After my third trip to the kitchen to trash-talk my little brother, Mamie threw her flour-covered hands up in the air in exasperation and told us that it was time for us to stop arguing with each other and time to be put to work.

Work?

What had happened to spoiling us rotten?

Had we just pushed our usually easygoing grandmother to the breaking point?

It sure seemed that way, because at that moment she handed each of us a large bucket and ordered us out the back door to pick the tomatoes with a stern warning for us not to fool around because she was on the clock to get all the pies prepared in time for the party.

While stuck outside plucking the tomatoes and dropping them in the bucket, we actually began to joke around and get along and nearly called a truce. But lo and behold, as the intense heat of the July sun started making us feel hot and sticky, and when the bugs started feasting on our sweaty skin, our moods quickly soured, and we started blaming each other for having to pick tomatoes in the god-awful heat.

Randy suddenly stood up, placed his hands on his hips, and informed me that this misery was all my fault because I was too bossy, and he was through being around me. He was going to go inside and watch game shows on TV, leaving me out in the sweltering sun to fill both buckets with tomatoes myself!

I don't know what possessed me, but his irritating tone got the best of me, and before I knew what I was doing, I found myself reaching into my bucket of ripe juicy tomatoes, grabbing a big fat one, and hurling it straight at Randy! It hit him square on the forehead, exploding in a wet, sloppy mess.

Randy's eyes popped open in surprise and he glared at me, still in shock as bits of the juicy tomato dripped down his face.

We both froze for a moment and stared at each other like two gunslingers, fingering the weapons in their holsters, about to draw in a duel. And then all hell broke loose.

Randy reached into his bucket and yanked out another big tomato and fired it off at me. I didn't duck in time, and it hit me in the nose, bursting apart, tomato juice blinding me as I frantically tried wiping it away. Before I had a chance to reach into my own bucket again, another one lodged in my mouth and I couldn't breathe. Randy was hurling them so fast and with such an impressive aim I could hardly keep up! The local Little League team surely lost a star pitcher the day Randy refused to go to the ball field and try out because practices were going to be held on Saturday morning during his favorite cartoons.

Once I caught my breath, I started firing back like Annie Oakley, hitting him in the chest, arm, legs, until both of our buckets were completely empty and we were covered in tomato skins and juice from head to toe.

We stared at each other for a long moment, and then collapsed onto the ground in an uncontrollable fit of giggles.

Unfortunately, we were so engaged in our tomato battle that we hadn't heard Mamie poke her head out the kitchen window and scream at us to stop! Grandpa did, however, and he ran around as fast as he could from the front of the house where he was mowing the lawn, to see what all the ruckus was about. As he rounded the corner, he failed to see the stack of buckets filled with tomatoes that Mamie had picked herself earlier that morning and plowed right into them, knocking them over, tripping over his own two feet. He fell facedown on the grass, crushing most, okay *all*, of the remaining tomatoes.

This was a disaster of epic proportions since there were only a handful of tomatoes left to pick. So poor Mamie had to rush to the IGA market for store-bought tomatoes in order to finish the pies. Store-bought tomatoes, of course, were a big no-no for the barn party, and we were sworn to secrecy.

The next day, luckily nobody seemed to notice the difference, except for Mamie's chief rival Vera Leland, with whom she competed every year at the annual Trenton Fourth of July pie baking contest. Vera clearly knew something was up when she tasted the pie, but Mamie kept giving her the evil eye, and Grandpa plied Vera with plenty of his signature highballs to the point where she must have made the smart decision to keep her mouth shut or she was just so drunk from the highballs she forgot where she was.

Despite all the drama, the annual barn party was a rousing success, and much to our relief, so were Mamie's delicious Tomato Casserole Pies. Grandpa's highball cocktail recipe was also a big hit with the adults because I don't remember the barn party ever getting so loud and out of control.

Randy wanted to try a highball for himself, but he was told by both Mamie and Grandpa that he would have to wait until he was grown up before he would be allowed to taste one. Well, eventually we both did a highball, and I must say Grandpa's recipe has remained a lifelong favorite. A good time is always had by all when serving Mamie's Tomato Casserole Pie and Grandpa's Whiskey Highball!

Grandpa's Whiskey Highball

2 ounces of your favorite whiskey
Ginger ale
Ice

Place 2–3 ice cubes in a highball glass, add two ounces of your favorite whiskey, and top off with ginger ale.

Needless to say, this is most refreshing on a hot summer's day—and not just the Fourth of July!

Mamie's Tomato Casserole Pie

1 pie crust, homemade or store-bought
3 large fresh tomatoes
8 grape tomatoes, sliced in half
1 cup shredded mozzarella cheese
½ cup shredded cheddar cheese
½ teaspoon salt
½ teaspoon freshly ground pepper
½ teaspoon garlic powder
½ teaspoon oregano
⅓ cup fresh basil leaves

Preheat your oven to 450°F.

Slice your tomatoes about a quarter of an inch thick and place them on paper towels. Lightly salt them and set aside to dry a bit.

Prick some holes in your pie crust with a fork and add ¼ cup of the mozzarella evenly over the crust. Bake 10 minutes. Remove and let cool completely.

Combine half your cheddar cheese and ¼ cup of the mozzarella in a small bowl.

Sprinkle the tomato slices with the garlic, oregano, and black pepper.

Layer half the tomatoes in the pie crust, then half of the cheese mixture and half of the fresh basil. Repeat with the rest of the ingredients and top with the sliced grape tomatoes.

Reduce the oven to 350°F and bake 35 minutes. Remove and cool before serving.

This casserole pie is best served at warm temperature so it is great for parties and when having friends over!

Chapter 20

Hayley could tell that Lex was surprised to see her standing in the doorway of the small caretaker cottage where he had been living since he was hired to work on the estate.

Hayley smiled. "I hope I'm not waking you up by dropping by so early, Lex."

"No," Lex lied, yawning and rubbing his eyes. "I was already up and just about to make some coffee. Come on in."

Lex waved her inside. He was wearing the same smoky jeans he had worn the night before when he and his men had put out the pantry fire, a ratty old T-shirt hung on his lean frame, and on his head was a Boston Red Sox ball cap that went a long way in covering his unruly dirty blond hair. He had obviously dressed in a hurry when she knocked on his door.

Hayley walked into the small kitchen, followed by Lex, who snatched the coffeepot off the stove, rinsed it in the sink, and set it into the maker, adding some ground coffee beans and pressing the start button. She felt awkward, not sure if she had made the right decision to just swing by when the sun had only just risen, but she wanted to catch him before he started working on the grounds with his crew.

"I just want to make sure you are all right after last night. You must have inhaled quite a lot of smoke yourself rushing in like that to save Lena," Hayley said looking him over, though he appeared to be fit and healthy.

"I'm fine," he said, smiling slightly, clearly happy she was so concerned.

"That was very brave of you, you and your men," Hayley said, sitting down at the kitchen table.

Lex shrugged, and Hayley remembered he was a modest man, not one to easily accept compliments. They made him supremely uncomfortable so he usually just quickly changed the subject.

"You hungry? I may have some bacon and eggs I can fry up in a pan," Lex said, throwing open his fridge and browsing his shelves and bins.

"No, thank you, I need to catch up on the sleep I missed last night from all the excitement. I don't know how you do it, up all night playing the dashing hero, and now about to work a long eight-hour shift."

"It's just a busy weekend. I'll have more downtime after the holiday," Lex said, pulling a package of bacon wrapped in plastic and a half carton of eggs out of the refrigerator, before closing the door shut with his back.

Hayley stood up to leave.

"You're not at least staying for coffee?"

Hayley shook her head. "Bruce is probably wondering where I am."

Lex nodded. "I see."

She hesitated, debating with herself whether to leave it alone or not, but she couldn't. She felt she owed him something given their past history.

"Lex, Bruce and I are not together."

"What do you mean? He's your boyfriend . . ."

"No, he's not. That's just a cover story."

"I don't understand."

"The only reason Bruce is here at the estate is because he smells a big story involving famous people and wants a front-page headline that might possibly go viral and help him get a better job at a big-city news organization."

"That may be so, but I've known Bruce a long time, and I'm betting that's not the only reason he talked his way into sharing a bed with you."

Hayley giggled. "Oh, come on, Lex . . ."

"I think there's more to it than Bruce just wanting a big story, that's all I'm saying."

"Seriously, there is nothing going on between us, and trust me, there never will be, and that you can take to the bank."

Lex smiled tightly.

She could tell by the expression on his face that he was not believing a word of it.

"No, really, Bruce and I are just work colleagues. That's it. I mean, yes, we dated for something like five minutes back in high school, but that was over twenty years ago. I have zero interest in dating Bruce now—"

"Hayley . . ."

"The very idea of us dating is hysterical. We couldn't be more polar opposites, and quite frankly, ninety percent of the time he's driving me up the wall—"

"Hayley . . ."

"I don't even find him all that good-looking anyway, not in the traditional sense like you, or Aaron my last boyfriend, after you, but Bruce? No, he's way too goofy and self-centered. I mean, can you imagine how high maintenance he would be if he was actually my *boyfriend* . . . ?"

"Hayley! Stop! You don't have to convince me. I'll take your word for it."

"I'm sorry, I don't know what just happened there," Hayley said, embarrassed by her unexplainable nonstop prattling about why Bruce Linney was not, and could not be, her boyfriend.

Was she trying to convince Lex or herself?

Hayley turned to go. "I'll see you later, Lex."

Something lying on the small coffee table in the living area suddenly caught her eye as she walked toward the front door.

It was a pipe.

Hayley stopped in her tracks, startled.

She had no clue Lex smoked a pipe.

He certainly had never touched one when the two of them were together.

"Anything wrong?" Lex asked, turning around from his sizzling bacon frying in the pan on the stove to see her still standing there, nowhere nearer to the front door.

"No, not a thing. Have a good day!" she chirped as she raced out the door and fled across the property toward the main house.

Hayley had believed that Conrad was the only one on the entire estate who regularly smoked a pipe, which would have explained why one was found lying on the ground near the scene of Conrad's fall.

But what if that pipe didn't belong to Conrad?

What if somebody else dropped it after pushing him off the cliff?

Could it have been Lex?

But that made absolutely zero sense.

Why would Lex have any reason to want Conrad dead?

Lex seemed perfectly content working for him and Penelope.

And what about Lena?

He certainly could not have had anything to do with locking her in the pantry, leaving her at the mercy of a roaring fire, because he was the one who gallantly led the team that heroically broke in and pulled her out.

When Hayley arrived back at her room, Bruce was there waiting impatiently for her.

"Where have you been? You had me worried!"

"Sergio and I had a talk with Penelope . . ."

"Great! Bring me up to speed. What did she say?" he asked, sitting on the edge of the bed, all ears.

"And then I stopped by Lex Bansfield's cottage . . ."

"Whoa. Wait. Why did you go *there*?"

"Because he risked his life last night to save Lena and I wanted to make sure he was okay."

"And was he?"

"Yes."

"Then why do you have that weird look on your face?"

"I don't have a weird look on my face!"

"Yes, you do. You always get it when you're holding something back from me," Bruce said. "So what is it?"

It bothered her that Bruce could tell when she was hiding something. It meant that he had been carefully observing her over the years, and that was, well, that was more than a little disturbing.

Hayley sighed and told Bruce about the pipe.

Bruce thought about it for a spell, maybe thirty seconds, then declared, "We should call Chief Alvares and have him arrested!"

"Bruce, don't be ridiculous! There is absolutely no proof to warrant an arrest. Just because he smokes a pipe, and a pipe was found at the scene, that doesn't mean Lex was the one who pushed Conrad off that cliff!"

"But you told me years ago he has a criminal record," Bruce said, springing to his feet while wagging an accusing finger at her.

"Yes, but it was all for juvenile offenses, and maybe one or two drunken bar fights, nothing serious, and they were a long time ago! You're just allowing the fact that you don't like Lex to cloud your judgment."

"Well, then we need to find out if that pipe you found at the crime scene belonged to Conrad or somebody else and then we will know for sure."

"No, we don't, because Lex Bansfield is *not* a cold-blooded killer. He's a good man. I know him intimately . . ."

Bruce's scowl said it all.

Hayley knew it was important at this point to revise her last statement.

"I know him well."

Bruce took this in, appeared at first to be satisfied, but then he just couldn't help himself. "*How* intimately?"

Chapter 21

Bar Harbor's Fourth of July celebration is world renowned for having been voted first in the nation by the *Today* show and ranked in the top ten in the United States by *National Geographic*. Every year the town teems with tourists from all over the world. The Fourth is packed with events starting with a sunrise blueberry pancake breakfast, followed by a craft fair, the famous Independence Day parade, a seafood festival, the YMCA annual lobster race, live music in Agamont Park, a free concert by the Bar Harbor Town Band in the Village Green, and finally, the spectacular colorful fireworks display over scenic Frenchman Bay.

Fourth of July was always one of Hayley's favorite days of the year, and she was a bit melancholy that she had already missed most of the events due to her commitment to spending the weekend at Penelope Janice's estate to help out with her TV show, not to mention dealing with the fallout from the hostess's husband taking a shocking dive to his death off a steep cliff and a purposely set fire that had left the life of a young woman hanging in the balance.

By sundown, Hayley, Bruce, and all of the other guests who were still gathered and thankfully accounted for at the Seal Harbor property were exhausted from all that had transpired during the previous few days, and were in desperate need of a break from being cooped up and endlessly questioned by the police.

Hayley was amazed that Gerard, Tristan, and Carol had not already bolted the island at this point, but all of them were career TV professionals.

At a somber cocktail party earlier that evening, Penelope apologized for any trauma she had caused them. When she had invited them to join her for her Fourth of July special, she hardly had expected such dramatic and heartbreaking events to unfold.

Penelope graciously encouraged everyone to head into town and enjoy the fireworks display. She even had Clara pack individual picnic baskets for them all, stocked with expensive bottles of wine, imported cheeses, and gourmet crackers to enjoy on the grassy knoll above the town pier, the perfect spot to get the best view of the fireworks.

When Tristan asked if she would be attending the fireworks with them, Penelope fought back tears as she nodded, promising to join them just as soon as she could. But first she was on her way to the hospital to check on Lena, praying her condition had improved from earlier in the day.

Hayley rode with Bruce into town, and they had to park the car at her house a mile away from the pier because the streets were jam-packed with people and there was nowhere in the vicinity to drive, let alone park. Bruce carried their picnic basket as they wove their way through the crowd swarming down Main Street toward the pier. They were lucky to find a small patch of free grass to set their basket down and unfurl a small wool blanket to sit on that Hayley had grabbed from a chest in her bedroom.

A few locals waved as they passed by, surprised to see Hayley and Bruce together, sitting side by side on a blanket, unpacking their wine and cheese. It certainly appeared to everyone that the two of them were on a date, and Hayley had no doubt in her mind that this little romantic scene would get a lot of local tongues wagging.

Suddenly Bruce threw an arm around Hayley's shoulder and drew her in close to him. The move startled her and she was about to shake free when she realized Carol Kay was sauntering by, and Bruce was just trying to play up the fact that they were supposed to be a couple.

Carol gave them a tight smile and a quick nod and continued on her way.

Hayley looked around for Gerard and Tristan, but couldn't see them in the crowd. The grassy knoll was getting so congested it was hard to even move.

Bruce uncorked a bottle and poured some merlot into two plastic wineglasses that had been packed in the picnic basket. He handed one to Hayley. He toasted her, trying to clink glasses, but the plastic didn't make much of a sound.

"To us," he said, grinning.

"Shut up, Bruce."

"Kiss me."

"What?"

"Penelope's on her way over here. Kiss me."

"No!"

"Come on, Hayley. We have to keep up appearances as long as we're both still staying at the estate."

Hayley sighed and leaned in and kissed him very lightly, their lips barely touching.

Bruce quickly snagged her by the neck and kept her face mashed up against his. It had to be the least romantic kiss she had ever experienced.

So why did it make her heart flutter for the briefest of moments?

When Bruce finally released her, she was flushed and fuming, but covered and smiled as Penelope approached.

Hayley also noticed their boss Sal and his wife sitting on a nearby blanket. Sal clutched a beer can in his hammy fist, slack-jawed at the sight of Hayley and Bruce smooching in public. His wife whispered frantically into his ear as she pointed at them. To their left were the Reverend and Mrs. Staples, also with stunned expressions on their faces.

This fake romance was causing quite a stir.

Penelope knelt down near the edge of their

blanket and checked her watch. "It's just after nine. The fireworks should be starting in a few minutes."

"Sit down and join us," Hayley offered, trying to make more room for her.

"No, I never like to be a third wheel. And besides, Hayley, you've been working very hard this weekend. You deserve some snuggle time with your man here and enjoy the fireworks without me around."

Bruce rubbed his nose on Hayley's shoulder like a loyal puppy dog.

Hayley fought hard not to laugh at his goofy overacting.

She then focused her mind on the distraught woman with the flaming-red hair in front of her.

"How is Lena?" Hayley asked quietly.

Penelope took a deep breath and shook her head. "The same, I'm afraid. Hanging on, but it doesn't look good."

"We just have to stay positive," Hayley said, reaching out and touching Penelope's arm.

"Yes! Lena is a young, vibrant, strong girl and she's always been a fighter. She'll pull through this," Penelope said in a valiant attempt to convince herself. "But seeing her hooked up to all those machines was devastating. Just the idea of losing her, I can't imagine anything worse happening to me!"

"Well, uh, there's your husband . . . who died . . . last night . . ." Bruce said in utter disbelief, astonished that he had to remind her of the *other* horrible thing that had happened in the last forty-eight hours.

Penelope gave him a blank stare.

It was as if she was processing what he was saying, and was now trying to figure out the proper response.

"Oh, yes, that too."

And that was it.

Her entire reaction to her husband's death.

In two seconds.

Giving up on trying to squeeze any tears out of Penelope over Conrad, Bruce was resigned and changed the subject to more mundane topics like the kind of cheese Penelope had packed in the picnic basket. This subject was infinitely more interesting to Penelope, and she rattled off a story about her travels to Paris and all the wonderful cheese shops she had visited.

Hayley glanced over to see Sal and his wife still staring at them, both astounded at having been witness to Hayley and Bruce, heretofore mortal enemies at the office, sucking face at the town pier, seconds away from having a colorful fireworks display exploding in the sky above them like the backdrop in the final scene of a schmaltzy romantic comedy.

She knew she owed them an explanation.

"Excuse me, I'll be right back," Hayley said, standing up and maneuvering her way through the throngs of people sitting on blankets in the grass, slowly making her way over to Sal and his wife.

When she reached them, Sal already knew why she was there. He held up a hand and bellowed for everyone in the surrounding area to hear, "What you do after work hours is your own business, Hayley!"

His wife snickered.

"It's not what it looks like," Hayley said.

"I've been a news reporter my whole adult life, Hayley, and I only deal in facts, and the fact is . . . you and Bruce make an awfully cute couple!"

"You're being sarcastic," Hayley said.

"I always knew you two were made for each other," he howled.

His wife could barely breathe she was laughing so hard.

Hayley spotted a whole congregation of locals nearby watching and smiling, riveted to the scene as she feebly tried to explain herself.

There was simply no use.

The rumor mill was already cranked up and there was no stopping it now.

Just east of the grassy knoll down by the shore path that wound around the harbor and out along the rocky coast of the island, Hayley spotted Gerard and Tristan. They were off by themselves, a good distance from the crowd, and they were in the middle of an intense and heated argument.

"I'll see you at the office on Tuesday, Sal, and we can continue this conversation," Hayley said, scurrying off down to the shore path, her eyes fixed on Gerard and Tristan.

"Just let us know where you two lovebirds plan on registering so we can buy you a nice gravy boat!" Sal yelled as his wife continued howling with laughter.

As Hayley approached Gerard and Tristan, she could see Gerard aggressively advancing upon his son, who slowly backed away, angrily wagging a finger in his father's face, his eyes blazing as he shouted something at him. The echo of the chattering crowd and the crashing waves against the shore drowned out their words, but as Hayley got close enough, she was able to hear Tristan yell at his father, "If you stay out of my love life, then I will stay out of yours!"

Gerard roughly grabbed his son's shirtsleeve and shook him, but Tristan yanked his arm away, and in a moment of raging brutality, gave his father a furious shove. Gerard stumbled back, luckily falling back against the railing that lined the path. Otherwise he would have toppled over and fallen ten feet, quite possibly smashing his head on the jagged rocks below.

Tristan tore off down a rickety flight of steps to the beach and ran off, disappearing in the darkness.

As Gerard stalked back toward the crowd on the lawn, Hayley spun around so her back was to him. He passed by her without a hint of recognition. Once Gerard was swallowed up by the crowd, Hayley darted back along the shore path, and then hurried down the steps to the beach in search of Tristan.

She had to know what he and his father were fighting about.

She had seen Tristan cavorting with Lena, so she could only assume that Lena was his object of desire.

But who on earth was his father involved with?

What was so interesting about *his* love life?

Tristan had no desire to talk to her before, so she saw no reason he would agree to speak with her now.

But Hayley hoped that if she caught him at the right moment, if he was still in a highly charged emotional state, maybe, just maybe, he might slip and say something useful.

It had proven to be an effective tool in the past, when Hayley tried to get reluctant people talking.

She searched the beach, but found no sign of him.

"Tristan?" she called out as the waves crashed and water raced up the narrow beach threatening to wash over her Nike sneakers.

Hayley walked farther down the beach, picking up her pace, her sneakers sinking into the wet sand of pebbles and shells as the tide slowly but forcefully made its way into the harbor.

Suddenly she heard a loud crack, like gunfire, and she nearly dove behind some rocks to hide.

The sky lit up with streaks of red, white, and blue.

It was just the start of the fireworks display.

She laughed at herself for being so jumpy.

And then out of nowhere someone grabbed her roughly from behind.

Chapter 22

Hayley struggled in the man's strong grip, elbowing him in the chest and trying to position herself to jab the heel of her sneaker into the top of his foot in order to break free.

"Whoa! Calm down, Hayley! It's just me."

She spun around, instantly recognizing the voice. Lex Bansfield.

"Sorry. I didn't mean to scare you like that. You were just walking so fast, and you didn't hear me calling to you so I had to run so I could catch up to you," Lex said, releasing her and raising his hands in the air.

"Lex, I'm so sorry, I was just . . ."

She looked around.

There was no sign of Tristan.

She turned back and smiled. "Never mind."

The fireworks burst into bright flashes of color above them, illuminating their faces with candescent light.

"I spotted you in the crowd back at the pier, but

it took me a while to push my way through to get over to you, and by the time I did you were gone so I walked around until I saw you down here on the beach."

"What do you want, Lex?"

His face soured slightly.

She hadn't meant for her words to come out like that.

Cold and rushed.

Slightly irritated.

But she was, at the moment, singularly focused on locating Tristan and finding out more about the argument with his father that she had just witnessed.

"I want to clear the air," he said.

"About what?"

Now she was slightly curious.

"You left the cottage in such a hurry. I could tell you were disturbed about something, and I think I know what it is."

The pipe she had noticed on the coffee table.

He must have seen her staring at it, and he knew one was found at the scene where Conrad fell off the cliff. Hayley was certain he must be thinking she suspected him of pushing his employer to his death for some still unknown reason.

"Lena Hendricks."

Hayley's mouth dropped open.

This was *not* what she was expecting to hear.

"Look, I know all about your hobby of investigating crimes. We were together for two years, so I had a front-row seat. And I know you are very much involved in what's been going on at the estate over the past few days."

"You mean one possible murder and one obviously attempted murder?" Hayley said, not the least bit comfortable just referring to them as "events."

"Yes. And I also know it's only a matter of time before you dig up the truth, so I wanted to come clean with you before you heard it from someone else."

"Heard what, Lex?"

"I was involved with Lena Hendricks."

Hayley stood there, letting the words sink in, before she nodded and said, "Okay."

"We met when I started working for Penelope and Conrad, and we hit it off. She asked me to dinner, and it went on from there."

"Were you still seeing her when you rescued her from the fire?"

"No. We only dated a few times over the span of a month, and then it just sort of sputtered out. It was obvious she was too young for me, and neither of us were looking to settle down, so we parted ways, promising to remain friends. That was pretty much it."

"And did you? Remain friends, I mean?"

"Yeah, I suppose so. I mean we didn't run into each other all that much. I was working outside, and she spent most of her time in Penelope's office helping her write her books. But when we did see each other, we were civil and polite."

Gloria and Rose, the young kitchen help who

had breathlessly told Hayley that Lena was seeing another man that sparked an intense jealousy in Conrad had been wrong.

The other man wasn't Tristan.

It was Lex.

"Why are you telling me this, Lex?"

"Because on one of our last dates, I took Lena to the Blue Hill Fair and we got into one of those photo booths and had our pictures taken, and she had one framed and came over to give it to me, maybe a day or two before we broke up, and I put it on my mantel in the living room and forgot about it. I realized it was still there when you stopped by the cottage earlier today. I just assumed you saw it, and that's what got you spooked, and why you left in such a hurry."

"No, Lex, I didn't see the picture."

"Oh," he said, surprised.

"I had no idea."

"Then why did I get the feeling you became upset about something when you were over at my place today?"

"I saw a pipe on the coffee table."

"My pipe?"

"So it did belong to you."

"Of course it does. Why?"

"Is it a new pipe?"

"Yeah, I went out and bought it this morning. How did you know?"

"Tell me what happened to your old pipe," Hayley

said quietly, her words nearly drowned out by the exploding fireworks in the air. "Did you lose it?"

"What are you trying to get at here, Hayley?"

"A pipe was found at the scene where Conrad fell . . . or was pushed . . ."

His face betrayed a hint of concern. "I thought the pipe they found on the ground belonged to Conrad. I heard he dropped it when he tripped and fell over the side of the cliff."

"It could have belonged to someone else," she said, eyes fixed on his face, studying him.

"It wasn't mine, Hayley."

Lex stared at her, waiting for her to say something, but she just stood there, not sure what to say.

And then Lex laughed.

"I'm sorry, I don't mean any disrespect, but do you think I . . . ?"

"It's not funny, Lex," she scolded.

"No, Hayley it is. I see how you're putting this all together. Look, I've heard the rumors too about Conrad's secret love affair with Lena, and as far as I know, they could be true, but I already told you, my relationship with Lena was a short-term fling. That's all! I'm not some spurned, jealous ex-lover out to get her back by any means necessary! I like working here, and I would never do anything to jeopardize that."

Hayley listened to his words carefully.

He seemed on the surface to be convincing.

She had known him a long time.

And she agreed he was not the jealous-lover type.

It was completely out of character for him to go to such an extreme as to push a man over a cliff in order to keep him away from the object of his affection.

It was a silly premise, in fact.

Hayley silently cursed Bruce for putting such thoughts in her head when he instantly accused Lex of being the killer after she told him about the pipe.

But the pipe still nagged at her.

"You never smoked a pipe when we were together," she said.

"Nope, never touched one in my life. Not until I started working here. I spent a lot of time with Conrad during the first few weeks I was on the job. He puffed on one constantly, so after a while I decided to try it, and unfortunately I got hooked pretty quick. Nasty habit. And expensive too."

Hayley watched him carefully.

He was nervous but still convincing.

"That night, when I had food poisoning, and I overheard a man and a woman in the hall talking about killing someone, the man was smoking a pipe."

"Wasn't me, Hayley. I've been trying to quit."

"Then why did you go out and buy a new pipe this morning after losing the old one?"

"It wasn't a real pipe," he said, pulling it out of his shirt pocket and handing it to her. "It's an e-pipe designed to look like a real one."

He handed it to her and she carefully inspected it.

It was hard to tell the difference but he was telling her the truth.

"I'm trying to wean myself off tobacco. It's working too. I misplaced the one I bought when I made the decision to quit, so I went out and picked up another one today after I went to check on Lena at the hospital and before I saw you at the cottage."

Well, if Lex was now just smoking an e-pipe, then it could not have been him in the hallway with Lena. The smoke she smelled from the pipe that night was a lot stronger than vapors from an e-pipe.

"Are we good?" he asked, genuinely concerned that their friendship might in some way be damaged.

Hayley hugged him.

"Yes, Lex, we're good."

The fireworks had reached a crescendo with bright bursts of red, white, and blue blazing across the beautiful night sky in a spectacular grand finale.

They held each other close.

It was a scene that could have easily jumped off the pages of a breathless Harlequin romance novel.

But Hayley knew in her heart that her relationship with Lex had long been over despite the attraction both of them obviously still felt for one another.

And because she was determined not to make any attempt to rekindle the flame that had been extinguished years ago, she slowly pulled away from his embrace, gave him a chaste kiss on the cheek, said good night, and dashed off down the beach back toward the town pier, her feet getting soaked from the waves that were now fast rolling in with the tide.

She could feel him watching her as she headed back up the ramshackle steps to the shore path, but she refused to look in his direction because there was a small part of her that was afraid she might go back to the spot where she left him.

And she could not allow that to happen.

Chapter 23

Hundreds of locals show up every year for Penelope Janice's Fourth of July barbecue.

It's now a time-honored annual tradition, and Penelope has deftly used the party to ingratiate herself with the island residents by plying them with lots of free food and booze.

When word that Penelope's husband Conrad had died in a tragic accident spread through town within hours of his body being discovered, most people assumed the barbecue, held this year on the Monday after the fireworks so locals didn't miss all the town-sponsored activities, would be quickly cancelled. But Penelope had no intention of depriving her dear "friends" of a festive time, even though she probably couldn't recognize by name even a small fraction of the attendees.

Penelope made the announcement on her Facebook fan page an hour after the fireworks ended that the barbecue would indeed go on as scheduled.

When the noon hour rolled around, cars began to fill up the side of the road outside her Seal Harbor estate and eager guests began filing onto the property to find rows of giant barbecues smoking with fleshy fresh meat, tables stocked with various salads and side dishes, and a full catering staff in matching white shirts and black slacks milling through the fast-growing crowd with trays of mimosas. A fully stocked bar on the far end of the yard, actually near the exact spot where Conrad took his fatal dive, had about fifteen people already lined up to get their hands on a stiff cocktail.

Hayley knew her time at the estate was finally coming to an end. She and Bruce and presumably the other guests were all scheduled to pack up and leave the premises immediately following the barbecue.

She had mixed feelings about getting booted off the estate. She was anxious to get home to her dog and her cat, Leroy and Blueberry, who had been under the watchful care of Mona since she had left them on Thursday morning, but she was also extremely frustrated that she and Bruce had not made any significant headway with turning up any useful information related to Conrad's death and the fire that nearly took Lena Hendricks's life.

Without access to Penelope and the property, Hayley feared the questions surrounding both incidents would ultimately fade away and never be answered.

Sergio had already concluded in his mind that

Conrad's death was just a hapless accident, the result of another stumbling, drunken night. The fire was more complicated given the cat food dispenser and chemicals found at the scene so that investigation would remain open even though there were still no plausible suspects or even a concrete motive that would explain why anyone would lock that poor girl in a pantry to die.

There were a myriad of suspects.

Gerard.

Tristan.

Carol.

Penelope herself.

And then there was Clara.

But just as Penelope had vehemently declared, Sergio had confirmed Clara was at home with an airtight alibi. Even if she had rigged the cat food dispenser, she could not have been the one who locked Lena in the pantry.

As for Gerard, Tristan, and Carol, they all claimed to have been sound asleep in their rooms alone so there was no one to back up their alibis, but there was also no one to dispute them either.

Hayley and Bruce lined up in front of one of the barbecues to load up on some freshly cooked chicken and beef slathered in Penelope's own bottled spicy barbecue sauce and were joined by Sergio, who was in shorts and a T-shirt, taking a much needed day off from his police-chief duties, and Randy, Hayley's brother, who was happy to finally have an entire day with his off-duty husband.

Randy instantly noticed Bruce's hand casually placed on Hayley's lower back and raised an eyebrow.

Hayley saw him staring at it and vigorously shook her head and mouthed the words, "It's nothing."

Randy clearly didn't believe her.

In fact, he snorted with laughter.

Sergio was too busy biting into a barbecued chicken leg and getting sauce all over his face as he rapturously chewed and swallowed the meat to notice much of anything.

"Delicious," Sergio moaned before pulling another hunk of meat off the bone with his teeth.

"Isn't he cute when he eats like a caveman?" Randy said, laughing.

Bruce, now with his whole arm around Hayley's waist, reflexively pulled her closer to him and asked, "I'm going to get us a couple of plates of potato salad and coleslaw. Wait here—I'll be right back, babe."

He trotted off to the table stocked with a multitude of side dishes.

There was an awkward moment as Hayley just stood there, dying inside, waiting for Randy to make some kind of remark.

It didn't take long.

"'Babe'?"

Hayley leaned in, whispering. "He's just acting like that so we give Penelope the impression we're a couple. Don't worry. It will all be over in a few hours."

Randy nodded, not believing a word of what she was saying.

"I'm serious," Hayley said emphatically.

"Look, I remember seeing Bruce Linney play Tevye in *Fiddler on the Roof* when he was a senior in high school, and believe me, he's not that good of an actor," Randy said, raising his eyebrow again.

Hayley wanted to reach out and grab that damn eyebrow of his and yank it back down but she resisted.

Violence never solved anything.

"We're just undercover!" Hayley declared, probably a bit too loud, and she caught herself and quickly lowered her voice. "He's just here to get a story!"

Randy nodded, and this time so did Sergio. Both of them had annoying grins on their faces.

"You two are impossible!"

"All I'm saying is, if it is just an act, Bruce is committing to the part one hundred percent!" Randy said, taking a long sip of the mimosa he was holding tightly in one hand.

Liddy and Mona wandered over to them. Mona had her dog Sadie on a leash because Penelope, a fervent animal lover, encouraged everyone to bring their pets. She even had a fenced-in designated play area just for dogs set up on the other side of the property.

"Where's Sonny?" Hayley asked Liddy.

Liddy rolled her eyes and threw up her hands. "Working! He's always working. Nobody works as much as that man does. You'd think he does it just to get away from me!"

There was another awkward silence.

Nobody wanted to say a word.

Except Mona, who was very obviously biting her tongue.

Mona fought to control herself, reaching down to scratch the top of Sadie's head, trying desperately to keep her mouth shut.

The golden retriever looked lovingly up at her master, tongue panting, sheer contentment in her eyes. Mona had adopted her from an old childhood friend, who had died unexpectedly some time ago near his home down east in Salmon Cove.

"How are my boys doing?" Hayley asked. "I've missed them so much."

"Leroy's been a good boy. He loves hanging out with Sadie and playing with my kids all day. But that bastard Blueberry is a nightmare. What a nasty cat. He hisses and growls all the time. Won't even let anyone pet him or even get near him, in fact. Only good thing he's done in the five days he's been at my place is scratch my husband Dennis for no reason. It was the first time I saw Dennis move in nearly a week."

"Do they miss me?" Hayley asked.

Mona paused, thinking about her answer very carefully.

"Yeah, sure they do," she lied.

Penelope suddenly appeared, looking bright and sunny in a lemon-colored sleeveless blouse and white pants. She was making the rounds, checking in on all the guests to make sure they were having a good time and had enough to eat and drink.

"I'm so happy to see you all here today," she said, acknowledging Hayley and Sergio, and smiling at Randy, Liddy, and Mona, none of whom she recognized nor cared to get to know.

"It's lovely to see you as always, Penelope," Liddy cooed, trying to create the illusion in her mind that she and the famous Penelope Janice were close personal friends.

Penelope stared at Liddy, trying to place her, and then gave up and turned to Mona.

"I have a special barbecue station set up cooking meat just for the dogs that are here. You should really take him over there at some point."

"I will, thanks," Mona said. "Nice party. I have to give you credit, I don't know if I could have pulled this off so soon after losing my husband."

And Hayley endured what was now the third awkward moment in less than five minutes.

Mona was never good at subtlety or discretion.

"Yes, well, uh, life goes on . . ." Penelope stammered, looking around for some other guests so she could excuse herself from them and go talk to someone, anyone, else.

But before Penelope had the chance to slip away, Mona struck again.

"So when's the funeral?" Mona asked, stabbing a piece of beef with her fork on her plate and shoving it in her mouth.

"Oh. I'm going to have him cremated and stored until I have time to plan some kind of memorial, probably after Labor Day when the weather isn't so nice and warm and there is less to do."

Welcome, awkward moment number four.

Penelope could tell by the looks on their faces that all of them were appalled by her cavalier attitude, so she tried to muster up some tears. When that failed, she tried to look somber and subdued, but it only lasted a few seconds until she saw someone she recognized and gave a friendly smile and wave.

Hayley never purported to be a good actress.

She could rarely hide what she was thinking.

And it was very clear to everyone by the look on her face that she was disgusted by what she was hearing.

"You don't approve, Hayley?" Penelope asked, zeroing in on her.

"What? No, it's your decision . . ."

"But you think I'm being cold and unfeeling . . . ?"

"No . . ." she said, failing at sounding the least bit sincere.

"I can tell what you're thinking. You don't like how I'm handling Conrad's death. You think I should act more like the stereotypical grieving widow, unable to go on, locked in my room crying into my pillow? Is that it?"

"I never said that, Penelope," Hayley said.

Randy, Sergio, Liddy, Mona, and even Sadie all stood frozen in place.

Gerard, who was standing close by and sensed Penelope's discomfort, swooped in and put a protective arm around her. "You're distressed, Penelope, I can tell. What's wrong?"

"Nothing, Gerard . . ." Penelope said, glaring at Hayley.

Gerard followed her gaze over to Hayley and grimaced. "Is she causing trouble again?"

Gerard gave Hayley such a disdainful, almost threatening look, Sergio stepped forward slightly to make sure he didn't slap her across the face or make some kind of other sudden move.

"No, no trouble. It's been nice having you here, Hayley. I'll be sorry to see you go later today," Penelope said with a fake smile.

She wasn't sorry at all.

She was just saying that to confirm Hayley's imminent departure so she would finally be free of her prying eyes and nosy questions and wild stories about sinister murder plots, all of which had in Penelope's mind spoiled her carefully planned weekend shoot for her stupid ratings-starved television show on the Flavor Network.

Penelope turned her back on Hayley and marched away.

Gerard lingered long enough to spit out under his breath, "Good riddance!"

And then he chased after his hostess.

Why was Gerard being so chivalrous when it came to the grieving widow?

Hayley was convinced there was more to it than a long-lasting friendship between the two.

And although the clock was ticking and her time on the estate was winding down and she was confident she would never be invited back ever again, she still had an hour or two left to find answers to some very disturbing questions.

Chapter 24

"Jillian Capshaw? What is *she* doing here?" Hayley asked Bruce as they stood in line waiting for more barbecued tri-tips, holding their plastic plates.

Bruce couldn't resist a lascivious smile. "Party's open to the public. Why wouldn't she be here?"

Jillian Capshaw bounced over to them, her ample breasts barely contained inside a skintight cream-colored halter top. Her denim shorts were riding up so high Hayley suspected they might be illegal in some states.

"This doesn't strike me as Jillian's kind of scene," Hayley said, watching her approach, waving at them, flipping her long curly blond hair back as every firmly heterosexual male in her vicinity stopped what they were doing and stared longingly at the nubile young woman.

Jillian Capshaw was a hell-raising, college-age, fresh-faced local party girl with a racy reputation in town.

She had also dated Bruce for five minutes when

he was going through a hardly surprising midlife crisis last year.

It had been unquestionably sad to watch.

Bruce trying to dress more hip to fit in with Jillian's young hipster friends.

Lots of tight-fitting T-shirts to show off the muscles he had worked so hard developing at the YMCA gym. Torn jeans. Black leather cowboy boots.

Hayley could always tell when Bruce had been out with Jillian the night before because he would swagger into the office, speak in a baritone drawl, and act as if he was God's gift to all womankind.

Two weeks later, when Jillian dumped him for a bearded biker from Dixmont who rode into town on his Harley for the weekend, Bruce was back to wearing his khaki pants, wrinkled L.L. Bean dress shirts, and scuffed brown Timberland shoes, along with a sheepish grin he wore to desperately try to mask his emotional pain.

The entire staff at the *Island Times* was enormously relieved Bruce's wild-man phase was officially over.

"Howdy, y'all," Jillian said, grabbing Bruce in a hug, which instantly discombobulated him, causing him to drop his plastic plate on the ground.

Jillian had started speaking in a Southern accent, even though she was born and raised on the island, after discovering that the majority of beauty pageant winners were from the Southern states. In her mind, if she was going to be a beauty queen in life, despite not having any sort of official title, she was going to speak like one.

Jillian turned to hug Hayley, but when she saw Hayley's whole body instinctively stiffen, she chose not to go in for one.

She simply said, "Hiya, Hayley."

"Hello, Jillian," Hayley said, mustering up as much politeness as she could. She certainly was not a fan of the flouncy hot little number, but it was not in her nature to be rude.

Jillian turned to Bruce. "So I did the research you asked me to do, and came up with a few interesting tidbits."

Bruce blanched and turned to study Hayley's reaction, which was perplexed. He then stepped out of the line, took Jillian by the arm, and guided her away from the eavesdropping crowd of people curious to know more. He led Jillian over to an open area, away from all the party guests, so they could speak privately.

Hayley was not about to miss out on their covert conversation, so she too left the line of people waiting for more tri-tips and joined them.

"Oh, hiya, Hayley," Jillian said as if she were just seeing her for the first time.

"I didn't want to miss this," Hayley said, staring at Bruce.

"Um, Jillian has picked up a few odd jobs to . . . uh . . . put herself through nursing school," Bruce sputtered.

"And Brucey has been kind enough to hire me on occasion to do some legwork for him," Jillian offered, flipping her hair again as if she were a model in front of a breezy fan for a *Sports Illustrated* swimsuit issue photo shoot.

"Legwork?" Hayley asked pointedly, eyeing Bruce.

"Yes, legwork! Doing online research for my columns, that kind of legwork," Bruce quickly explained. "Try to keep your mind out of the gutter, okay, Hayley?"

Jillian scrunched up her face, at first not getting the double entendre, but once it dawned on her, she burst out into a fit of giggles. "Oh, that's funny! I'm not sure exactly what it means, but it's funny! Oh God, who would want these awful legs wrapped around them? They're *so* ugly!"

Hayley glanced at Jillian's legs.

They were, in fact, perfection.

Bruce started perspiring, and not from the heat. He was suddenly nervous. "I had Jillian do a little digging into Lena Hendricks's life and background."

"What did you come up with?" Hayley asked.

"Well, I checked her Instagram, Twitter, and Facebook accounts, pretty much all of her social media outlets, and it was pretty obvious that she didn't want to spend the next ten years ghostwriting for Penelope Janice. This girl wanted to *be* Penelope Janice. She was building her online presence hoping to create her own following. I found a ton of posts and videos about her life and aspirations that gave some insight into what's been going through her mind lately."

Okay, Jillian might be a wild party girl with a

questionable reputation, but she also had promise
as an effective private investigator.

"She also shared a lot about her personal life.
There were a slew of videos about her relationship
with a man she referred to as just 'L'!"

Lex Bansfield.

It had to be Lex Bansfield.

"Well, there was one video she posted that was
quite emotional. She was crying, actually sobbing,
and it was hard to make out everything she was
saying, but she told her followers that her relationship with 'L' was kaput. Over. Done. She broke it off
because she realized he was never going to get serious with her. She felt he was stringing her along
because he didn't want to hurt her, but she could
tell he wasn't that into her. Then she went on and
on about how men can't be trusted, you know the
drill, I've said it a thousand times to my girlfriends,
I just never post it online."

"I'm surprised you've ever gone through anything like that, Jillian, since you're the one who
breaks men's hearts, not the other way around,"
Bruce said with more than a trace of bitterness.

Hayley tried not to laugh.

On some level, she actually enjoyed seeing Bruce
so worked up over having been unceremoniously
discarded by this vision of youthful beauty.

"Oh, Brucey, don't you start! Anyway, I watched
all the videos after that and she suddenly stopped
talking about the men she was dating, but you could
tell there was someone else in the picture. She

must have decided she was oversharing so she didn't mention any names or anything."

Conrad.

Maybe Tristan.

Or both.

Jillian's information corroborated Lex's story.

He had been involved with Lena.

But it was just a fling and it was now over.

Hayley felt an overwhelming sense of relief.

Lex was telling the truth.

"I'm still going through her Twitter feed. The girl likes to tweet more than Donald Trump! But I wanted to swing by and give you what I've found so far."

"Good work, Jillian, thank you," Bruce said, still obviously smarting from his temporary Girl Friday's stinging rejection.

"Thanks. Do you have my check?" Jillian asked, now all business and more serious than she had been since her arrival.

The girl wanted to get paid for her efforts.

Bruce pulled out his wallet and rifled through it. "I wasn't expecting you to show up here so I didn't bring my checkbook."

Jillian held out her hand. "Cash is fine."

Bruce pulled out a couple of twenties and gently placed them in the palm of her hand. She glanced at them, hardly satisfied, and raised her eyes to meet his, glaring at him.

He quickly grabbed the rest of the cash in his wallet and pressed the bills in her hand. She closed her fist, stuffed the money in the tiny pocket of her tight denim jeans, and smiled again. "Thanks, Brucey."

"You're welcome," he said, scowling.

"Now I got a much better party to get to, not as many old fogies. Bye y'all!" she sang as she bounced away.

Hayley watched Bruce, who looked as if he wanted the ground to open and swallow him up whole.

He was supremely embarrassed.

And Hayley was loving every minute of it.

"You are a saint, Bruce, for helping put that bright young girl through nursing school out of the goodness of your heart."

"Don't start with me, Hayley," Bruce warned.

"Are there any other pretty young girls in Bar Harbor who are the lucky recipients of the Bruce Linney College Scholarship Program?" she asked.

"Oh, nice, Hayley! That's a good one!"

"I'm sorry, Bruce, I just can't help it!" Hayley said, laughing.

"Try!"

Hayley attempted to get more serious. "No, honestly, I think it's swell what you're doing. Helping a young person advance their education is a noble cause . . . as long as it's done for the right reason."

"And what's a *wrong* reason?" Bruce demanded to know.

"Well, if I had to come up with one, I guess I'd have to say . . ."

"I'm listening . . ."

Hayley suddenly realized she was swimming in uncharted waters.

She and Bruce rarely spoke of their personal lives.

Since when did his activities outside the office become any of her business?

"Nothing. Forget it," she said.

"No, tell me."

His eyes bored into hers.

He was angry because he knew where this was going.

And suddenly she regretted the thought even popping into her head.

"Never mind, Bruce. I didn't mean to imply anything—"

"You think I'm hoping that girl might be so grateful to me for helping her out, she might decide to fool around with me again, is that it?"

"I didn't say that."

"You were thinking it!"

"Bruce, please, let's just drop it. I didn't mean to start something."

"Well, you did. Are you *jealous* of her?"

"Am I *what*?"

"You heard me!"

"What could I possibly be jealous of, besides her pretty face and gorgeous body? Those attributes, I do admit, make me a little jealous."

"I think you're jealous that Jillian and I had

some harmless fun together in the past, and now you're trying to make me feel bad about it!"

"Bruce, I don't care what happened between the two of you . . ."

"I don't believe you!"

"It doesn't matter to me whether you believe me or not, I'm just telling you the truth."

"Well, I think you're lying! And I am hurt that you would think I'm such a disrespecting sleazeball that I would use that girl, bribe her with money for school, just to get her into bed with me!"

"Bruce, I'm sorry . . ."

She knew he was right.

That was exactly what she was thinking.

And now she felt horrible.

"I'm outta here!"

Bruce stalked off, charging through the sea of guests toward the garden and rocky cliffside beyond.

At first Hayley decided to just let him go so he could cool off.

She promised herself she would find him later and apologize.

But the argument kept nagging at her because she knew she was the one who had started it by needling him in a way that it was unavoidable for him not to notice she was judging him.

She couldn't allow this to go on and fester.

She had to deal with it now before it damaged their friendship beyond repair.

Hayley marched through the party, scanning the crowd, asking the guests if they had seen which direction Bruce was heading. When she got to Mona, who was walking Sadie around the grounds away from all the hoopla of the barbecue, Mona told her she had just spotted Bruce heading along the ocean path down toward the rocky beach in front of the estate.

Hayley thanked her and jogged along the path, shielding her eyes from the glaring sun with her hand as she set out in search of Bruce.

After fifteen minutes of looking, there was still no sign of him.

She was about to turn back when she heard some rustling behind her.

She started to turn around, expecting to find Bruce, but instead someone shoved a white cloth over her face, locking her in an iron embrace with his arm around her waist. She struggled for a few seconds before breathing in the paralyzing toxic smell of a strong chemical.

Chloroform.

Someone was drugging her with chloroform.

This realization sent a shiver down her spine and she started fighting her assailant, pounding her fists on his chest, but he was big, brawny, and sturdy and much stronger than she, and her attempts to free herself proved fruitless.

Finally she was overcome by the noxious fumes and succumbed.

She stirred awake a few minutes later.

Her arms were outstretched as someone gripped her by the wrists, dragging her across the wet sand.

Her whole body was numb and she was barely conscious.

When she opened her mouth to cry for help, no words came out.

She felt dizzy and disoriented.

And then everything went black again.

Island Food & Spirits
BY HAYLEY POWELL

This summer has been such a whirlwind of activity that I've barely had time to tend to my small garden that I grow out in my backyard. It's nothing fancy, mind you, just some tomatoes, sweet peppers, cucumbers, and of course, my favorite, zucchini. Zucchini is a must, since every year my brother Randy and his husband Sergio throw their August Birthday Party Bash for themselves, having been born less than a week apart in the dog days of August. I always bring my world-famous (okay, maybe not *world*-famous, let's go with *locally* famous) Zucchini Lasagna!

Randy and Sergio live in a beautiful old rambling house nestled near the famed Shore Path, a narrow gravel path that stretches along the Eastern Shore of Mount Desert Island that is trodden by tens of thousands of tourists and locals alike every summer so they can take in the breathtaking ocean views and picture-postcard sunrises and sunsets. Those lucky boys, Randy and Sergio, wake up to extraordinary beauty just outside their window every morning. Needless to say, they have the perfect party house so all of their friends and family look forward to their big, boisterous summer gala every year that boasts plenty of food, cocktails, and music.

Last year's party, however, was a double celebration. Not only was it their birthdays, it was also the fifth anniversary of the month they bought their gorgeous home, and moved in to start their life together as an official married couple. They decided to throw their biggest party to date. Out went the DJ, usually a friend who fancied himself a hip club spin-meister, and in came a local rock band hired to play live music. Gone was a cardboard table with a few liquor choices and some plastic bottles of soda mixer and in came a full-blown bar complete with a handsome young bartender. No crepe-paper decorations were bought at the last minute from the local party store. Instead they ordered a full range of fresh flower decorations. And especially exciting for everyone, no potluck dishes. We were going to be treated to a fully catered sunset dinner!

However, there was one item not on the caterer's menu that the boys insisted be served—my Zucchini Lasagna! And I was more than happy to make it. In fact, by the time I had finished, I had baked six large pans of it and delivered them to the caterer's shop the day of the party.

Since the boys were being so generous, a few of us wanted to do something special for them so we chipped in and bought an enormous six-tier birthday cake that was almost as tall as I was! We also splurged on a giant ice-sculpture fountain that would be flowing with champagne, which we had stored in the back of a refrigerated truck parked a few blocks away. The sculpture would be wheeled in at precisely 10 P.M. for a champagne toast.

Randy and Sergio were so busy dancing and socializing with all of their guests, they never noticed the flurry of activity just a few feet away as the champagne fountain and cake were being set up.

Their best friend Alex from Los Angeles, who had flown in for the event, took to the makeshift stage where the band was playing and grabbed the microphone, requesting that Randy and Sergio come forward for the toast. The boys were shocked and delighted at all the effort we had put into this very special moment.

As the champagne and cake were handed out to all the guests, we suddenly heard a woman's frantic voice yelling, "Tiny! Tiny, come back!"

Everyone paused for a moment and glanced around to see what was happening. And then, all eyes fell upon an adorable furry little gray kitten scampering between people's legs and meowing softly, before landing at Sergio's foot. He bent down and picked the cute kitty up in his arms and everyone laughed and applauded.

Unfortunately, this was *not* Tiny.

Not even close.

The disembodied woman was still yelling, "Tiny! Tiny, no!"

That's when all hell broke loose.

Suddenly, without warning, like an earthquake or lightning strike, the biggest black-and-white spotted Great Dane you have ever seen plowed right through the crowd, panting and drooling, and then launched himself straight at the kitten, which Sergio was cuddling in his arms.

The kitten spotted the dog and then, terrified, jumped out of Sergio's arms and climbed right up his chest and over his face, leaving kitty scratch marks on his cheeks and forehead before leaping onto the table where the cake was displayed and hiding behind it.

We all watched the disastrous scene unfold as if it was in slow motion. Randy vaulted in front of the ice fountain and held out his arms to protect it while Sergio, with all of his police training, leapt in front of the cake like a human shield, as if protecting a by-stander from a stray bullet, screaming at Tiny to stop. But Tiny wasn't about to listen. He was too focused on getting to the kitten, who was peeking out from behind the cake, eyes as big as saucers.

Tiny took a giant leap into the air and slammed right into Sergio's chest with such force, it knocked them both over and they landed with a giant thud right into the six-tier cake! All six tiers shot up into the air and then came crashing down with a large splat on top of Sergio, covering his entire head and face with chocolate cake and gooey sticky frosting. Tiny stopped to lick some of the frosting off Sergio's face, slobbering him with slime before he got dis-tracted by the kitten making a fast getaway by running down the middle of the table. Tiny continued his frenzied and relentless pursuit, and we all cringed as we saw dishes and champagne bottles smash to the ground.

Finally, a rather rotund, red-faced woman stepped in front of Tiny, and he suddenly stopped his ram-page when she screamed, "Tiny, HEEL!"

He did as he was told, allowing her to grab the end of his leash that had been trailing behind him.

Order was restored, but not before we all heard a loud cracking noise and turned to witness the table holding what was left of the cake, and Sergio, who was lying on top of it, give out under the weight and collapse. Randy rushed forward to catch his husband, but tripped and crashed into the table holding the ice fountain, which up to this point, amazingly, was still in one piece. But then, the ice fountain tipped over and crashed to the ground, exploding into a million pieces and spraying champagne, soaking everyone in the immediate vicinity. Both Randy and Sergio got the worst of it, however, and were covered from head to toe in a sticky mess of cake and champagne.

The boys began howling with laughter and everyone joined in, and the dog's owner, Julie, who was visiting her family's summerhouse just a few doors down until Labor Day, was invited to stay and join the party. Even Tiny was forgiven. The kitten turned out to be a stray, so the boys adopted him and called him Tim and spent the next few weeks hanging out on their porch with Julie, sipping champagne cocktails, while Tiny and Tim, who remarkably became best friends, played on the lawn. Who says dogs and cats can't learn to get along?

So with preparations already under way for this year's annual birthday party at the boys' house, let me share with you my recipes for a new champagne cocktail, and of course, my world—ahem, *locally* — famous Zucchini Lasagna!

Sparkling Pear Champagne Cocktail

Makes 4 servings.

> 1½ cups of your favorite champagne, chilled
> ⅔ cup pear liqueur, chilled
> 8 pear slices

Pour the chilled pear liqueur into four glasses and divide the chilled champagne between the four glasses. Add 2 slices of pears to each glass and sit back, relax, and enjoy a beautiful sunset.

Hayley's Zucchini Lasagna

2 zucchini, chopped
1 yellow onion, chopped
2 gloves garlic, minced
2 tablespoons olive oil
1 32-ounce container of ricotta cheese
2 16-ounce tubs of fresh baby spinach
1 egg
1 teaspoon kosher salt
1 teaspoon freshly ground pepper
16 ounces shredded mozzarella cheese
2 25-ounce jars of your favorite marinara
     sauce, or homemade
1 12-ounce box of no-boil lasagna noodles

Preheat your oven to 400°F.

Add one tablespoon of olive oil into a large skillet and heat on medium heat. Add your spinach, and cook until it is soft and wilted. Remove the spinach to a separate bowl to cool.

In the same skillet, add the rest of the olive oil and cook the zucchini and onion 7 minutes on medium heat, or until soft. Then add your garlic and stir another 30 seconds, or until you can smell the garlic. Remove from the heat and set aside.

Combine your egg, ricotta, cooked spinach, salt, and pepper in a medium bowl. Stir to combine and set aside.

Spray a 9-by-13-inch baking dish and layer tomato sauce, noodles, ricotta mixture, zucchini mixture, and mozzarella cheese. Continue layering in that order, ending with mozzarella cheese.

Place the baking dish on a cookie sheet to catch anything that may drip and cover with aluminum foil. Bake 45 minutes, remove foil, and bake 15 minutes more, or until the cheese is melted and starting to brown.

Remove from oven and let it sit at least 15 minutes before serving.

Chapter 25

Hayley felt her whole body hurtling through the air, rolling round and round before a sharp jagged object stopped her momentum and a piercing jolt of pain shot through her lower back from the sudden impact.

She wanted to scream, but her mouth was full of salty water and the more she inhaled, desperately trying to breathe in air, the more she choked and gagged. She then dropped to the ground and found herself facedown in a soggy mix of pebbles and sand, and when she tried to sit up, she was coughing up so much water, her body erupting in a fit of spasms, she lost all control.

Hayley managed to lift her head up ever so slightly and pop her eyes open just in time to see a rushing torrent of water crash to the ground just a few feet from her, the power of the surge knocking her back again and driving her into the hard rock wall behind her.

She knew enough to keep her mouth closed this

time and hold her breath to stop herself from taking in any more water, but as the waves receded once again, leaving her drenched and cold and lying in the wet sand, seaweed entangling her arms and legs, she finally managed to quickly glance around at her surroundings.

She was in some kind of sea cave.

Her heart began beating faster as she realized the only way out was through the large opening in front of her, but with the tide rushing in, it would be nearly impossible for her to get out by fighting against the force of the ocean waves rolling in fast and furious, filling the cave every few seconds.

When the water receded again, Hayley made a mad dash forward, her head down, praying she might make it out before the next large wave crashed down in front of her and seawater poured into the cave.

But she was out of luck.

She barely made it to the edge of the rocks that led outside to fresh air when suddenly another wave crested and broke and the tide gushed in, filling the cave and knocking her back again.

She held her breath at least twenty seconds this time while splashing around and waiting for the water to mercifully recede.

She had no idea who it was who had drugged her with chloroform and dragged her here, but his or her intention was chillingly obvious.

Hayley was put here to drown.

And she was determined not to spend the last

few minutes, last few seconds of her life trapped in a watery grave.

There was no way she was escaping through the large opening of the sea cave.

Her only choice was to climb out from the top.

Hayley looked up at the rock ceiling and spotted a small blowhole where a ray of sunlight was streaming through. It appeared as if it might be wide enough so she could squeeze her body through, but she wasn't absolutely sure.

Hayley swiftly crawled up the rock wall, using the jagged edges as footholds, until she could not climb any higher. Another wave crashed and water filled the cave.

Hayley gripped the sides of the rock wall and closed her eyes as the water rose up almost to her shoulders. She waited for the water to recede, and then continued climbing until she was close enough to the blowhole where she was able to stretch her arm toward the opening. She managed to reach up far enough where her fingers were just underneath the hole, but the sides were too smooth and there was nothing to grab on to in order to hoist herself up and out.

Desperate and on the verge of panicking, Hayley screamed at the top of her lungs while clinging to the rocks.

She screamed for what must have been at least five minutes.

With the thunderous roar of the crashing waves drowning out her voice, Hayley's efforts appeared hopeless, and she fought back tears as she slowly realized her chances of escaping this deadly ocean trap were fading fast.

And then, she heard a voice.

A man's voice.

He was calling her name.

She screamed a few more times, praying whoever was out there would hear her frantic cries for help.

She waited five more minutes, yelling every few seconds, trying to draw attention to her whereabouts.

Minutes passed.

There was no response.

Had she imagined the voice?

Was her desperate mind playing tricks on her?

Another few minutes passed.

She kept up her screams for help.

Her voice was hoarse, her vocal cords strained from the constant shouting.

Suddenly a shadow fell over the hole blocking out the sunlight.

"Hayley! Hayley!"

It was Bruce.

"Down here!" she cried.

Bruce stuck his face as far down the blowhole as he could and spotted Hayley waving frantically at him as the water below her rushed into the cave, rising up, this time to her neck.

In a few more minutes, she would be completely underwater.

Bruce shoved his arm down into the hole to grab Hayley.

She reached out, her fingers touching his, but she just wasn't close enough to get a good grip.

They both groaned as they kept trying, stretching mightily, but it was useless.

Bruce finally withdrew his arm and disappeared.

Hayley called to him a few more times, but he didn't answer.

She couldn't stop herself from crying anymore because her situation was now dire and her chances of getting out of this alive didn't look good.

Suddenly Bruce returned, shouting, "Hold on!"

He stuffed a long narrow tree branch down through the opening of the hole. It was thin enough to make it through but sturdy enough so that it just might hold Hayley's weight.

"Grab on to it, Hayley!" Bruce yelled from topside.

She extended her arm, slapping at leaves, which broke off and fluttered to the raging water below that was starting to fill up the cave again.

After a few tries, she finally got her hands around it and was able to hold on to the end.

"You got it?"

"Yes, Bruce! Hurry!"

With all his strength, Bruce tried raising the branch back up through the hole, but Hayley could tell he was struggling as she hung there, looking down at the water now swallowing her feet, legs, torso, neck, and face. She held her breath, her cheeks bursting, as she tightly hugged the branch, totally immersed in seawater.

The power of the rising tide slowly and miraculously lifted her up, and as the water drained out again, she felt the smooth sides of the blowhole wall scraping her body.

Hayley closed her eyes, praying she would not get stuck halfway through. But then she felt a pair of hands latch on to her wet clothes, and she was pulled the rest of the way up and through the top of the hole. She mercifully felt the warmth of the blazing midday sun cascading over her face.

Hayley opened her eyes, and found herself collapsing into Bruce's muscled arms.

She was coughing and shivering from the cold water, still in a state of shock.

Bruce hugged her tightly, holding her close to him, rubbing her with his hands to warm her up.

After a few minutes, he gently lowered her until she was lying on the ground and he was hovering over her, worriedly checking to make sure she was all right.

Bruce Linney had just saved her life.

He gently slid a hand underneath her head and raised it just high enough so their eyes met. "I thought I was going to lose you."

She tried to speak, but coughed up water instead.

Bruce tenderly sat her up, and patted her back until she got it all out.

Hayley wiped her mouth and they stared at each other for a few moments.

And then she reached up, grabbed him by the neck, pulled his head down and kissed him.

On the lips.

He was startled at first, hardly expecting such a bold move.

But then he smiled and kissed her back.

What was happening?

What were they doing?

Hayley ultimately broke the spell by trying to stand up.

But she was still wobbly, her body half-frozen from the relentlessly cold seawater.

Bruce helped Hayley to her feet, and she used his body as a crutch to limp slowly back to the main house.

They made the short journey in silence.

Not speaking about the momentous kiss they had just shared.

As if it had never happened.

Chapter 26

Hayley's lumpy old bed had never felt so good. She snuggled deep inside the covers to get warm. She could feel Leroy's curled-up furry little body sleeping soundly next to her.

When she had arrived home late yesterday after speaking with police about her ordeal and enduring the skeptical looks from Penelope, Gerard, Carol, and Tristan, all of whom had trouble believing someone would go to the trouble of smothering her with chloroform and dragging her unconscious body to a remote sea cave to leave her there to drown.

But that was Hayley's story and she was sticking to it.

She didn't care what any of them thought.

Penelope's annual day after Fourth of July barbecue had been winding down anyway, so Hayley wasted no time in packing up her things and bolting from the property for good.

She had no intention of ever going back there.

But she was still determined as ever, as was Bruce, to keep digging, keep investigating until they came up with some answers as to what really happened to Conrad and who it was who locked Lena Hendricks in that pantry to die in a well-timed fire.

But all of that could wait.

Hayley, whose nasty cold had returned with a vengeance after Bruce so heroically pulled her up through that blowhole, just wanted to stay in bed all day and recover.

But she knew that was a fantasy.

After almost a week out of the office, she was scheduled to report back to work today. Sal was acting nonchalant about her long absence, but she could tell by the sound of his voice on the phone that they had been lost without her.

He was nice enough to offer her half the day off given the distressing circumstances she had endured the day before, and so she was allowed to sleep in late. She was not expected to report to the office until noon.

Hayley intended to take full advantage of her morning off by staying in bed until the last possible second. She closed her eyes and was about to drift off to sleep again when the meowing started.

Leroy shifted his body, sighing deeply, annoyed by the disturbance.

Hayley rolled on her other side, clutching the pillow, praying her cat Blueberry would just give up and go away.

But the meowing continued.

She knew his bowl downstairs was empty.

And he was hungry.

And he would not budge from the doorway of the bedroom where he sat meowing at the top of his lungs until Hayley got her butt out of that bed, walked downstairs, and fed him his breakfast.

Hayley threw off the covers, burying Leroy in an avalanche of wool blankets and wrinkled white sheets, tossed on some sweats and a T-shirt, and made her way to the kitchen, sniffling and coughing the whole way as Blueberry chased behind her.

She pulled a box of dry food from the cupboard and poured it into a bowl decorated with tiny paw prints. Blueberry stopped eyeing her with scorn for taking so long and focused on devouring his Friskies Tender & Crunchy Combo.

Hearing the commotion downstairs in the kitchen, Leroy excitedly jumped from his mattress throne and scampered down to receive his own breakfast. Hayley had already anticipated his move, so his food was already poured and ready for him. He eagerly began chomping it down so fast that bits and pieces flew out from his bowl and onto the floor.

Hayley was filling the coffeemaker when she glanced out the kitchen window and noticed a police cruiser parked on the street next to her driveway. She could see someone inside the car watching the house.

It was Sergio.

She knew exactly what he was doing.

Sergio was worried about her safety given the events of the day before, so he was keeping watch over the house to make sure nobody showed up and tried to attack her again.

She had never had police protection before.

Hayley whipped up some scrambled eggs and bacon, buttered some toast, poured hot coffee into a Styrofoam cup, sealing it with a lid, and placed it all in a brown paper bag and walked outside to the cruiser.

Sergio was half-asleep when she knocked on the passenger side window.

He jumped in his seat, startled, and then smiled when he saw her, and unlocked the door. She hopped in the squad car's passenger seat and handed him the bag.

"I thought you might want some breakfast."

"You're too good to me."

"I could say the same about you. Have you been out here *all night?*"

"Randy insisted."

Hayley knew that was only partially true. Sergio loved her like his own sister, and would do anything to make sure she stayed safe.

"Well, I appreciate your concern and I'm touched that you would stake out my house all night, but I suspect that whoever was behind pushing me off the boat and knocking me out and dragging me to that cave is done trying to get rid of me now that I'm no longer snooping around on the estate. I'm a lot less of a threat now that I've been exiled and away from all the action."

"Better safe than sorry," Sergio said as he pulled the plastic container of eggs, bacon, and toast out of the bag and started stabbing at his yellow scrambled eggs with a silver fork Hayley had provided. "I'll drive back to the station once you're safely at the office. I have a nine o'clock appointment with Penelope Janice."

"What are you meeting with her about?"

"We examined Lena Hendricks's cell phone and discovered a text from Penelope asking Lena to refill the cat food dispenser in the pantry. The text came in about five minutes before Lena went to the pantry, where the dispenser exploded, causing the fire."

Hayley gasped.

She couldn't believe it.

"But Penelope said it was Clara's job to refill the cat food dispenser."

"Right, but Conrad had fired Clara so she wasn't there to do it . . ."

"So Penelope asked Lena . . ." Hayley said, her voice trailing off.

Hayley's mind raced as she shifted in the passenger seat toward Sergio, who was crunching on a piece of bacon. "Why didn't Penelope mention that to you before when you questioned her?" she asked.

Sergio swallowed his bacon and patted the sides of his mouth with a white napkin. "There's no plausible reason except that maybe she was setting her up to be killed and didn't want the police knowing about it."

"But she must have known the text would be on

Lena's phone. Penelope is a smart woman. I'm sure she would have thought of that."

"Maybe, maybe not. Either way it's a pretty incremental piece of evidence."

"Incriminating."

"Yes. That's what I said. Incremental."

"No, the correct word is incriminating."

"Yes," Sergio sighed, annoyed. "Incremental."

Hayley decided to let it go.

"So you believe Penelope was furious over her husband's affair with Lena, rigged the cat food dispenser with chemicals and a timer, and then lured Lena to the pantry with a text while she was lying in wait to lock her inside so she couldn't escape when the dispenser exploded?"

"It's a working theory. But it makes sense."

Hayley looked at the digital clock on the car's dashboard.

It was 7:45 A.M.

"I'm not due in the office until noon today," Hayley said. "So I was going to stay home until then. You can't very well watch my house *and* have your meeting with Penelope at the station at the same time so there's only one thing to do . . ."

"Hayley . . ."

"I'll come to the station with you and hang out there until it's time to go to work," Hayley said. "I know your primary concern is that I remain safe and under the watchful care of a competent law enforcement officer.

Sergio shook his head.

He knew exactly what she was doing.

She wanted to be around so she could hear what Penelope had to say about the evidence Sergio was about to present to her.

"I'll just take a quick shower and be back down in twenty minutes," Hayley said, jumping out of the car before he could protest. "Enjoy your breakfast!"

"That is the most preposterous, bogus, unsubstantiated load of bull crap I have ever heard in my life!" Hayley heard Penelope scream from inside Sergio's office.

When Penelope had arrived, Hayley had decided it might not be a good idea for the food maven to see her hanging around, so she slipped into Officer Donnie's cubicle and buried her face in a magazine, concealing herself from Penelope's view as she made her grand entrance into the station and marched inside the police chief's office for questioning. But Sergio had strategically left his door open a crack so Hayley would be able to hear their conversation.

Their very prickly and tense conversation, as it happened.

"It is hardly unsubstantiated, Mrs. Janice," Sergio said calmly. "We have your text on Miss Hendricks's phone."

"But it wasn't from me! I didn't send any text to Lena that night! I swear on my life!"

"The text came from your number."

"Well, then someone must have gotten ahold of

my phone and sent that text to Lena so Lena would think it was from me!"

"Well, who do you think would have done that?"

"I have no idea!" Penelope wailed.

"Who else in the house has access to your phone?"

There was a pause.

Hayley was frustrated.

She wanted to be in Sergio's office, studying Penelope's face to see if she could tell if she was lying or trying to hide something.

"No one!" Penelope declared.

"You hesitated," Sergio said quietly.

"I was thinking! You asked me who had access, I was running names through my mind and I came up with no one! Nobody else has access to my phone! I keep it on my person at all times in case the network, or production company, or my managers call me. I am a very busy woman!"

"Please don't leave town, Mrs. Janice," Sergio said sternly. "At least until we get this all sorted."

"I don't believe this! You're treating me like a common criminal!" she screeched.

"I'm just trying to get to the bottom of all this," Sergio said.

Penelope stormed out of the office in a huff and marched down the hall right past Hayley, who covered her face with a copy of *People* magazine. Penelope blew by and out the door, slamming it behind her to make the point she was not leaving a happy woman.

Hayley peered above the top of the magazine to

make sure she was really gone before jumping up and bolting into Sergio's office.

"Well, what do you think?" Hayley asked breathlessly.

"When I asked her who else had access to her phone, I could tell she was thinking of someone specific, but she didn't dare say the name."

Who?

Who was Penelope protecting if she was not the one who sent that text to Lena?

Sergio's phone rang and he scooped up the receiver. "Chief Alvares."

Hayley watched Sergio's face as he listened to the caller.

His stony expression melted, replaced by surprise and concern. He nodded solemnly, thanked whoever was on the other end, and hung up.

"What's wrong?"

"Lena Hendricks didn't make it. She died earlier this morning," he whispered.

Hayley wasn't expecting this. She thought of Lena as so young and strong. She just assumed that she would somehow pull through this.

But she was wrong.

And now they were dealing with a homicide.

Chapter 27

Hayley knocked on Bruce's office door at the *Island Times*, and without waiting for permission to enter, breezed inside. She stopped dead in her tracks at the sight of a smiling, bright-eyed Jillian plopped comfortably down in a chair opposite Bruce's desk.

"Hi!" Jillian chirped, waving at Hayley.

"Hello," Hayley answered evenly, not sure why she was so thrown by Jillian's unexpected presence.

Hayley turned to Bruce. "You wanted to see me?"

"Yes, come in," Bruce said, feet up on his desk, hands clasped behind his head. "I came across some very interesting information I think you will want to know about."

Hayley entered the cramped office, but there was nowhere for her to sit down because Jillian was occupying the only chair, so she stiffly leaned up against the wall and awkwardly folded her arms across her chest.

"My old college roommate Steven Farley is a

business reporter at the *Times* in New York," Bruce said, sliding his feet off his desk and leaning forward, typing a few keys on his computer.

"He's a real cutie! Bruce showed me his picture on Facebook," Jillian cooed. "But he's not as adorable as you are, Bruce."

"Aww, you're so sweet," Bruce said, cheeks blushing a rosy red, turning his computer screen around so Hayley could see a photo of Steven on his Facebook page.

He was handsome, she had to admit.

"Is that the big news you wanted to tell me?" Hayley asked, quickly losing patience.

"Of course not," Bruce said. "Steven tracks and writes all about corporate business mergers, and last night when we were on the phone planning our upcoming college reunion weekend next month, I casually mentioned that I had spent the weekend at Penelope Janice's estate investigating her husband's nosedive off that cliff. Well, he told me about a proposed merger that is very close to getting federal approval between Penelope's company and, wait for it, Gerard Roquefort's company."

"They are going to become business partners?"

"Individually their companies are very successful, but together they will instantly become a mega-sized cooking and lifestyle empire!" Bruce yelled, slamming the palm of his hand down on his desk.

"Oh, Brucey, I love watching you get all excited over a story!" Jillian interjected, staring goggle-eyed at Bruce before turning to Hayley. "He's like a little boy on Christmas morning who gets the train set he really, really wanted, right, Hayley?"

"So cute," Hayley said, barely managing to put a lid on her sarcasm.

Bruce scowled at Hayley before he continued. "And that's not all. Apparently, according to Steven's sources, the merger isn't *just* in the boardroom."

"They're having an *affair*?" Hayley gasped.

Jillian gasped too just so she could remain included in the conversation.

Bruce nodded. "While they were both in New York for merger talks, they were spotted together all over the city, holding hands at *Hamilton*, having a romantic dinner at Gramercy Tavern, and according to one source, they even shared a suite at the St. Regis."

"So they aren't exactly being discreet," Hayley said.

"The word Steven's source used was 'flagrant,'" Bruce said.

Jillian raised her hand.

Hayley and Bruce exchanged a look and then Bruce said, as if calling on a student in the back row of a classroom with a question, "Yes, Jillian?"

"What's *flagrant* mean? I've never heard that word," Jillian said shyly, embarrassed she had to ask.

"Blatant, as if flaunting their secret relationship, very open about it in public . . ." Hayley said, trying to help.

After a few seconds, the word finally registered with Jillian and she slapped her forehead with the palm of her hand. "Oh, okay! I get it! Well, it sounds like they were! *Flagrant,* I mean."

"I can't believe it. We've been so focused on Conrad's extramarital affair with Lena that we completely ignored the possibility that Penelope may have been cheating as well," Hayley said, shaking her head.

"So here is what we have so far. Penelope was cheating on Conrad with Gerard. And Conrad was cheating on Penelope with Lena," Bruce said.

"If Conrad opposed the merger and wanted to stop it because he was threatened by Gerard coming in and having undue influence over Penelope's company stocks and cash reserves because they were sexually involved, one way to do that is to plot Penelope's murder with his mistress Lena, which is *exactly* what I heard happening the night I got food poisoning," Hayley said.

"And maybe after you alerted Penelope, she was the one who gave her husband a hard shove off that cliff before he had the chance to carry out *his* plot to kill *her,*" Hayley said, her mind racing. "But then who tried to kill Lena?"

"That's where Jillian comes in," Bruce said proudly.

Jillian smiled, and then as a thought popped in her head, her eyes nearly bulged out of their sockets. "I didn't kill her!"

"We know, Jillian. I'm talking about what you came here and told me this morning. I want you to tell Hayley," Bruce said patiently.

"Oh, right," Jillian said, sitting up straight in her

chair, adjusting her breasts slightly, and slapping a very serious, businesslike expression on her face. "Well, as you know, Hayley, I work part-time at the Bar Harbor Banking and Trust . . ."

"I didn't know that," Hayley said.

"No? I've been there about eight months. My Aunt Cissy works there. Gosh, she's probably been there something like twenty, maybe thirty years. She's in charge of hiring tellers, and so she brought me in part-time when one of the girls, Elise, went on maternity leave . . ." Jillian said, before lowering her voice to a whisper. "Elise got knocked up by one of the married vice presidents, but that's all on the down low, if you know what I mean. The official story is the baby was fathered by some ex-boyfriend from Boston who was in town one weekend, but we all know that man doesn't even exist—"

"Jillian! Sweetheart! Hayley doesn't care about any of this!" Bruce yelled, exasperated.

"Actually I'm riveted, but maybe you can finish telling me about all that over coffee sometime," Hayley said.

"Oh, I'd love to! I've always thought we'd make great friends!" Jillian said. "We have so much in common!"

Besides Bruce, Hayley couldn't think of one thing.

"Jillian," Bruce said through gritted teeth.

"Oh, right! Well, Elise came back recently, but Aunt Cissy still calls me to fill in when a teller is out sick, which was what happened last week. I was asked to confirm some deposits on a few accounts, and one very large amount stuck out to me because it was over ten thousand dollars, and whenever we record a deposit over ten thousand dollars we have to get approval, which I did. But when I pulled up the account on my computer at the request of the customer who wanted to make sure the money was available for withdrawal, I noticed there were several more deposits in that same amount."

"Lena Hendricks!" Hayley guessed.

"Well, I'm really not supposed to *say* any names, because private banking information is strictly confidential . . ." Jillian said. "But . . ."

She began nodding her head up and down vigorously.

"And were the deposits *from* Penelope Janice's account?" Hayley asked, eyes fixed on Jillian.

"Well, like I said, I'm not supposed to *say* . . ." Jillian said.

She was now nodding so hard it would be a miracle if her head didn't hurt.

"Were the ten-thousand-dollar deposits in addition to her regular income as Penelope's assistant and ghostwriter?" Hayley asked.

"They seemed to be, yes," Jillian said, before clasping a hand over her mouth and looking around to make sure no one outside Bruce's office had heard her. "I mean . . ."

Jillian nodded wildly as if having some sort of seizure.

"So you believe Lena was blackmailing Penelope . . ." Hayley surmised before turning to Jillian.

"When did the large deposits start appearing in Lena's account?"

"A few weeks ago," Jillian said, not realizing she was now speaking and not just nodding her pretty head with the perfectly coiffured hair.

"Well, that blows a hole in your blackmail theory because Penelope was handing over these large sums of money long before Conrad died," Hayley said, frustrated.

"Maybe she was blackmailing her about something else. What about the affair with Gerard? Lena could have been having a secret affair with Conrad while at the same time extorting money from Penelope with the secret she knew about her boss's own affair with her future business partner," Bruce said.

"You guys are *so* smart!" Jillian said, looking from one to the other, beaming.

Bruce offered Jillian a dismissive smile before turning back to Hayley. "Let's say Lena was blackmailing Penelope and threatening to expose her affair with Gerard to Conrad. She was receiving cash payments to stay quiet. And maybe she was also sleeping with Conrad on the side, and Conrad wanted Penelope out of the way so he could be with Lena and inherit all of his wife's money before the merger. But then you alerted Penelope to what they were up to, which led to her giving Conrad the ole heave-ho off that cliff while he was drunk."

"Lena either saw Penelope kill her husband or had proof that she did the deed, so the blackmailing continued," Hayley said.

Bruce jumped in. "That would give Penelope a

very strong motive to get rid of Lena! *She* rigged the cat food dispenser with the chemicals, texted Lena to go feed the cat, and then locked her inside just before the timer was set to go off. It all makes sense. But we have no evidence to prove any of this."

"I still feel Penelope is too smart to text Lena from her own phone," Hayley said, starting to pace back and forth in Bruce's cramped office, but the space was so tight she finally gave up.

"How do we prove that any of this speculation is true?" Bruce asked.

A lightbulb suddenly went off in Hayley's head and she smiled. "I know a way!"

Both Bruce and Jillian leaned forward, filled with curiosity.

Hayley turned, a conspiratorial look on her face. "What if we caught her in the act of trying again?"

Chapter 28

Hayley was understandably nervous. She was back at Penelope Janice's estate, after all that had happened. She never dreamed she would ever return here after being accused of making up wild stories, shunned by the VIP guest list, twice attacked by some dangerous, marauding assailant. If she never set foot near this place again, it would be too soon.

But she had to come. She was on a mission, one that she had carefully planned out with Police Chief Sergio Alvares and, to her surprise, a remarkably supportive Bruce Linney. And yes, to some extent, the plucky and excitable Jillian.

When Hayley called Sergio after leaving Bruce's office with the new information she had, Sergio immediately was on board with what Hayley had in mind, although he was worried about the very serious risk.

Hayley tried putting his mind at ease by brushing aside his concerns. She could handle it. Besides,

nothing was going to stop her from finding out
the truth, and she felt strongly in her bones that
they were getting very close to some long-awaited
answers.

Pam, the perky maid who had first welcomed
Hayley to the Fourth of July celebrity potluck weekend, wasn't so perky now. In fact, as she led Hayley
to the kitchen, she was scowling, which began the
moment she answered the door and saw Hayley
standing on the stoop. The household staff had
believed they had seen the last of her and her disruptive antics, and were probably hoping without
her around anymore the household could return
to a sense of normalcy.

But no such luck.

Pam sighed and waved Hayley inside. She was
rather curt with her when she told her Penelope
was cooking in the kitchen and did not want to be
disturbed. Hayley insisted it was important that
she speak with her, and after a flurry of phone calls,
Penelope's permission had been granted, and they
were finally making their way there.

Pam stopped just short of the kitchen and ges-
tured for Hayley to enter. When Hayley passed her,
Pam did an about-face and scurried off, having no
intention of being included in what promised to
be a very tense conversation given the circumstances of Hayley's unceremonious departure the
day before.

Penelope was braising some beef with loyal and
devoted Clara at her side when Hayley quietly
walked toward them. Penelope slowly raised her

eyes to Hayley, gave her a slight nod, and went back to what she was doing, leaving Hayley just standing there, arms folded in front of her, waiting.

Penelope took her sweet time, whistling a tune, making a silent point of letting Hayley know that she was not at the moment even close to being a priority. Penelope finally decided the beef looked moist enough so she slid the roasting pan over to Clara, who picked it up and carried it to the oven.

Penelope casually brushed the front of her apron with her hands, and finally glanced up, tossing her hair back, and with a hard look, said, "Yes, Hayley? How can I help you?"

Hayley cleared her throat nervously.

More for effect than from actual nerves.

She wanted to give Penelope the impression that right now she had the upper hand.

"I just want to apologize for everything," Hayley lied.

She knew there was nothing she had done that warranted an apology.

Penelope softened slightly, took her apron off and folded it up, then set it down on one of the counters.

"I see . . ."

"I've been going over everything in my mind, and maybe you were right that I wasn't thinking clearly when I was ill from food poisoning . . ."

She noticed Clara flinching as she slid the roasting pan into the oven.

"I may have let my imagination run wild a bit . . ." Hayley said apologetically.

Penelope watched her silently, trying to gauge her sincerity.

Hayley worked hard to pretend this was not a well-rehearsed performance. "And then I got so paranoid, like everybody was out to get me, and well, oh, Penelope, I just feel awful about all that's happened!"

"Well, you can't blame yourself for *everything*. You may have gotten a little carried away with your stories, but it's not your fault Conrad fell off that cliff or that poor, poor Lena got caught in that horrific fire . . ." Penelope said solemnly, wiping a stray tear away as it ran down her cheek.

"You must miss him so much . . ." Hayley said.

"Who?"

"Conrad."

Penelope caught herself and nodded quickly. "Yes, of course. We were married for a long, long time."

Her words were mechanical, rehearsed.

Hayley hoped that she was giving a much better performance than the rather stiff and unconvincing Penelope Janice.

"And Lena . . . what she must have gone through . . . I keep imagining what she was thinking, trapped inside the pantry, unable to get out, black smoke consuming her . . ." Hayley said, shaking her head.

Another tear shot down Penelope's cheek.

And then another.

In Hayley's mind, they almost seemed genuine.

Unlike Penelope's wooden, graceless words about

her pain of a late husband. The only kindness she could muster about him was to note how long they had been married.

A long, long time.

That was all she could come up with to express her grief.

"Well, as difficult as it is losing a spouse, you must find some solace in knowing Lena's going to make it . . ." Hayley said.

Penelope, who only moments before had appeared lost and hopeless, suddenly snapped to attention. *"What?"*

"Lena's going to recover."

"I don't know where you get your information, Hayley," Penelope spit out, aghast. "But I heard directly from the hospital that Lena had passed away earlier today."

"Oh, gosh, you didn't hear about the mix-up? Apparently Nurse Tilly McVety was given the wrong information. A Mrs. Laura Henderson died, not Lena Hendricks. She was in the next room in the ICU, and there was a mistake in the recording of the room number, and well, Nurse Tilly made a couple of calls before it all got corrected. Nobody called you back to tell you?"

"No!" Penelope yelled as she whipped out her phone and called the hospital. She was frantic as she demanded to be put directly through to Nurse Tilly. Once Tilly was on the line, Penelope asked her point-blank what exactly was going on, and Tilly explained, along with an avalanche of apologies—

probably with Police Chief Alvares at her side coaching her on exactly what to say.

Penelope listened, a shocked look on her face, and then she put her phone down on the counter and stared into space, not angry or worried, just stunned.

"I'm so sorry . . . all this time you thought . . ."

Hayley let her words trail off.

Penelope didn't look at her, or wave her away, or acknowledge her in any way. She just stood next to her oven, a hand over her mouth, shaking slightly, processing the fact that Lena Hendricks was still alive.

"I should go," Hayley said, turning on her heel, and creeping out.

Her work here was done.

The wheels of her plan were in motion.

Now they just had to wait.

Island Food & Spirits
BY HAYLEY POWELL

Every so often I come up with a new casserole recipe, bake it the night before, and take it with me on my routine early-morning walk before work with my dog Leroy. Our daily route takes us right past the local police station so whenever I have a casserole in hand, I stop in and present it to my brother-in-law, Police Chief Sergio Alvares, and any other officers who happen to be on duty at the time. They sure do appreciate it, especially during the busy summer months when the town is bustling with hundreds of tourists, including campers, off-loaded cruise-ship passengers, and of course all the visitors who drive onto the island and fill up the motels and hotels. You can scarcely spot a "Vacancy" sign until well after Labor Day.

You can only imagine how many calls regarding fender benders, lost children, and minor thefts the police department receives when the town is so packed.

With all of this activity, our boys and girls in blue hardly have any spare time to slip away and get themselves something hearty and homemade to eat, so it warms my heart to see such appreciation on their faces when I drop off my casserole dish at the station.

One particular morning I presented my Summer Squash Taco Casserole, a Mexican twist on an old favorite. I also brought along a plastic container of my refreshing Sparkling Lemonade for the officers to wash it down with, confident that both the casserole and the lemonade would be a big hit with all those hardworking police officers.

Stopping by the station reminded me that today was Wednesday, and like clockwork, every Wednesday I received the Police Log email that we would print in the Thursday edition of the paper. I have to admit, I love reading the Police Log! It's like gossiping with your girlfriends on the phone, or in person over a cocktail! The log is filled with all the dirt, summing up in little snippets all of the trouble the locals and tourists have gotten themselves into over the past week.

I could spend the next twenty columns discussing the various crimes and misdemeanors of our local population, but I'd much rather focus today on the out-of-towners, the oblivious tourists from all over the world who seem to lose their minds the minute they land on our beloved, picturesque island paradise.

Today's Police Log featured a treasure trove of craziness! For instance, on Friday, a group of college-age men arrived from New York and set up an illegal campsite in the woods. Well, they polished off more than a few bottles of bourbon and vodka and Lord only knows what else, and actually thought a game of hacky sack was a good idea. For those of you who have never played hacky sack, let me explain. The game consists of two or more players standing in a circle, and everyone tries to keep a small round ball filled with sand or pellets from hitting the ground by kicking it around. Sounds harmless enough. Except that these boys decided to use a hatchet instead of a ball filled with sand! When a park ranger happened upon the scene, drawn by all the screaming and hollering, he found the drunken young men with deep cuts all over their feet from their hatchet–hacky sack game gone wrong. The ranger had to call for medical attention, despite the men's protesting that they were fine. When they sobered up, however, and they could actually feel the pain, well, it was quite a different story!

On Sunday, the police arrived at a local campground after receiving several complaints that a woman would not stop screaming at her husband and disturbing the other campers. When Officers Donnie and Earl arrived they discovered the poor husband had locked himself in the car. His wife was trying to break in the windows with a tent pole to get at him. Apparently the husband had refused to set up their tent that night because he was too tired after their long drive from Worcester, Massachusetts, and he insisted that they should just sleep in the car for the night. Well, the wife had other ideas and began screaming at him to erect the tent at once because she was not sleeping in a car! One thing led to another and the situation quickly escalated, resulting in the wife beating her husband with the tent pole until he locked himself in the car to protect himself! The wife was arrested for assault, and yes, you can assume alcohol was involved. Fortunately, the husband sobered up by morning and refused to press charges since they were on the island to celebrate their twenty-fifth wedding anniversary.

On Tuesday, a crying, inconsolable woman arrived at the police station to report that she had left her campsite to head into town and buy a few groceries, and upon her return, was shocked to find that her husband, three children, and RV were missing and no one on the campground had seen them leave! Police Chief Alvares managed to calm the woman down long enough for her to tell him which campground the family was staying at, and with blue lights flashing, the chief raced to the scene to investigate. Surprisingly, when he arrived, he discovered the husband, three children, and RV all present and accounted for, all safe and sound.

Well, after a little digging, the chief was able to determine that after grocery shopping, the woman returned to the wrong campground, one that was a couple of miles down the road! The chief was happy to reunite the poor woman with her "lost" family.

Okay, to be fair, I should also share a few items from the Police Log that did involve our colorful local population that week. One irate man called the police to report that his neighbor's car alarm had been going off for the past hour and all the racket was disturbing his sleep. On arrival, the officers discovered the car's alarm had a faulty wire causing it to honk incessantly, and the car was registered to none other than the irate man who called the police!

Then there was the elderly woman on Wednesday who called the station to complain of trespassers on her property. She also noted that this was not the first time these lawbreaking delinquents had trodden on her land and plants, and she wanted the police to come out immediately and speak to them. Well, when the officers pulled up, they were shocked to discover that the trespassers were four cows from a neighboring farm.

One frantic man called to report that there were

two men loitering on lower Main Street trying to light a fire. When the police arrived, they found two men casually just trying to light a big cigar on a windy day.

I could go on and on, but I better save a few stories to share in a future column. Right now I want to share with you my delicious Sparkling Lemonade and Summer Squash Taco Casserole!

Sparkling Lemonade

¾ cup sugar
½ cup water
¼ cup lemon peel strips (about 2 lemons)
¾ cup lemon juice (3 freshly squeezed lemons)
1 cup club soda, chilled

In a saucepan, heat up your sugar and water over medium heat, stirring to dissolve all of the sugar. Stir in the lemon strips. Bring to a boil. Reduce the heat and simmer 5 minutes. Cool 10 minutes. Pour into a pitcher. Stir in your lemon juice. Cover and refrigerate until chilled.

Remove the lemon strips and stir in the club soda and serve over ice on a hot summer day.

For an adult beverage, just add your favorite vodka for a little added kick!

Summer Squash Taco Casserole

2 cups thinly sliced summer squash
1 14½-ounce can diced tomatoes
1 pound ground beef, cooked and drained
1 tablespoon chili powder
2 teaspoons paprika

2 teaspoons cumin
2 teaspoons onion powder
1 teaspoon garlic powder
Pinch of kosher salt
½ teaspoon cayenne pepper (or more if you
  like heat)
2 cups shredded cheddar cheese

Preheat your oven to 350°F.

Add your diced tomatoes and seasoning in the
skillet with your cooked meat and simmer about
10 minutes.

Place the sliced squash on the bottom of a 13-by-
9-inch baking pan. Spread the meat mixture over
the top of the squash and top with the shredded
cheese.

Bake 30 minutes. Remove and enjoy with a
refreshing glass of lemonade!

Chapter 29

Hayley could hear the repetitive beep of the ventilator in the ICU as she lay flat in the bed, the covers pulled all the way up over her face. She remained still, not moving, waiting. When Officer Donnie had radioed Sergio to let him know that a car had left Penelope Janice's estate, and that he followed it all the way into Bar Harbor and it was heading in the direction of the hospital, she knew the time was near.

Hayley had raced up to the ICU from the cafeteria where she was having coffee with Sergio, and taken her place in the bed just as they had discussed when hatching this plan.

Hayley's phone buzzed and the light illuminated under the covers. She turned it over and looked at the screen.

It was a text from Sergio.

Car on Wayman Lane. Heading to hospital guest parking.

She turned the phone back over to snuff out the light.

Hayley couldn't believe what she had earlier considered a cockamamie plan, even though it was her own, was actually working. But if all unfolded as expected, they would soon have Lena Hendricks's killer in custody.

Hayley waited for what felt like an eternity.

It was uneasily quiet.

Just the persistent beeping from the ventilator.

She took a deep breath and exhaled, calming herself, mentally preparing for what might happen next.

And then she heard the door to the ICU room swing open with a whoosh.

Footsteps approached the bed.

Hayley's nose suddenly itched and she resisted the urge to reach up with her finger and scratch it. She tried twitching her nose around to get some relief, and thought she must look like Samantha Stevens from those old *Bewitched* reruns she used to watch religiously as a kid.

Hayley felt a presence hovering above her, staring down at her, and then there was some fumbling and she felt a yank on the IV drip she was holding in her hand.

The door suddenly opened again, this time with a bang, and she heard Sergio bark, "Hold it right there!"

Hayley threw off the covers and gasped.

It wasn't Penelope standing over her.

It was Gerard Roquefort.

In one hand he gripped a syringe and in the other the IV tube.

He was about to inject the tube with a liquid.

Something to stop the heart no doubt.

Gerard looked surprised but resigned.

Sergio ordered him to drop the syringe, and he immediately complied, setting it gently down on the bedside table.

Hayley sat up, eyes blazing. "I suppose Penelope sent you here to do her dirty work? Finish the job she thought she botched?"

Gerard's eyes widened and he shook his head. "What? No. Penelope knows nothing about any of this."

"I highly doubt that," Hayley sneered.

"I'm telling you the truth. Penelope is completely innocent," he said, looking around at Sergio, who was blocking the door.

"Then how did you come to believe Lena was still alive?" Sergio asked.

"Penelope told me. After you left earlier today. But she had no idea I was the one who . . ."

"Killed Lena!" Hayley spat.

Caught red-handed, Gerard sighed, knowing the truth would come out eventually, so he started to talk.

Quite a bit, in fact.

"Penelope and I were in the middle of merging our companies, a fact I'm sure you already know, but the whole deal was being complicated by

Conrad. He had a major stake in it, but refused to go along with the merger because he suspected Penelope and I were having an affair," Gerard said.

"And *were* you?" Hayley asked pointedly.

"Yes," Gerard whispered.

"Go on," Sergio ordered.

"Penelope wanted a divorce, but she knew if she filed for one, Conrad would get half of her fortune, and the whole merger would be thrown into disarray. But there was a clause in their prenuptial agreement . . ."

"Let me guess," Hayley interjected. "If Conrad committed adultery, he would waive his rights to any of his wife's fortune in the divorce proceedings."

Gerard nodded, bowing his head.

"Penelope is a smart, observant woman. She knew Conrad was attracted to her assistant Lena, so she paid her to start a clandestine relationship with him," Hayley said, sitting up in the bed, the pieces now falling into place.

Hayley turned to Sergio. "That would explain the large deposits in her bank account unrelated to her regular work. Lena was desperate to please Penelope because she had so much to learn from her. In fact, she wanted to *be* her, so she agreed to the plan, anything, even starting a relationship with Penelope's husband, to make her boss and role model happy."

"The plan worked. We set up a camera in Lena's room. We got the proof we needed," Gerard said.

"Then why not just expose the affair, file for

divorce, and be rid of him once and for all?" Hayley asked.

"Because Conrad was never going to go away. He was always going to be a thorn in our side. The bastard hired private investigators to dig up some dirt on me, a couple of past business ventures that you might possibly describe as 'slightly shady,' contracts that went belly up and cost a lot of people a good deal of money, deals that would threaten the merger if they came to light . . ." Gerard said, rubbing his tired eyes with the back of his hand.

"So that's where the murder plot came in," Hayley said, glancing at Sergio who at this point looked totally confused.

Gerard nodded. "I encouraged Lena . . ."

"Encouraged?"

"I told Lena," Gerard said, noticing the skepticism on Hayley's face. "Okay, ordered her to draw Conrad into a fake murder plot to get rid of Penelope so they could be together."

"What made you think Conrad would go for it?"

Gerard chuckled. "Are you kidding? He despised Penelope and was head over heels in love with Lena. He would have done anything she wanted. Including bumping off his own wife. If they made it look like an accident, then not only would he get Lena, but he would also get Penelope's fortune."

"So I take it Lena recorded their conversations discussing the plot, including the one I overheard the night I had food poisoning and stumbled upon them in the hallway?"

Gerard nodded. "We were going to use the tapes

to blackmail Conrad into leaving town quietly, never to return, so the merger could move forward without any more interference from him, and my previous business deals would stay buried. Everything was going according to plan until he got rip-roaring drunk and fell off that cliff."

"So you *didn't* push him?" Sergio asked, trying to muscle his way into the conversation since he was, after all, the official investigating officer in the room.

"Of course not," Gerard hissed, appalled at the notion even though they had just caught him trying to do away with Lena Hendricks, who he thought was still alive. "But needless to say, we were ecstatic. The problem had suddenly taken care of itself. The deadbeat husband was finally out of the picture."

"Except Lena was the one loose end who could ruin your carefully laid plans for a prosperous future together," Hayley said.

"We weren't worried at first. She was so loyal and devoted to Penelope. But she got it into her head that we were the ones who did away with Conrad, pushed him to his death, and no matter how hard we tried to convince her that we had nothing to do with his falling off that cliff, I could tell in her eyes she didn't believe us. She was *never* going to believe us!"

"So you took matters into your own hands," Hayley said quietly.

"I was afraid she would go to the police and tell them about the blackmail scheme and our involvement. It might have spooked our board of directors and threatened the merger, and I just couldn't let that happen."

"So you rigged the cat food dispenser, and then you used Penelope's phone to text Lena, which I assume you had access to since you obviously snuck into her room late at night when Conrad wasn't around. You pretended to be Penelope and asked her to refill the dispenser with cat food so Sebastian wouldn't go hungry during the night. Then you followed her down to the pantry and locked her inside seconds before the explosion was timed to go off."

Gerard's head was bowed.

He didn't have to answer her.

It was clear she had nailed down what had really happened.

"And when Penelope mentioned that there had been a mistake, and Lena was still very much alive, you raced over here to finish the job."

"My God . . ." a man's voice said from behind Sergio.

Sergio glanced over his shoulder and then stepped aside.

Gerard's son Tristan stood in the doorway, eyes fixed on his father, a bouquet of fresh flowers in his hand, trembling.

"Dad, what have you done?"

Chapter 30

"Tristan, son, what are you doing here?" Gerard gasped.

"I was looking for you at the estate, and Penelope told me that Lena had made a miraculous recovery so I rushed right over . . ." he said, his words trailing off as he stared glumly at his father, dropping the flowers in his hand onto the floor.

"How much did you hear?" Gerard asked, his face stricken.

"All of it."

There was a long, agonizingly tense silence.

No one knew quite what to say.

Hayley sat up higher in the bed as Tristan stepped into the hospital room and moved closer to Gerard.

He pointed a finger in his father's face. "*You* killed Lena?"

"Son, let me explain—"

"I don't want to hear it! I don't want to hear anything you have to say! I loved her, Dad, don't you get it? I was in *love* with her!"

This caught Gerard by surprise.

It was obvious from his reaction that he had no idea the extent of his son's feelings for Lena Hendricks.

"I know she didn't feel the same way about me. She told me she didn't have time for a relationship because she was too focused on her career and where she wanted to go. She said as sweetly as she could that I just wasn't a part of that plan. I got it. I totally did. But that didn't change how I felt about her even knowing deep down she would never want me . . ."

"Tristan, I didn't realize . . ."

"How could you, Dad? How could you do it?"

"It was for you, son! I was securing your future! You were going to be sole heir to a whole cooking empire! You were going to be rich beyond your wildest dreams!"

"Becoming a billionaire was *your* dream, Dad, not mine! You took away the only thing I really cared about! I pretended to be like you. Pompous and arrogant, the loudest voice in the room! I tried really hard! But it just isn't me! I hate acting like that! I hate trying to be *you* all the time! I just wanted to find a girl and get away and live a simpler life. I was hoping when I came here for the weekend that girl was Lena, but . . ."

"Tristan, I'm sorry . . ."

Another long, uncomfortable silence followed.

Tristan's eyes darted back and forth as his mind detonated with thoughts flying in all directions.

And then, he slowly raised his head and gazed at

his father. "Were you the one who pushed Hayley overboard during our sailing trip on Saturday?"

Gerard didn't answer him.

He didn't have to because it was obvious he was the guilty party.

"It *was* you, wasn't it?"

Finally, with Tristan, Hayley, and Sergio all glaring at him, he crumbled. He slowly nodded his head and then folded his arms across his chest, hugging himself. "I wanted her to stop asking nosy questions. Lena was already spooked, believing I was the one who pushed Conrad off that cliff, which is *not* true, and with Hayley constantly poking around, upsetting everyone, I wanted to send her a strong message that she should just stop. She was on the verge of torpedoing the merger with her big mouth!"

Hayley took umbrage at that last part.

But she didn't interrupt him to defend herself.

She decided to let Gerard continue babbling.

He was doing a pretty good job of torpedoing himself without any help from her.

"But she didn't stop! She stubbornly kept bringing up questions, especially after Lena . . ." Gerard choked, his eyes brimming with tears.

Tristan's eyes bored into his anguished father. He spoke in a low, flat voice. "So you knocked her out and dragged her to that sea cave to drown so you would finally be rid of her and you wouldn't have to deal with any more questions!"

Gerard glanced at Hayley, who remained stone-faced.

She wasn't about to give him the satisfaction of a response, be it anger, fright, or despair over his heinous, despicable actions.

Tristan raised a shaky hand to his mouth and looked at Gerard as it dawned on him what his father was doing in this hospital room. "Dear God, Penelope told you Lena was still alive like she told me, and so you came over here to . . . Oh my God . . ."

Tristan was inconsolable now.

He recoiled as Gerard moved toward him with an outstretched hand.

Tristan turned to Hayley, who had quietly crawled out of the bed and was now standing next to the sobbing young man. She took him in her arms and hugged him, trying to comfort him, but knowing there was very little she could do to make him feel better after all he had just learned.

Gerard took another baby step forward, but Sergio blocked his path, unhooking a pair of handcuffs from his belt.

"I think we better go down to the station and get you booked," Sergio said.

Gerard nodded, held both hands out to Sergio, forming fists as if to capitulate to the chief's orders and allow himself to be handcuffed.

But before Sergio had a chance to snap one of the cuffs on Gerard's wrist, he catapulted one fist upward, clocking Sergio underneath the chin, momentarily disorienting him and allowing Gerard to push him across the room into Tristan and Hayley, who were still hugging.

All three of them tumbled to the ground.

Gerard bolted from the hospital room.

Sergio rubbed his chin as he sprang to his feet and chased after Gerard.

Tristan was curled up in a ball crying as Hayley jumped to her feet and rushed out the door after Sergio.

She heard a nurse scream, no doubt startled by the two men running past her, the whoosh of air sending papers flying up off the reception desk.

Hayley followed, spotting Nurse Tilly on her feet, hand to her chest, face flushed.

She pointed down the hall. "They went that way!"

Hayley sprinted down the long corridor past rows of hospital rooms and down to the cafeteria where she saw several panicked visitors and staff hurrying out, the swinging doors flapping behind them.

She knew that's where she would find Sergio and Gerard.

When she crashed into the cafeteria, there was no sign of them. The whole room had been abandoned. Just half-eaten Jell-O and mushy meatloaf and lumpy potatoes on trays, cups of coffee, and even a purse left lying on one of the tables.

Then she heard plates smashing in the kitchen.

Hayley swiftly ran through the swinging doors into the kitchen in time to see Sergio backed up against a stove, hands up to defend himself, as Gerard gripped the handle of a sharp butcher knife, waving it around, threatening to stab the chief.

"Come on, Gerard, you're facing enough charges

already! You don't need to add assaulting a police officer to the list!" Sergio barked.

But there was no reasoning with Gerard.

He had lost everything.

His son.

Penelope.

The merger.

His entire livelihood.

He had nothing left and there was no telling what he was going to do.

Sergio caught Hayley's eye and directed her toward a frying pan lying on the counter. Without wasting another second, Hayley dashed forward, grabbed the pan by the handle, reared back and cracked it hard against the back of Gerard's head.

He dropped faster than a sack of potatoes, releasing his tight grip on the knife, which clattered to the floor just before Hayley kicked it clear across the room safely out of his reach.

And then she gave Sergio a hug, who certainly appeared as if he needed one.

From the way he hugged her back, Hayley could tell that she had been right.

The man needed a hug.

Chapter 31

A week after Gerard Roquefort's arrest, the murder of Lena Hendricks was still very much on everyone's mind. Bruce had written a front-page story on the whole sordid affair, detailing the merger, the secret trysts, and all the schemes that had unfolded within the walls of Penelope Janice's estate.

Penelope herself had pretty much holed up in her seaside castle, talking to no one on the outside, least of all a rabid press eager to get her side of the story.

There was an ongoing discussion at the Hancock County district attorney's office over whether or not charges should be filed against Penelope for her role in the fake murder plot, but no one seriously expected anything to come of it. Lena was the one who had lured Conrad into agreeing to off his wife so they could be together, but it never got farther than the planning stages, and Conrad died before it ever got to the point where Penelope actually used the recorded conversations to blackmail her husband into leaving town quietly. Even if there was intent, Penelope's celebrity status was enough to squash any talk of a possible indictment.

But there were still a lot of people who thought Penelope should be punished, not because she was in any way legally responsible for Lena's death, but because in many minds, her calculating, cold, highly immoral actions did in fact play a significant role.

The irony was, Penelope's brand didn't suffer much at all, at least in the short term. Sales of her cookbooks and cutlery and bedding and towels all skyrocketed because of the salacious details of her affair that were splattered all over the papers, gossip websites, and cable news channels. Her company stock soared.

Scandal was definitely good for business.

Hayley was just happy to be home, with her pets, back to living a quiet, decidedly non-celebrity life. She relished the routine of feeding Leroy and Blueberry, picking up her morning cup of coffee at the Big Apple gas station on her way to work, and spending the day behind her desk at the *Island Times*, enjoying a relatively obscure existence.

A flurry of interview requests poured in those first few days, but she refused to take the bait, and answered each call and email with a firm and final "No comment."

* * *

It was a Friday morning, and Hayley stood in her kitchen, staring out the window, reliving the events of that fateful Fourth of July weekend one more time, hoping this time would be the last, and that she would finally be able to put it all behind her and move on.

But so far she hadn't been able to do that.

She had foolishly thought the same thing the day before, and the day before that.

Something was still nagging at her.

Hayley just couldn't shake the idea that there was one last piece of the puzzle still missing.

She had no clue that today would be the day that last piece would fall so perfectly into place, and that the startling revelation would haunt her forever.

It was eerily quiet as she watched tiny raindrops splash against the window. The only sound in the house was Leroy gulping down his breakfast so fast he was pushing his plastic bowl with his wet nose, causing the bowl to scrape across the linoleum floor. She was about to turn and grab her umbrella to take to work in case she had to run errands at lunch when she saw a police cruiser pull in to her driveway.

Sergio got out, slammed the driver's side door shut, and jogged around to the back. She was waiting for him as he rapped his knuckles on the wood door quickly before coming inside.

She had told him a hundred times he didn't need to knock.

He was family.

But he never listened.

His beautiful Brazilian mother had brought him up to always knock.

"I would have made breakfast if I knew you were going to stop by," Hayley said.

"I'm good," he said. "I was going to call you last night, but it was late and I didn't want to risk waking you so I thought I would just swing by this morning on my way to the station."

"What's up?" she said, suddenly curious.

"I closed my investigation into Conrad's death. I am officially ruling it an accident."

He could tell from Hayley's troubled expression that she was not satisfied with his final conclusion.

"There was just no clear evidence that anyone pushed him," he said, still trying to convince her. "But there were plenty of clues that suggest he fell, like the rain making everything slippery and the fact that he was drunk, three times the legal limit, in fact, according to the coroner."

"What about the pipe found at the scene?"

"I don't know. I suppose it must have belonged to him."

Hayley nodded, praying that the feeling in the pit of her stomach would just go away, but it only got worse when she heard what Sergio had to say next.

"It wasn't even a real pipe."

"What?"

"It was one of those fake pipes. What do they call them?"

"E-pipes," Hayley answered.

"Right. I assume Conrad was using it to try and kick the habit."

"But he *wasn't* trying to quit. Believe me, the night I had food poisoning, he was smoking real tobacco. The smell of it made me sick all over again."

Sergio shrugged, dumbfounded. "Then I just don't know."

Hayley did.

She knew exactly who the pipe belonged to, but she couldn't bring herself to say it, not just yet.

"I need to get to work," Hayley said mechanically.

Sergio noticed her sudden change in tone.

"Are you okay?"

"Yes, fine," she lied, checking her watch. "I just don't want to be late."

Sergio gave her a hug and turned to leave, glancing back one more time to check on her.

She kept a mask of calm on her face as if nothing was wrong, even though inside she was falling apart.

After Sergio slid into his cruiser, backed out of the driveway, and sped off, she grabbed her keys off the counter, walked outside in the rain, got behind the wheel of her car, and drove to Seal Harbor, staring at the road ahead of her, the flapping windshield wipers holding her in some kind of hypnotic trance.

When she arrived at Penelope Janice's estate, the gate was open and she drove straight past the main house down to the caretaker's cottage.

When she pulled up, she saw Lex sitting on the front porch alone, looking out at the vast ocean, lost in his thoughts.

She got out of her car and walked slowly toward the porch, taking in deep breaths, trying not to burst into tears.

He looked at her, a slight smile on his face, happy to see her.

"It *was* you . . ."

The slight smile on his face suddenly disappeared.

"*You* were the one who pushed Conrad."

Lex Bansfield.

A man she thought she knew, a man she had once loved and been intimate with, this man, rocking back and forth in a chair in front of her, was a killer.

"Tell me I'm wrong," she said, her voice quivering.

Lex stood up. Tears streamed down his face as he slowly nodded. "You're not wrong. It was me. I killed him."

Chapter 32

"Lex, no, I can't believe it," Hayley whispered as if the wind had just been knocked out of her. "Not you. You're not capable of harming anyone. I know you. I know your heart."

Lex stepped toward her, his hands shaking. "It *was* an accident. A stupid, preventable accident. When Conrad found out I had briefly been involved with Lena, he went wild with jealousy. It consumed him, and suddenly after months of him complimenting me every day on the job I was doing, suddenly everything I touched wasn't good enough. And anything that went wrong around the estate was somehow my fault. It quickly became clear he wanted me gone, so he tried to make me miserable enough so I would quit."

"He didn't want you on the property for Lena to pine after," Hayley said, watching him try to keep it together. "And he couldn't fire you because Penelope would want to know why, and Conrad didn't want to risk her finding out about his affair with Lena."

Lex nodded solemnly.

Hayley could see that he was about to fall apart.

Living with this had clearly taken an emotional toll on him.

He looked drawn and tired.

Nothing like the ruggedly handsome man he had been when they first met.

"So he was stuck with me," Lex shrugged. "But every time he saw me working in the garden, or mowing the lawn, or fixing a window, all that jealous rage came roaring back, even though he knew Lena and I were no longer an item."

"What happened that night, Lex?" Hayley asked, bracing herself.

"Normally I would know how to avoid him since I'm pretty familiar with his habits and schedule, but that fateful night, the night he died, I thought he would stay late at the dinner. I didn't expect he would be out by the cliff smoking his pipe until much later, so it was a surprise when I decided to get some fresh air that night and I ran right into him."

"He was drunk and surly and upset about what had happened at the dinner, and he took it out on you," Hayley said.

"Yes. He started yelling about how I still had feelings for Lena and he kept poking me in the chest with his finger and spitting at me and calling me names, and so I just gave him a little shove backward. Well, that didn't sit well with him and he suddenly charged at me and started throwing punches and hollering and I got him into a headlock to try and calm him down. But that just made him madder, and he punched me in the kidney, which nearly took me off my feet, but I managed to steady myself and then . . ."

Lex stopped talking.

His face flinched as he relived the painful memory of that night.

"And then *what*, Lex?"

"He ran at me, and we collided and stumbled back, and I knew we were getting close to the edge of the cliff, and so I dropped to my knees to stop the momentum, and he accidentally tripped over me, and the next thing I knew he was grasping at the grass near the edge, but before I even had a chance to grab him, he let go . . . and then he was gone . . ."

Lex's eyes welled up with tears.

He was a tough man.

Hayley knew the last thing he would ever want would be for anyone to see him like this.

A bawling mawkish mess.

But he had always felt comfortable around her, and so he didn't hide his face or turn away.

He simply allowed her to witness him crying.

Lex sniffed, wiped his nose with his forefinger. "I thought my eyes were playing tricks on me, that he really didn't fall, that I was just imagining it, but then I got closer to the edge and I saw him down there, his body all broken, and I knew for sure he was dead."

"What did you do next?"

Lex sighed. "I panicked."

Hayley knew this was the hardest part for him.

The part where he allowed his fear to dictate the course of events.

His face was full of shame and despair as he cleared his throat and continued. "I ran back to the cottage. Apparently I must have dropped my e-pipe near the scene either during the struggle or as I ran away, but it doesn't matter. I never should have left. I was a coward, and I'm going to have to live with that the rest of my life. I didn't sleep a wink that night and by morning I was so filled with guilt I decided to turn myself in . . . but I didn't. When the body was discovered, there was so much to do and the whole estate was like a circus with the police and forensics people, and Penelope seemed so much more concerned with leaving on the boat trip on time than with making sure her husband was shipped off to the morgue. It never felt like the right time. And then, as the hours ticked by, and then the days ticked by, it became harder and harder to say anything. I knew everyone would want to know why I took so long to come forward, and the more time that passed, the less I could bring myself to confess to what I had done."

"I can see how the guilt has been eating away at you . . ."

Lex took her by the arms and drew her close.

"I want you to drive me into town so I can turn myself in to Chief Alvares," he said grimly.

"Wait . . ."

Lex gave her a puzzled look.

"Lex, I won't say a word. I promise. We can keep this secret just between us," she said, trying in vain to convince herself that this was the right way to go. "It was an accident. You're no criminal, Lex. No one has to know."

She couldn't believe she still felt strongly enough about Lex Bansfield that she was willing to make a secret pact never to discuss the real sequence of events at Penelope Janice's estate.

Lex smiled sadly and stroked her cheek. "Thank you. But no. It's time I did the right thing, Hayley."

He took her by the hand and led her over to her car, and opened the door for her. She climbed in the driver's side, and once she was settled, he slammed the door, walked around the other side of the car, and slid into the passenger's seat.

A gush of tears flowed down her face as she drove Lex to Bar Harbor, and at one point she almost had to pull over because she couldn't see anything in front of her.

Lex, with a resigned and impassive look on his face, gently took the wheel to assist her while reaching into his pocket, withdrawing a handkerchief, and handing it to her, which she used to wipe the moisture away from her eyes.

She offered him a wan smile, acknowledged that she had the driving under control again, and his hand let go of the wheel.

They spent the rest of the ride in silence.

Except for the sniffles that kept escaping from Hayley as she fought back the flood of tears.

Chapter 33

When Lex Bansfield turned himself in to Police Chief Alvares, it didn't take the local press long to pounce on the story, especially Hayley's own *Island Times* paper. The *Times'* rival publication, the *Bar Harbor Herald*, went with a more salacious view of events highlighting Lex's torrid affair with the gorgeous and doomed murder victim Lena Hendricks and all the backstabbing and scheming that went on at the Penelope Janice estate, while Hayley insisted—pleaded, rather—with Sal to give a more balanced view of what really happened despite Sal's instincts to go big.

Lex was well known and liked all over town, but this was a big news story, and could sell a lot of papers not to mention garner an avalanche of clicks online.

But Sal was well aware of Hayley's history with

Lex and so he made sure the coverage was at least somewhat fair.

Lex quickly made a deal with the county prosecutor.

Involuntary manslaughter.

According to Liddy's boyfriend Sonny Lipton, who, as a lawyer, boasted a number of contacts in the legal community, Lex was exceedingly cooperative, appropriately remorseful, and willing to make any necessary reparations. This led to the judge's sentencing him to six months in jail although most experts predicted he would be out in two.

And they were right.

Lex was quietly released eight weeks later with very little fanfare. Within three days, he had packed his belongings in the back of his truck and left town. He wanted to escape the memories of what had happened. He always had a road trip to Key West for some fishing on his bucket list, so that's where Hayley assumed he went. She had visited him twice during his time in jail, but stopped when it became painfully clear it bothered him that she was seeing him locked up.

She waited until he got out and called to invite him over for dinner, but he made up an excuse, too much to do to get ready for his trip. And before she knew it, he was gone. Mona had spotted his truck barreling across the Trenton Bridge early one morning while she was on her way back from Ellsworth after buying some new lobster traps for her business, and that was the last time anyone saw him.

Lex Bansfield was gone for good, ready to put all

the tragic events of the past summer behind him and start over somewhere else.

Hayley hoped she would one day see him again, but she wasn't going to hold her breath. Lex was very proud and independent, he wasn't much of a communicator, and he rarely showed any kind of strong emotion.

But most of all, Lex Bansfield was a loner.

Always had been.

Always would be.

Which was a big part of the reason it didn't work out between him and Hayley in the long run.

Hayley sat at her desk at the *Island Times* lost in thought, wondering if Lex had really gone fishing in Florida, or if that was just a story he told to keep people from trying to locate him.

It was past five o'clock, her quitting time, so Hayley shut down her computer and reached underneath her desk for her bag. Sal was still toiling in his office, but otherwise, everyone else was either out covering a story or had gone home for the day.

The door suddenly blew open, and much to Hayley's surprise, a rather regal woman in a stylish hat, carrying a sophisticated air about her, breezed inside the office.

It took Hayley a moment to recognize her.

Penelope Janice.

It had been months since the events that unspooled so dramatically over the Fourth of July weekend.

Penelope appeared fresh-faced and relaxed, as if she had just spent a week at some high-end spa in

Arizona getting massages and facials and mud baths, rejuvenating herself and putting all the unpleasantness of her scandal-plagued summer behind her.

There was still no word on any kind of memorial for Conrad. His parents were already gone and he was an only child and he and Penelope never had children so his cousins held a small service for family and friends in his hometown of Dayton, Ohio. But that was pretty much it. Penelope barely mentioned him on her show. It was as if he never existed.

Penelope did, however, establish a scholarship program in Lena's name for aspiring writers going to college and was about to make the first sizable donation.

"Hello, Hayley, how have you been?" Penelope asked, flashing that megawatt smile that had been on the cover of so many lifestyle and cooking magazines and, in recent weeks, tabloids.

"Fine," Hayley said quietly.

"I'm glad I caught you. I've been meaning to call, but I've just been so busy flying back and forth between here and New York where I have been taping new episodes of my show."

Hayley politely nodded.

She didn't care if Penelope called or not.

She had been so worried about Lex the last thing on her mind was maintaining any kind of friendship with Penelope Janice.

"I have a proposition for you," Penelope said, a

twinge of excitement in her voice. "Remember that casserole cookbook I announced over the summer I wanted to publish?"

"The one you were going to co-write with Conrad?"

There was a flicker of discomfort on Penelope's face as if the last name she wanted brought up was her late husband's, but she held it together and offered a tight smile.

"Yes, that one. Well, I don't want to write the whole thing by myself, and on my flight back to Bar Harbor this morning I had an epiphany. I want *you* to be my partner on it. We'll write it together and split the royalties."

Hayley was floored.

Co-authoring a book with Penelope Janice, a *New York Times* best-selling author whose last nine books had hit number one during their first week of release?

"Are you serious?"

"Absolutely. You proved yourself an excellent cook this summer. I love the way you write in your columns here at the paper. You're very personable so I'm sure you would do very well on the talk-show circuit when we do the promotional tour. It makes perfect sense!"

Sal was being unusually quiet in his office in the back bull pen. Hayley knew he was eavesdropping on their conversation. It wasn't every day a major TV celebrity swung into the *Island Times* office.

Hayley sat back in her chair, clutching the scuffed faux-leather bag in her lap. With the money she would probably make from writing a book with Penelope Janice, Hayley could buy a brand-new bag.

Maybe a Hermès or Marc Jacobs.

The offer was tempting.

But she already knew her answer.

"I appreciate the opportunity, Penelope, I really do, and I'm flattered that you would think of me, but I'm afraid I have to say no. But thank you."

Penelope stared at her, flabbergasted.

It was the very rare occasion when anyone, least of all a local yokel who struggled to pay her property taxes like Hayley, said no to Penelope Janice.

"Oh," she managed to get out. "I see."

"But good luck on the book. I'm sure it will be another best seller."

Penelope nodded, turned to leave, but then stopped by the door and turned back to Hayley. "May I ask why? You're turning down a lot of money."

Hayley thought carefully before she answered.

She didn't want to upset Penelope, or cause a scene, or in any way make an enemy out of her, so she simply said, "Sometimes it's not about the money."

Penelope was not satisfied with her answer, but she realized that was all she was going to get so she left the *Island Times* office, still in a daze over being so resoundingly rejected.

By a nobody, no less.

Sal raced out of his office after she was gone and hovered over Hayley's desk. "So what was that all about?"

"Come on, Sal, you were back there hanging on every word," Hayley laughed.

"Okay, okay, but why did you turn down that sweet offer? I thought Penelope Janice was your idol!"

"She was. Until I actually spent time with her and realized the depths she would go to to keep building on her fame and fortune. At the expense of other people. Sometimes it's not a very good idea to get such a close-up look at your heroes. They're bound to disappoint you."

Sal thought this over and seemed to agree because he nodded slightly, but she could tell he still wasn't completely getting it.

"Penelope may not have committed a serious crime, at least one she could be convicted for," Hayley said, trying one more time to explain. "But her behavior wasn't worthy of anyone's admiration."

"You're something else," Sal said. "Saying no on principle like that. I may never get my head around you turning down all that money from what was sure to be a best-selling book!"

Hayley smiled.

"You're a good person, Hayley," Sal said, putting his arm around her as she stood up from her desk.

"Not really."

"Yes, you are," Sal insisted.

"Really, I'm not."

"Why do you say that?"

"Because I am about to burst into tears thinking about all that money I'm never going to see," Hayley said, her lip quivering.

Sal burst into laughter and led her toward the door. "Come on, I'll buy you a drink at your brother's bar."

"It may have to be more than one," she said, sniffling.

"As many as it takes. Don't worry. I will do my best to help you forget this ever happened."

And with his fatherly arm around her shoulder, they walked out the door.

Chapter 34

Sal was true to his word.

By the third round at Drinks Like a Fish, Hayley was feeling much better. She rarely went out drinking with her boss.

And she often wondered why.

Sal was rough around the edges and sometimes moody, but overall he was a fun guy.

The bar was buzzing with activity, and she barely saw Randy, who stayed mostly in the kitchen cooking items from his new happy-hour food menu. Michelle, his loyal bartender of nine years, was desperately trying to keep up with all the drink orders. All of the tables were full and there was only one stool at the bar that was not occupied.

Sal and Hayley sat at the far end of the bar, with a clear view of the front door. When Bruce entered and stopped at a nearby table to say hello to some friends, Hayley tried catching his eye, waving at him, but he was engaged in conversation and didn't see her.

"You really want Bruce to join us?" Sal asked, staring at the bottom of his glass before swallowing the last of his bourbon.

Hayley reacted, surprised. "Yes. Why? You don't?"

"Bruce is all right. I just didn't think you two got along. I'm not the only one at the office who thinks that."

"No, we get along just fine," Hayley said, suddenly curious about the gossip obviously flying around the office about her and Bruce. "Whatever gave you, and the entire *Island Times* staff apparently, that impression?"

"I don't know. Maybe the fact you spend most days arguing like an old married couple."

Married couple?

Well, that was just ridiculous.

"Bruce and I have had our differences in the past, but we've managed to settle into a pleasant, low-key tolerance of one another. He's mellowed a bit over the last couple of years, and isn't so much of a self-involved jerk anymore."

"High praise indeed."

"No, really. I've grown fond of him."

"I see," he said, smiling at Michelle, who refilled his glass with bourbon. He splashed the bourbon around in his glass before taking a healthy swig.

"So what else does the staff think of me and Bruce?" Hayley asked.

"We better not get into that here."

"Why not?"

"Because he's heading over in this direction right now."

Hayley spun around on her stool to see Bruce approaching, a laconic smile on his face as he politely asked Buster, a grizzled fisherman with a beard that went all the way down to his belly button, to slide over to the empty stool next to him so Bruce could sit next to Hayley. Buster begrudgingly agreed, snorting a reply as he downed his beer, leaving foam in his beard as he moved.

"Evening," Bruce said, glancing back and forth between Hayley and Sal, dying to know why they were out together and why he had not been invited to join them.

Sal raised his glass. "Bruce."

Bruce flagged down Michelle and ordered a bottle of Stella Artois.

Michelle turned to Sal. "Another bourbon?"

"No. I'm out," Sal said, gripping the edge of the bar and sliding his bulk off the stool. "Wife's got dinner waiting at home."

"Was it something I said?" Bruce asked, a slight frown on his face.

"Nope, not at all. It's a school night so I have to get out of here before I have the one that gets me to the tipping point where I end up staying until last call. You two have a nice night," Sal said, winking at them.

What was he up to?

Why was he leaving so suddenly?

He never mentioned racing home to dinner *before* Bruce's arrival.

"See you tomorrow, Sal," Hayley said.

Sal clapped Bruce on the back. "Good luck, Linney."

He ambled out of the bar.

"What do you need luck for?" Hayley wanted to know.

Bruce didn't answer her.

Michelle dropped off Bruce's Stella Artois and he gulped half of it down, his Adam's apple popping in and out as he swallowed.

Hayley laughed watching him guzzle down his beer so fast.

He appeared so nervous and she couldn't understand why.

And then, without warning, he blurted out, "Do you want to have dinner with me?"

"Tonight? It's kind of late . . ."

"I don't mean tonight. I mean this weekend like Saturday night," he said quickly.

"Saturday?"

"Yes, Hayley, Saturday, this coming Saturday, if you're free I'd like to take you to dinner."

"You're *paying*?" she asked incredulously.

This was definitely a first.

"That's right. I'm paying. Like a real date."

Hayley's heart nearly leapt into her throat.

An honest-to-goodness date with Bruce Linney.

She never could have imagined it two years ago.

They had been at odds since high school.

But lately she had developed a soft spot for the ambitious, often exasperating crime reporter at the *Island Times*.

But going on a *date* with him?

Sure, the kiss they shared when he rescued her from the sea cave gave her a tingle. Well, okay, maybe more than just a tingle, but this was a big step, and she just wasn't sure it was a good idea, especially since they both worked in the same office.

Hayley had made it a firm rule never to date a coworker.

"So how long are you going to keep me hanging in suspense? It's a simple yes-or-no question."

Hayley finished her Jack and Coke and sputtered, "Yes."

He didn't smile or jump for joy or celebrate her answer in any way. He just downed the rest of his beer and gave her a fast nod. "I'll pick you up at seven."

And then he jumped off his stool and flew out the door, grateful to be done with the whole thing.

Hayley replayed the entire scene in her mind.

Sal knew.

Bruce must have confided in him, asked his opinion, set her up by pretending to believe, along with the rest of the office, that she and Bruce didn't get along.

But that was all just an act.

Sal and the rest of the *Island Times* staff must have suspected something happening between them.

Especially after the Fourth of July fireworks display.

Had she been the *only* one still in the dark?

Randy raced out of the kitchen with a plate stacked with thin crispy onion rings and delivered them to a table of four women, who dove into them before the plate had even hit the table.

On his way back, he swung around to check on Hayley. "Need anything, sis?"

"Bruce just asked me out on a date," Hayley said, still a bit bewildered.

"Finally! Took him long enough," Randy chuckled before zipping back into the kitchen.

So Randy knew too.

And she guessed that if she called Liddy and Mona, her two BFFs who knew more about her than possibly anyone else in her life, they would also claim to have known.

Hayley leaned forward on her stool, elbows on the bar, and shook her head, amazed at how she was the last one to know.

She was even more amazed that she was excited about Saturday night.

And what the future might hold.

Who knows?

This could be the start of a whole new chapter.

Island Food & Spirits
BY HAYLEY POWELL

Recently I was sorting through all of my favorite recipes that I have collected over the years in a card file. I sometimes pick out my favorites and set them aside to try again one day soon. I've been sharing my recipes for quite a while now, and I've been encouraged by my friends to write my own cookbook.

Well, needless to say, I'm no Rachael Ray or Penelope Janice, with huge social media followings and cable TV shows, nor do I aspire to be famous, but a cookbook I could share with my family and friends and future generations has always been a dream of mine since I picked up my first baking dish at the age of twelve and followed the instructions on a recipe card my grandmother had given me—a Summer Corn Casserole.

The Summer Corn Casserole was a huge hit with my family and so I made my fair share of them over the years. I knew if I ever wrote that cookbook, the Summer Corn Casserole would be on page one, as the moment I first discovered my love of cooking.

The Summer Corn Casserole was not just the first recipe I ever tried. It was also the favorite dish of a close friend of mine. I was going to change his name to protect his privacy, something like "Rex," but let's face it, on Mount Desert Island everybody pretty much knows everybody else's business so there's really no point in trying to hide his identity. Yes, I'm talking about Lex Bansfield.

I'm not going to discuss the big scandal of last summer that happened on Penelope Janice's estate during Fourth of July weekend. By now, everyone knows all the sordid details and Lex's role in the whole affair. It was all well documented in the local papers, the *Island Times* included. Lex was recently paroled and left town for parts unknown. I won't speculate on where he might have gone out of respect for his privacy.

But I have to say, I miss him. We had a very color-ful history. Many of you might recall the time we first met, when I hit him with my car. That's right. I plowed right into him and he wound up on the hood. Luckily after I rushed him to the hospital, he checked out okay, no broken bones, and once he was given the all clear to go home, he asked me out on a date. It's not every day you go out with someone you just ran over with your car. But that was Lex. He said it was a sign we were supposed to get to know each other. And we did.

Of course, everyone also knows the relationship ran its course and ended, and now years have gone by, and I am proud to say we have remained friends. The other night as I was making his favorite Summer Corn Casserole, all my happy memories of Lex came flooding back, so I made myself a lovely cocktail creation given to me by my brother Randy's friends Ivan and Stephen from Bristol, England, called the "Last Word." That cocktail also reminded me of good old Lex because when we were together and had our occasional disagreement, he always accused me of having to have the "last word!"

True or not, it's a yummy cocktail.

But I was still melancholy from Lex leaving town without even a quick visit or call, or even email to say good-bye.

Maybe he was afraid I might try talking him out of moving away and didn't want me to have the last word and try to change his mind.

I thought I would forever remain in the dark about whatever happened to Lex Bansfield.

Well, a few days later, on a Saturday morning after running a few errands and taking Leroy for a walk, I stopped to grab my mail out of the mailbox, and glancing through the small stack as I strolled up the driveway, I suddenly noticed a postcard with a beautiful tropical ocean scene on the front. I couldn't help thinking to myself, "Who sends postcards?"

I flipped the card over and on the back was scribbled one word—"Aloha!" I started to laugh as I stared at the Hawaiian word that means both "hello" and "good-bye."

Well played, Lex Bansfield, well played.

You finally got the last word.

On a hot summer day or any day for that matter, you are just going to love Ivan and Stephen's refreshing Last Word cocktail!

Ivan and Stephen's Last Word Cocktail

1 ounce gin
1 ounce green Chartreuse
1 ounce maraschino liqueur
1 ounce lime juice

Shake all ingredients in a cocktail shaker with ice, and enjoy!

Summer Corn Casserole

2–2½ cups fresh corn off the cob (about 5 ears);
    you can also substitute frozen or canned
1 can cream-style corn
1 8.5-ounce box Jiffy corn muffin mix
1 cup sour cream
1 stick butter
1 cup shredded cheddar cheese

Preheat your oven to 350°F.

Combine both your corns, Jiffy mix, and sour cream in a mixing bowl.

Melt your butter and add to the bowl and mix all together.

Pour the corn mixture into a greased casserole dish and bake for 45 minutes. Remove and sprinkle the shredded cheese on top and bake 10 more minutes, or until cheese is melted.

Remove from oven and serve.

Have a happy Fourth of July, everyone!

Recipe Index

Hayley Powell returns in 2019 in
Death of a Wedding Cake Baker.

**In the meantime, Lee Hollis will be debuting
a new mystery series,**

POPPY HARMON INVESTIGATES,

in summer 2018.

Lee Hollis begins a delightful new series in which Poppy Harmon and her friends find that life after retirement can be much busier—and deadlier— than any of them ever anticipated . . .

When Poppy goes from complacent retiree to penniless widow in a matter of weeks, the idea of spending her golden years as the biggest charity case in Palm Springs renders her speechless. With no real skills and nothing left to lose, Poppy uses her obsession with true crime shows to start a career as a private eye . . .

But after opening the Desert Flowers Detective Agency with help from her two best friends, Violet and Iris, Poppy realizes that age brings wisdom, not business—until she convinces her daughter's handsome boyfriend, Matt, to pose as the face of the agency. It's not long before Matt's irresistible act snags a client desperate to retrieve priceless jewelry burglarized from an aging actress at the Palm Leaf Retirement Village. Or before Poppy stumbles upon the bloodied body of the victim's archrival . . .

In a flash, Poppy's innocent detective gig is upstaged by a dangerous murder investigation riddled with slimy suspects and unspeakable scandal. As she and her team uncover the truth, Poppy must confront the secrets about her late husband's past and swiftly catch a killer lurking around the retirement community—even if it means turning her world upside down all over again.

Read on for an exciting sneak peek of

POPPY HARMON INVESTIGATES

coming soon wherever print and e-books are sold!

Chapter 1

Poppy frantically banged on the door of the house but there was no answer.

She waited a few moments and then tried again.

Still no answer.

A foreboding sense of dread filled her entire body.

She had learned from a very young age to trust her intuition.

Something was seriously wrong.

She jiggled the door handle.

It was unlocked.

She sighed, making a quick decision, then pushed the door open slightly and poked her head inside.

"Hello? Anyone home?"

The single-level house was eerily quiet except for some soft music playing from somewhere not far away.

She couldn't tell who was singing because the volume was too low.

Poppy pushed the door all the way open and slipped inside, looking back to make sure none of the nosy neighbors saw her sneaking into a house where she did not live.

"Hello?" she tried one more time, but there was still no answer.

She was hardly surprised.

Poppy had guest-starred on enough TV crime shows in the '80s to know this was usually the point in the show where an unsuspecting woman found herself in the wrong place at the wrong time, and suddenly fell prey to a mad killer or treacherous villain seconds before the commercial break.

Still, her burning curiosity won out over her innate cautiousness, and she shut the door behind her and slowly, carefully, moved farther into the foyer, looking around to make sure no one was lying in wait to suddenly jump out at her with a rag soaked with chloroform, or worse, a sharp weapon like a carving knife or a rope cord from the curtains which he could use to loop around her neck and choke her to death.

Again, she had played a lot of damsels in distress during her years of acting in film and TV.

So her imagination tended to run wild.

There was hardly that kind of violent crime to be found in Palm Springs, her home for the last ten years.

And yet, there were alarm bells going off in her head.

She never felt such a strong sense of imminent danger.

She followed the sound of the music into the living room until she was finally able recognize the familiar voice belting out a song on an old CD player set up in a corner on a small wooden desk next to the fireplace.

It was Elaine Stritch.

The brassy, ballsy late Broadway legend.

The song was "The Ladies Who Lunch," from the hit 1970 Stephen Sondheim musical *Company*.

How appropriate, Poppy thought, given the majority of women who resided here in the Palm Leaf Retirement Village, most of whom spent their days golfing during the morning and enjoying cocktails in the afternoon during their typical three-hour lunches.

She moved farther into the living room in order to turn off the CD player when she caught something out of the corner of her eye.

Poppy spun around, gasping, her right hand flying to her chest.

She struggled to steady herself as she stared at the body lying facedown on the floor next to a cracked coffee table.

A small pool of blood seeped slowly into the pristine white carpet.